MW01245049

Our Little Secret

By Donald Ward

Death Takes the Stage
Our Little Secret

Our Little Secret

Donald Ward

St. Martin's Press
New York

Grateful acknowledgment is made for permission to quote from the following songs:

"Across the Alley from the Alamo." Words and Music by Joe Greene. Copyright © 1947 Michael H. Goldsen Inc. © Renewed 1975 Michael H. Goldsen Inc. Used by permission.

"Mam'selle." Words by Mack Gordon and Music by Edmund Goulding. Copyright © 1947 renewed 1975 Twentieth Century Music Corp. Rights assigned to EMI Catalogue Partnership. All rights controlled and administered by EMI Feist Catalog Inc. International copyright secured. Made in U.S.A. All rights reserved.

"Near You." (Francis Craig, Kermit Goell). Copyright © 1958 (Renewed) WB Music Corp. & MCA Music Publishing All rights reserved. Used by permission.

"(There'll Be Bluebirds Over) The White Cliffs of Dover." Words by Nat Burton and Music by Walter Kent. Copyright © 1941 Shapiro, Bernstein & Co., Inc. New York. Copyright renewed. Used by permission.

Design by Dawn Niles

Library of Congress Cataloging-in-Publication Data

Ward, Donald.
Our little secret / Donald Ward.
p. cm.
ISBN 0-312-05942-6
I. Title.
PS3573.A72809 1991 91-7392
813'.54—dc20 CIP

First Edition: June 1991
10 9 8 7 6 5 4 3 2 1

For
O.K.W.

Our Little Secret

1

The sun had not quite set. Its last rays penetrated the taller larches and jack pines on the horizon and continued to light up the mine buildings at the eastern end of town, washing the white asbestos cladding on the mill and headframe with a coat of vivid salmon pink and transforming each window into a miniature golden spotlight aimed directly at his eyes. Instinctively he retreated deeper into the thick bushes, rousing a swarm of mosquitoes to join the ravenous hordes already hovering about his face and arms.

Grateful for the comparative protection afforded by a lavish coating of insect repellent, he stooped lower down to obtain a clearer view of the house across the road. Not that the repellent worked as well as it should. There always seemed to be several brave storm troopers in every swarm capable of withstanding its vile creosote scent. And even after two summers of acclimatization, he still broke out in itchy red bumps, unlike the local children who seemed to get through the long biting season with no ill effects whatever. And that was only the mosquitoes. When it came to the man-eating black flies who took over the day shift—

He started and shifted his gaze from the window directly opposite him to another window farther to his left, near the end of the house facing an empty plot of land where blueberry, willow and Labrador tea bushes grew amid taller evergreens and the occasional pin cherry tree. Both windows appeared perfectly blank behind the gray metal mesh of their summer screens. Perhaps he had imagined it, that quick flash of white in the living room, glimpsed out of the corner of his eye. He continued to stare at the window, but nothing moved behind it and no sound emerged to disturb the sleepy twitter of birds settling down for the night in the surrounding trees.

They had to be out. On a bright Friday evening, with little hope of clear radio reception for another two hours, no adult in town not actually working underground or providing some necessary surface support would dream of missing the weekly motion picture at the recreation hall. Especially tonight, he thought, when the powers that be had actually managed to book in something worthwhile. *The Lost Weekend* was just the kind of picture he liked—serious, intelligent and totally unsuited to the tastes of the noisy children who occupied the front rows and chattered ceaselessly through comedies, musicals and westerns. But he had seen it two years ago while passing through Toronto on his way back from overseas in the autumn of 1945. And he had other plans for tonight.

Picking up the sack at his feet, he moved sideways through the bushes until he could see past the black tarpaper porch tacked incongruously on to the otherwise white house like a hastily added afterthought. This position enabled him to look down the narrow lane leading across town toward the river. No one. He glanced up the sloping, dusty road past two other identical houses, and down toward the post office at the bottom of the hill. All seemed deserted. His moment had arrived. He pulled the pants and jacket out of the sack and slipped them on over his regular clothes, tucking the ends of the pants into his black rubber boots and securing the jacket with a broad belt. Then a final look round, and with a quick sprint across the road he had gained the side of the porch, where he finished dressing.

In adjusting the hat, he experienced a pang of impatience as his hands encountered the lower half of his face. The beard, alas, had to remain, a necessary evil. At least until—but he mustn't think about that yet. Fixing his mind on the present, he slipped around the porch and let himself quietly in through the screen door.

Safe now from the prying eyes of any passerby, he tried the door to the house, turning the knob slowly and pushing it gently. The door swung open. Odd, this small-town disdain for locks. He smiled and stepped into the kitchen, closing the door quietly behind him.

Since almost every house in Crow River followed the same plan, he could have found his way through it blindfolded. Directly ahead lay a door down to the cellar. To the left, the kitchen, leading through to the rest of the house. To the right, a small bedroom. He turned right, pushing open a door that had been left just a little off the latch.

She lay on the bed, apparently asleep except for a tiny glint of light escaping from under her eyelashes.

He gave a low chuckle and said, "Hello, Ellie."

The eyelashes parted and a sleepy smile flickered onto her lips. "I thought maybe you weren't coming."

He opened his eyes wide. "Not coming?"

"Because you were too busy."

"Never too busy for you, Ellie." He sat down on the side of the bed. "You're very special."

Smiling into her eyes, he softly lifted the bedclothes and pushed them to one side.

She had on a pink nightdress with tiny roses running down the front. Very good. She raised her head a little off the pillow.

"Did you bring it?"

Not trusting himself to speak over the pounding of his heart and the sudden rush of weak dizziness, he nodded dumbly.

"Can I see?"

"My, aren't you in a hurry. And we're still getting acquainted."

One foot protruded from under the nightdress, riveting his attention with its sturdy brown ankle and small curling toes. He stretched out his hand to investigate. She giggled and pulled her foot away.

"When?"

He withdrew his hand and arched an eyebrow. "Maybe if you're *very* good and get out of bed and stand *right* here . . ." He helped her rise and placed her directly in front of him. "Hands up." Deftly he slipped the nightdress off over her head, wafting with it a light scent of unwashed hair.

"Why did you do that?"

"It's all right." He leaned closer to breathe in the perfume.

Her eyes lost their momentary glint of alarm and she giggled again. "Your beard tickles."

"Are you ticklish?" He ran the beard over her bare shoulders and neck.

"No, no, no," she laughed. "No, stop."

"Ellie," he said. "Look."

The silver heart glinted in his hand, its delicate incised pattern catching the light as he swung it to and fro on its silver chain. She reached out automatically.

"No, no, no," he echoed, to tease her, holding the locket out of reach. "It's just to look at."

She was so lovely. Her skin had a bloom like velvet and he yearned to touch it, very lightly so as not to alarm her. He wanted to let the feverish weakness build up inside him as his hand roved over her soft legs and belly until his head began to pound and his mouth became dry and he could hardly breathe.

She was staring at him. "You look funny," she said.

"Come sit here." The words came out as little more than a gasp, but he managed to pat his knee in a brisk, reassuring manner.

She twisted about and became coy. "No."

Bitch. He twinkled at her. "Not even if I let you hold this?"

The locket worked its usual magic.

"All right."

He held his breath as the little girl climbed up on his knee.

"Good," he said after she had wriggled into place. He let his right hand curl quite naturally around her hip as his left brushed her thigh. He closed his eyes and continued to explore.

"Now tell old Santa what else you want for Christmas," he whispered. "Anything you can think of. Anything at all . . ."

2

Curiouser and curiouser. The familiar phrase sprang into Tilly's head the moment she woke to find herself in an atmosphere of soft muffled darkness and a bed certainly not the one in which she had just fallen asleep. She could remember quite clearly retiring as usual in her own room and growing drowsy while her mother read aloud from *Alice in Wonderland*, by request, for the third time. But now, through some mysterious agency, she seemed to be swaying gently along in the berth of a Pullman car on her way to some destination that, try as she might, she could not bring to mind.

This was odd, because she could still summon up every detail of last year's trip to Toronto, although she had been only seven at the time. She remembered lying down fully dressed on top of a bed in the little three-story hotel where they had taken a room after traveling out from the mine in a bumpy seaplane. And she remembered being wakened in the night and bundled into the only taxi in Sioux Lookout for a brief ride to the tiny station where, trembling by the tracks in an ecstasy of anticipation, she had seen a tiny pinpoint of light transform itself into a hissing black monster, huffing and chuffing as if it could barely restrain itself long enough for the porter to put out a yellow metal step and help them into a long, silent railway car where people slept stacked up behind thick green curtains, each decorated with its own number.

Now here she was again, a number herself, slipped in between cool, taut sheets and lulled by the persistent rhythm of clacking wheels, occasionally augmented by the soft patter of footsteps on carpet and a sharper swish against the outside of her curtain as some other sleepless traveler lurched unsteadily down the rocking corridor. Close by in the dark, she could feel her clothes swaying to and fro on a captive wooden hanger while, above her right ear, the tip of a light switch glowed green and an open air vent tickled her nose with its heady mixture of coal smoke and steam. Tilly took a deep breath of perfect contentment, convinced that heaven itself could offer nothing as perfect as a night in a berth aboard a C.N.R. sleeping car.

Not that she had the slightest intention of wasting even a minute on sleep. There would be plenty of time for that when they got to their unknown destination. What she needed to do now was discover if she had been relegated to a windowless upper berth or whether, by some happy chance, they had put her downstairs. No sooner had the thought crossed her mind when a thin, flickering band of light materialized out of the darkness, a short distance ahead to her right. Sitting up carefully to avoid hitting her head on whatever type of low ceiling might happen to lie above it, Tilly stretched out her hand until she could feel first the yielding surface of a lowered window shade, then a pair of metal tabs. The tabs were stiff, but by taking a firm double-handed grip on them and exerting all her strength, she managed to squeeze them together. Instantly, and without any effort on her part, the shade rolled up.

As she had expected, the window revealed nothing more than blurred gray bushes and low deciduous trees flashing by against a slower-moving background of spiky evergreens thrown into dark relief by a starry night sky. The endlessly unrolling scene rapidly became monotonous. But just as Tilly began to contemplate deserting her post in favor of a walk to the end of the car for a drink of iced water from an ingeniously pleated waxed paper cup, the tedious panorama whisked away and reappeared on the far side of a lake stirred by some passing breeze into a dancing cloud of silver spangles.

Here the train slowed down as it negotiated the winding shoreline. Tilly immediately noticed the dark shape of a dock projecting out into the lake and, floating on pontoons at the end of the dock, a small seaplane with silver wings that glimmered like a glow-in-the-dark picture in the light of a full, round moon. As she watched, the plane spun its propeller into a shimmering disc, taxied away from the dock and, in one smooth movement, lifted itself off the water, drawing her along in its wake like a piece of thistledown caught on a rising current of air.

Up from her berth she sailed, through the window and into a fresh, cool night scented with evergreens, damp vegetation and the first falling leaves of autumn. Higher and higher she rose, until the lake below appeared as a tiny bead among thousands of others, all caught in a gigantic web of water that stretched across the limitless woods of northern Ontario like mercury spilled from a giant thermometer. Traveling fast and smooth, she watched rivers turn into lakes, then back to rivers again, all the while hunting through the great tangled design for the thread that led home to Crow River and the particular stretch of it she knew by heart, from the power dam at one end of town to the flooded shallows, half an hour upstream by canoe, where in summer the weathered skeletons of partly submerged trees kept guard over floating meadows of yellow marsh marigolds bordered by purple iris and bushy cattails.

But summer had almost vanished now. Only the dead trees remained, their smooth, gray branches shining up like arrows to point her on toward the first unprepossessing outposts of civilization, now advancing toward her on the right-hand bank of the river. First came the garbage dump, home to a year-round population of dapper ravens, followed by the hills and hollows of the gravel pit. These gave way to flat, gray deposits of hardened waste left over from the gold-smelting process. Then more forest. Then at last there they were, laid out before her like Monopoly houses on a sand table: the headframe, the mine buildings, the swimming dock, the green and orange rooftops of Crow River.

A still, sleepy silence hung over the town. Indeed, it seemed to Tilly that the whole world had tucked itself up for the night. Not a breath of wind whispered in her ear. No cat wailed, no dog greeted the moon. No one passed through the circles of gold cast by the town's few street lights, and no miner burned a late lamp in any of the three bunkhouses lining the road to the mine. Only a sudden "gonk, gonk" from the hoist signal reminded her that work never ceased underground; and, by banking gracefully around the top of the headframe, she could even catch the sudden hum of the hoist motor as heavy wire cable reeled off a giant winder in the powerhouse, soared to the top of the tower and then plunged a fragile cage full of men down into a narrow black mine shaft like the one where they found—

A safety valve in the back of Tilly's mind sounded an alarm. She had entered dangerous territory. To dwell even for a second on Ellie and the mine shaft was to run the risk of being dragged deep into the earth and lost forever in a terror of tunnels and caverns and clammy darkness. Exerting her will to the utmost, she wrenched her thoughts upward, back into the air, and flew off on a course that took her across the river, then followed a boxed-in pipeline up the side of a steep hill to a clearing where three houses sat in a row along the crest of a ridge overlooking the water.

She passed quickly over the first two houses and brought herself to a halt over the third, which stood apart from its neighbors by virtue of a half-finished picket fence around its backyard—a family summer project devised by Tilly's mother. It also boasted a substantial extension on its far side, where Tilly's father maintained law and order as set forth in the regulations of the Royal Ontario Police, with the help of a barred lockup from which abashed miners sometimes appeared for breakfast after reveling too aggressively in the hotel beer parlor the night before.

Tilly smiled to herself. How pleasant it was to be out flying by night. And how surprised everyone would be if they could see her this very minute, watching over the house while they slept. The moon drew sharp purple shadows on the ground, and she could easily translate the elongated shapes into familiar landmarks: the clump of trees in the corner of the backyard, the two swings that her father had built last year, and even the exact spot where they had all tired of nailing pickets on the fence. Strangely, though, the outline of the trees seemed to be moving. A bulge formed at one side and then, to Tilly's horror, detached itself from the main mass and slipped silently across the yard to the side of the house.

No, she thought, this isn't the way it's supposed to be. Again she strained to pull back from danger, but for all her efforts the dark shape continued to move slowly and relentlessly around the house, pausing at each window until it had passed the kitchen, the living room, her parents' room, and come at last to the end of its search. No! The cry resounded in Tilly's head but refused to emerge. Unhindered, the shape melted through the wall into her bedroom.

And there it hung, a tall, shrouded figure in the corner opposite her bed, perfectly still and black, with only a deeper blackness to mark the place where its face should have been under the folds of its heavy hood. Its eyes were hidden, too, but Tilly knew that they stared constantly at her, never wavering for a moment, just as she stared back through closed eyelids, fighting to keep her breathing shallow and regular (in, out, in, out) so that the creature suspended there in the shadows would think her still asleep.

It was important to fool the Shadow, for then it would be content to merely watch and wait. Wait for the smallest flicker of an eyelid or the slightest sound, even the ghost of a sob, by which it would know that she was shamming and not asleep at all. If she could keep it up (in, out, in, out), if she could maintain the pretense, she would be safe. She had managed before, but it was hard, hour after hour through the long, slow night, when she felt so afraid and alone and her parents were so far away—an endless run out the door, across the kitchen and through the living room, all the time never knowing what might be following at her heels, reaching out to catch her before she could reach the safe haven of her mother's bed.

In, out, in, out. Could she do it? She tried to remember whether her door had been left open or closed. If she could throw off the covers, jump out of bed and get through the doorway, all in one quick motion, she might escape. But if she lost time by having to fumble with the doorknob—no, it was impossible. An action like that demanded courage, and all hers had drained away. Somehow, she would have to last out the night until dawn washed the darkness away from the room. She must lie there aching for a deep breath of air (in, out, in, out), lie with her heart pounding, body rigid, nerves about to crack—

Before she knew what she was doing, she found herself out of bed, in front of the door. It was open. She ran.

3

John Henry was back. Even with one ear buried in her pillow, Kate could hear his thin, high-pitched wheezes as they floated upward from among the old shoes and oil canvases gathering dust under her bed. She found the noise reassuring. Life could hardly be easy for an asthmatic mouse. And, after a week's silence during which he had been written off as missing, presumed dead, it was good to know that John Henry still held his own against heavy odds. It was also good to have a legitimate reason for putting off the major housecleaning blitz she had been promising her conscience since last spring. Far be it from her to upset John Henry's bedroom. And, in any case, more important matters awaited her attention.

The forthcoming Crow River Dramatic Club winter production, for instance, sat heavily on her mind. It seemed unfair that this would be the first in years not to bear the words "Directed by Kate Taggert" at the bottom of the program. And the worst of it was, she had only herself to blame. Despite reliable reports of plans for a rival production by Gloria Lewis, she had wasted too much time deciding between *The Pirates of Penzance* and *Oklahoma!* as a follow-up to last year's triumph.

For it was she who had dragged the committee away from its boring reliance on one-set, low-royalty formula farces chosen from the back of the Samuel French catalog, and she who had brilliantly pointed out that since no one in Toronto or London knew or cared what happened in a tiny gold-mining camp in the woods of northern Ontario, they might just as well forget about royalties altogether and shoot for the moon. Gloria had objected, naturally. But initiative won out, and it was Kate who, in the middle of the curling season, rounded up a cast, coaxed twelve unwilling men into the chorus, persuaded all of them that they could sing, whipped an efficient production staff into shape, coped with a neurotic pianist and, at the end of it all, at an increased ticket price of seventy-five cents, filled the recreation hall for two nights running with her ambitious, illegal extravaganza still referred to by her facetious husband as *The Hot Mikado*.

With all this to her credit, then, had she been wrong in expecting to lead the Dramatic Club on to further, greater endeavors? Apparently so, since it was not to be. Gloria had moved faster than expected and announced imminent rehearsals for *Nellie's Night In*, a farcical romp to be performed by a surreptitiously assembled company with Kate's Yum-Yum and Nanki-Poo or, as it might have been, Laurie and Curly cast in the leading roles. Gloria certainly knew how to twist the knife.

Now I'm being unfair, Kate told herself. No stone tablet existed with a chiseled commandment saying that she should direct every play in town. Others deserved a chance, too, even if the results wouldn't be nearly as—well, it wasn't worth getting upset about that. And as far as casting the leads went, who else could Gloria have chosen? She had made a sensible decision and good luck to her. But, thought Kate with a mental sigh, it would be almost impossible to find another winter project at this late date. Opportunities in Crow River were as scarce as good actors, and she needed something really convincing if she hoped to avoid being shanghaied onto a curling team for an interminable winter of sweeping ice and throwing heavy granite stones that always refused to follow their intended path. With another sigh, she turned over on her back, narrowly avoiding a direct collision with Veronica, the amber-eyed family cat, who had recently taken to spending her nights indoors. Veronica vocalized a sleepy question mark, then rearranged herself into a compact ball and dropped off again before reaching the end of a drawn-out purr breathed into the base of her tail.

Opening her eyes, Kate ran a hand along Veronica's curved back and looked across the tiny bedroom to see if her husband had returned from late-night patrol duty. A single open window admitted enough light to reveal a massive black shape stretched along the full length of the twin bed in the opposite corner. This was not Jerry but Sam, acting on his conviction that any bed privileges granted to tortoiseshell cats should be extended equally to Newfoundland dogs. Jerry would be wedged out of sight in a narrow stretch of mattress between Sam and the wall. Kate smiled and tuned her ear until she could pick out Jerry's somewhat squashed breathing from Sam's heavier sighs and, nearer to home, John Henry's tranquil snores. It's a full house tonight, she thought, just as her daughter burst into the room and, shivering miserably by the side of the bed, begged to be let in beside her.

Kate's well-thumbed book on the care and feeding of children contained a paragraph on how to handle exactly this type of situation. As frequently happened, she chose to ignore it.

"But just for a bit," she warned, by way of throwing a sop to her conscience. "Then we'll put you back to bed and I'll leave the light on in the kitchen. Anyhow," she added in a confidential whisper, edging Veronica over to make room for Tilly, "you're supposed to be too old for bad dreams like that."

"I wish I was," came a small voice from under the covers.

Kate planted a kiss on the inch of forehead left showing above the blanket edge and ran through her standard list of potential trouble spots.

"Are you feeling all right?"

"Yes."

"You're not worried about going back to school, are you?"

"No."

"I saw Miss Walter the other day. She says you'll walk through the third grade."

"I hate Mona Meade!" announced Tilly, with feeling. "She's always picking on me."

Sallow, thin and tall for her age, Mona Meade had recently become a terror to the younger children, surprising no one by this behavior. The ladies of Crow River knew only too well what to expect from a minister's only child. They had their own ideas about policemen's daughters as well. But, so far, Tilly had refused to conform to type.

Kate could play the Mona tune by heart. "Do you and your friends tease her?" she asked.

"Not much."

"What's 'not much'?"

Tilly wriggled uncomfortably. "Sometimes we call her Stringy."

"That's mean. And you're just asking for trouble. Leave her alone."

"She won't leave us alone!"

"Shh. Don't wake up your father."

"She picks on me because I don't have anyone to play with." This in a lower voice, ending in a sniff. "I miss Ellie."

"I know." Kate gave her daughter a hug. "You'll find someone else. There's Joey . . ."

Tilly sniffed again. "It's not the same. Ellie was . . . she was . . ." She stumbled to a halt, then went on in a rush. "She was going to get a silver locket from Santa Claus and let me wear it!"

Kate held back any sound of a smile in her voice. "I thought you and Ellie decided you didn't believe in Santa Claus."

"We did, but Ellie . . ." There came a small rustle as Tilly turned her head on the pillow. "It just isn't fair. Why did it have to happen?"

A dark hole with ladders, caved-in platforms and, far below, something white caught in a wedge of rotten two-by-fours, with a nail—

Kate fought to keep the image from leaping again into her imagination. She failed and shuddered. The nail was a new touch.

"It didn't *have* to happen," she said, speaking carefully until the sick feeling had gone away. "Sometimes bad things can't be helped and it's nobody's fault. They . . . they just happen," she ended lamely. "Still," she went on in a more confident tone, "if Ellie had listened to her parents . . . You've been told over and over to keep away from the old mine shaft."

"Yeeess," said Tilly slowly. "But Ellie wouldn't have gone there. She was afraid. And anyhow, there's a big padlock on the door."

Except someone managed to break it off just in time for a little girl to—

"How do you know about the padlock?" Kate's sudden twist in bed brought forth a grumpy protest from Veronica. "Did you and Ellie—?"

"Just once," Tilly interrupted hurriedly. "Just to look at the shed. But Ellie kept saying someone's going to catch us, so we went away and we never went there again. Couldn't you talk to Mr. Meade and get him to make Mona leave me alone?"

Kate accepted the change of topic with relief. "I'll see," she hedged. "It can't be easy for him, bringing up Mona all by himself. And it's hard on Mona, too. You have to make some allowances."

"Mmm." Tilly sounded unconvinced. "I heard Mr. Meade talking to Miss Walter in the store today. He wants her to combine the school concert and the Sunday school recital and do a Christmas pageant this year."

"That sounds nice." A spark of hope flickered on Kate's bleak winter horizon. "What did Miss Walter say?"

Tilly yawned. "She said fine, but she couldn't write it, and Mr. Meade said he couldn't either. What's a pageant?"

"Just the story of Christmas," Kate replied absently. "It shouldn't be hard to write at all."

In fact, I could probably lift most of it straight from the Bible, she continued to herself. The costumes would be easy: white gowns for the angels and stripy robes for everyone else. And a kind of basic set with an upper walkway, and lots of Christmas carols instead of talking. And maybe something lighter to follow, with toys and elves and Santa Claus. Which reminded her . . .

"What?" Tilly asked in a fuzzy voice from out of her pillow.

Kate repeated her question. "I said, how did Ellie know in the summer what Santa was going to bring her for Christmas?"

"Oh . . ." Tilly nuzzled deeper into the pillow. "He promised . . ."

"What was that?"

". . . secret . . ." The faint words trailed away.

"He promised?"

But Tilly had slipped the conversational thread and drifted off to sleep. Kate prepared to do likewise.

Probably one of their games, she told herself. Nevertheless, she must remember to ask about it again in the morning—and tackle Harriet Reese right away about playing the piano for the pageant, which wouldn't be easy after her reaction to *The Mikado*, and all those doctors' certificates afterward. But with Harriet sewn up, she could make the offer to Miss Walter (who would naturally be delighted to get out of so much extra work) and start writing the script and designing the set and costumes. Then a lot of rehearsing with the children, and organizing everyone to sew and paint . . . It would be an enormous job, really. She could see it taking up all her spare time and more until mid-December. Long past the start of the curling season.

Kate's plans ran seamlessly on into happy dreams.

4

"Tilly had another of her bad dreams last night."

"Poor old Til." Jerry Taggert put down his fork and marveled, not for the first time, at his wife's ability to judge the exact moment when he had consumed just enough scrambled egg, toast and coffee to be in the mood for conversation.

They were seated in the living room, one at each end of a maple dining table pushed up against the wall nearest the kitchen. On the wall, over the table, hung one of Kate's oil landscapes. Opposite the landscape sat Sam, yearning, with the tip of his chin resting on the table, his eyebrows contorted into twin peaks of anguish and one thought only in his head. Tracking Jerry's fork from plate to mouth and back to plate again with unwavering concentration, he wondered how much more of this exhausting silent pressure need be applied before the plate got placed on the floor to be wiped clean with one sweep of his large, pink tongue. The thought made his mouth water, and from time to time an overflow of saliva hit the floor with a reproachful plop.

Jerry reached for a pot of wild raspberry jam. "Is she worried about anything?"

"Just the usual." Kate gave the jam a push across the table. "Mona Meade. And of course Ellie Hayes. She can't understand what happened."

"That makes two of us." Under Sam's watchful eye, Jerry turned his attention to the spreading of jam on toast.

Kate idly stirred the tepid coffee at the bottom of her cup.

"Jerry, is there anything you haven't told me?" She hesitated for a moment. "Did Ellie really fall in there all by herself or do you think someone . . ."

Jerry swallowed with a gulp and a cough. "Isn't this a jolly conversation to be having first thing in the morning? Where's Tilly?"

"Next door with Joey and Davy. I was wondering—did Doug say—were there any—?" Kate turned pink. "Any signs? Oh, you know . . ."

Jerry regarded her with the steady gray-eyed stare that seemed almost as much a part of his official persona as the brown uniform on which he had just spilled jam. "If you mean was she interfered with, Doug says no. Of course, he's not an official coroner, but he's a good doctor and his opinion is that she got into the shack under her own steam and died from the fall. Now let's please change the subject." He returned to the last of his eggs.

"It was just—"

A thin, plaintive note, pitched almost beyond human hearing, floated out over the table. Sam had reached breaking point. Kate changed the subject.

"You're not going to eat all of that, are you?"

Jerry looked up, then down again at his plate. "Why not? I'm still hungry."

"You can't be. I put in an extra egg for Sam. Look at that poor tragic face."

They both stared at Sam, who, sensing a battle won, immediately exchanged his woebegone expression for one indicative of hope, trust and gratitude.

With a sigh, Jerry set his plate down on the floor, where the remains of his breakfast vanished in one wet inhalation.

"That's it," he announced as Sam prepared to resume yearning. "Look. All gone."

Having verified the truth of this statement, Sam waved his tail and padded off into the kitchen for a noisy drink of water. A moment later, the screen door creaked and slammed behind him.

Kate poured herself more coffee. "You must have come in late last night. Any trouble?"

"Nothing much. I had to drive over to Springford and break up a fight in the beer parlor." Jerry offered his cup for a refill. "Jack McCallister was there begging drinks."

"Did you see him eat a glass?"

Jerry shook his head. "I think that's an apocryphal story. They probably started calling him Glassy Jack because of the way he looks when he knocks back a few too many. Anyway, he was in one of his guilty moods."

Kate made a face. "That means you'll probably find him sleeping it off in the lockup."

"Just as long as he doesn't lock himself in and throw away the keys again." Jerry yawned and scratched his head. "I'm not feeling up to another search behind the filing cabinet."

"Did you have a bad night?" Kate bit her tongue. The question had come out too quickly.

"No." And of course Jerry had noticed. "Have I been waking you up again?"

"No, not for months." For which, thank God. "I just wondered if the dreams . . ."

"Uh-uh." Jerry grinned at her. "I guess the war's really over. But I did have an idea."

Kate grinned back. "So did I."

"If it's anything like the picket fence . . ."

"You won't have to lift a finger."

"I like it already."

"I'm going to put on a Christmas pageant with the schoolchildren."

"Lordy, there's nothing you won't do to get off the curling team."

Kate's expression of blank innocence crumbled at the corners of her mouth. She gave up and laughed. "It'll be fun. Just minimum story and lots of Christmas carols. I spoke to Harriet about playing the piano before you got up."

"She never said yes!"

"Well, of course not—I got the whole routine about her nervous system and the doctors' certificates. But she thought I was talking about another big musical for adults, so when I told her that it was going to be for the children—you know how she is about sweet little children—she got all flustered and confused, which was my cue to say 'Think it over' and get out before she said no."

"Poor Harriet. She doesn't stand a chance."

"Jerry! Of course she does. She's a grown-up woman. Still"—the corners of Kate's mouth turned up again—"somehow or other I'll get her to say yes. Now what's *your* idea?"

"Cassoulet."

"Cassoulet?"

Jerry adjusted an imaginary pince-nez. "A French casserole, my dear, composed of beans, pork, sausage, lamb—"

"I *know* what cassoulet is."

"For our Christmas party. I was reading your mother's book on French country cooking and it's just what we need. Enough to feed an army and all the cooking done ahead of time. We could use the big enameled basin—"

"That goes under Tilly's bed when she's sick. She throws up in it."

"We could use the wine crock. And with some of your nice rolls, a salad, a few bottles of vintage blueberry vino from that great year 1947 . . ." Jerry kissed his fingertips. *"Magnifique!"*

"Sounds *délicieux*." Leaning both elbows on the table, Kate cradled her chin in her hands. "And does all this 'we' mean that you're going to help in the kitchen?"

Jerry looked wounded. "Of course. Not only that, but I shall take it upon myself to provide a goose for that final authentic touch."

"Surely a chicken . . ."

"Kate, I'm shocked, truly shocked that you could even think of making a cassoulet without a goose." Jerry tilted his chair back from the table and became expansive. "In a couple of months we're going to have thousands of the creatures landing on Beaver Lake, and when they do, I shall be waiting."

"Official police revolver in hand . . ."

"Borrowed rifle at my shoulder, trusty bird dog at my side—"

"Sam isn't a bird dog."

"Well, he always tries to drag Tilly out of the water when she goes in swimming. He can do the same for the goose. And if you speak to me very nicely, I'll let you and Tilly come along to wonder at my marksmanship."

"Darling, I wouldn't miss it for anything. And the cassoulet's a wonderful idea. Now if you're all finished . . ." Kate stood up and began to stack plates.

Jerry rose too. "Actually, that wasn't my main idea. I had another." He hesitated and turned red. "I . . . um . . . I was just thinking that, you know, since I wasn't having those dreams anymore, that maybe"—he cleared his throat—"maybe it might be time for us to put the beds back together again. What do you think?"

Kate opened her mouth, but found herself unable to speak a word. She set down the plates.

Moving around the table, Jerry reached out and ran his hand through the unfashionably short brown hair framing his wife's face. A few lines now decorated the almost comic puckish features, and the brown curls seemed to have acquired a little gray, but essentially it was the same devastating combination he had fallen in love with ten—was it ten years ago?

"What do you think?" he repeated.

Kate swallowed. She said, "I haven't thought of anything else," and then, "Oh," as her husband pulled her into an unexpected embrace.

"Did you say Tilly was out?" Jerry murmured, a little later.

Kate nodded.

"And Veronica?"

"Mm-hm."

"And Sam, too." Still keeping his arms around her waist, Jerry leaned back to look into his wife's eyes. "We could put those beds together now."

Kate smiled. "Why not?"

A long-drawn-out moan wafted into the room from somewhere beyond the kitchen.

"Oh, dear," said Kate.

"I been bad! Terrible bad!"

They looked at each other ruefully.

Having drawn attention to his presence, the moaner began to wail. "Scum of the earth! Satan's disciple!"

Jerry sighed. "If he's lost the key again . . ."

"Lock me up!" bellowed Satan's disciple. "Lock me up forever! Throw away the key!"

"Happy hunting." Kate detached herself from her husband's arms.

"Show no mercy. Feed me on bread and water!"

Jerry executed a mock bow. "Mr. McCallister wants his breakfast."

"Starve me!"

"I'm tempted," said Kate grimly as she gathered up plates and headed into the kitchen.

" 'A policeman's lot is not a happy one,' " quoted Jerry on his way through to the lockup. He paused in the passageway. "Any more news before I start my constabulary duties?"

"Well . . ." Kate thought for a moment. "We're going to have kittens."

"Amazing! And we haven't even got the beds together."

"Veronica, idiot."

"Are you sure? She doesn't look it."

"No, but she's become kind of quiet and she's spending her nights on my bed. I know the signs."

Jerry pointed a firm finger. "I give you fair warning—I shall never drown another kitten. Either you find them homes or we keep them." He sagged dramatically against the wall. "They'll discover us when we're very old, quite mad, with a house full of newspapers and cats."

"Don't worry. We'll get homes for them."

"We?"

"All right—I." Kate began beating milk and eggs for French toast.

"In that case, you can give the little mother-to-be my heartiest congratulations."

And, with a kiss blown into the air, Jerry sauntered off to work.

5

The amount of concentrated energy necessary to shame his family into parting with a few insignificant morsels of food never ceased to amaze Sam. Wearied by his recent efforts, he now lay fast asleep in his favorite retreat, under the back porch steps next to the garbage cans, while a grumpy Veronica kept watch over his slumbers from a cramped perch on the outside ledge of the porch window. She resented this self-imposed task because she had planned on a nap of her own under the peony bushes on the sunny side of the house and because she knew perfectly well, in some deep-seated reasoning part of her brain, that Sam neither wanted nor needed her protection.

Unfortunately for Veronica, her feeling for Sam had very little to do with reason. From his earliest puppy days, when she first made the mistake of regarding him as an oversized, backward kitten, he had aroused maternal passions in her far stronger than any she could summon up for the tiresome offspring whose appearance disrupted her life with clockwork regularity. Not that Veronica ever fell short in her duties as a mother: she had supplied more households in Crow River than Kate liked to remember with kittens perfectly instructed in all the feline accomplishments. But kittens grew up and went off into the world to make lives of their own, while Sam lingered on in perpetual adolescence, her greatest challenge and, so far, her only failure.

No matter how hard she tried, Sam stubbornly refused to profit by either lesson or example. Veronica had repeatedly washed his head until her tongue gave out, but his attempts at personal hygiene remained as perfunctory as ever. Every day she demonstrated how to manage human beings by simply ignoring them, but Sam persisted in overwhelming all comers with a seemingly inexhaustible supply of moist, uncritical affection. He could not be played with or even used as a warm pillow without the risk of accident, and he had transformed mealtimes into an unseemly race to bolt down her dinner before Sam appropriated it for dessert. He was rowdy, noisy, smelly, uncivilized—and she adored him.

But even the most selfless devotion has its eventual rewards and, for Veronica, Sam possessed one virtue that far outweighed all his faults: he could be relied on to challenge any dog unwise enough to enter what he considered to be his own private backyard. This happened very seldom, since all the local dogs respected each other's territorial rules. Occasionally, however, some rash newcomer would swagger through the unfinished fence, only to find himself under attack by a combination of forces guaranteed to exceed anything conjured up in his worst dreams. For Veronica loved nothing better than to join Sam in battle and had evolved an infallible technique for finishing any fight he chose to start. Her present mood therefore improved vastly when a strange dog emerged from the woods opposite the Reese house and began to show signs of interest in the discreet wooden enclosure where the Reeses kept their garbage cans.

The newcomer sniffing the air at the edge of Harriet Reese's hard-won lawn was of medium size with short black fur, yellow eyes, pointed ears and a long narrow tail that normally curved over his back but now hung down at a cautious, propitiatory angle. Attached to a passing tribe of Indians, he knew almost nothing of town life, understood only Ojibwa and, just at this moment, felt very much out of his element. He had no name and expected to be addressed merely as Dog on those rare, alarming occasions when anyone bothered to speak to him at all. He therefore kept himself ready to bolt at the first sound of an angry voice.

Friendly, willing and, when it came to the ways of town, as innocent as an egg, Dog earned his keep during the winter months by pulling a sled in harness with seven of his friends and relations. In summer, however, his employers expected him to fend for himself; and, after four months of a monotonous diet based on small wildlife interpersed with an occasional berry, he yearned for a touch of variety. Harriet Reese's garbage cans promised just such a change of menu for, as Dog had learned from his human companions on their rare passages through town, these fascinating containers often yielded much that, while considered worthless by those with plenty, could still be of value to those with little.

Today, Dog inclined toward something in the nature of a nice, ripe stew or, better still, a well-aged bone. He moved stiffly forward a step or two and took another sniff. Yes, he could detect a faint scent of food. Made bold by hunger, he approached the wooden enclosure, inserted his nose into the gap between the hinged top flap and the wooden side, and breathed. Instantly the faint scent became an odor heady with promise. Heaven awaited. He pushed his nose farther and the flap began to rise. One more heave and—Dog froze in mid-push at the sound of a screen door swinging suddenly open on the opposite side of the raised wooden landing behind the garbage enclosure.

Still with his nose wedged firmly under the flap, Dog raised his eyes to peer over its edge. He found himself gazing at a pair of feet, each decorated with what appeared to be the rear end of a rabbit. Above the fluffy white pom-poms loomed a stout lady wielding a stick with dried grass tied to one end. As expected, she began to yell, and although Dog could make nothing of her words and had never before set eyes on a broom, he understood quite well what they intended to convey. He therefore allowed the flap to fall shut and trotted rapidly over to the yard next door.

The house before which he hesitated also ran to the luxury of two garbage pails, fully as enticing as the first pair, with the added advantage of being free from any impediment to easy inspection. But Dog knew better than to rush into any precipitous action. After the irate lady with the stick had retired from the field, he stood quietly and took note of his new surroundings. The sound of Tilly and the Wilson boys playing on the other side of the house presented no threat. Neither did the small domestic animal wedged into a window frame on the house to his right. Of a breed unknown to Dog, the creature seemed to be spherical in shape, legless and asleep. Beneath it sat two more garbage pails filled to overflowing. Dog decided to pay them a call after exhausting the Wilsons' hospitality.

Shifting her weight imperceptibly to get a better purchase on the window ledge, Veronica watched Dog through the narrowest of slitted eyes and possessed herself in patience. A slight snuffle from below the steps informed her that Sam slept on. She began to knead the soft wood under her feet. Everything was coming together splendidly.

Harriet Reese shut the screen door with a bang, marched out of her spotless kitchen into her gleaming living room and plumped down into her favorite chair, a low, round, well-upholstered echo of its owner. Why, she wondered, did things never turn out the way she planned? When Edward announced his intention of spending all day at the office and dropping in at the cookery for lunch—on the theory that a mine manager should occasionally be seen eating the same food as his unmarried staff—the ingredients for a perfect day sprang instantly into her mind: first, breakfast in bed (tea and toast, on her grandmother's hand-painted china), followed by a dainty lunch (chicken sandwich, ditto) and then, to crown it all, a full afternoon at her beloved grand piano tackling one of the more difficult Debussy *Préludes*. But Kate's visit had dimmed the pleasant glow engendered by the tea and toast; and, after chasing the scrawny mongrel away from her garbage cans, she found that the prospect of a dainty lunch had lost much of its appeal. And how, with her mind in a turmoil at the thought of performing again in public, could she hope to give her full attention to the wicked demands of *Feux d'artifice*?

For Harriet harbored a talent that, but for one unfortunate failing, might well have lifted her far above the ranks of the mere amateur. She possessed an excellent technique, supported by considerable powers of interpretation. She practiced faithfully and never begrudged the hours spent polishing a piece of music to bright perfection. Nor did she really require that her husband leave the house while she did this. It was only with regard to the rest of the world that her nerves presented a problem—specifically, a tendency toward cold sweats and vomiting if called upon to sit down at the piano in the presence of anyone not directly related by blood or marriage. She had doctors' certificates to prove this.

Harriet knew to her cost that Kate never allowed anything as fragile as a simple refusal to stand in the way of her objectives. This was why she had reluctantly agreed to provide the piano accompaniment for last year's *Mikado* and why she had immediately thereafter taken the precaution of obtaining official papers forbidding her to undertake anything resembling a repeat engagement. The papers made this point quite clearly and should have been accepted without question. But they were not.

"Don't say no just yet," said Kate, poised halfway out the door. "Think of all the fun we had last year at rehearsals and all the friends you made. We'll talk about it again." The door had swung shut at this point, but the parting shot passed through it with devastating clarity: "And don't forget—it *is* for the children."

How did she know? wondered Harriet, feeling like a worm that had just barely escaped the bill of a beady-eyed robin. How could anyone know of her silly secret fantasy in which, like Snow White in the forest, she would look up from the piano to discover a rapt audience, not of small woodland animals, but of just a few—two or three would do—local children? It certainly didn't seem too much to ask. But she had tried and failed. Neither virtuoso showpieces nor fairy scherzos had ever drawn Tilly Taggert or Joey Wilson to linger beneath her open windows or interrupt their play for more than a moment.

Now, as Kate had so astutely pointed out, here she had a chance to bring music into the lives of all the little ones who, but for her, might reach adulthood with no exposure to the finer things of life beyond radio, movies and the recreation hall jukebox. Harriet shuddered. It was almost too horrible to think about. She tried to think about it and instantly suffered pangs of doubt. As the only competent pianist in Crow River, she alone had the power to expose those innocent minds to the wonder of music and coax song from those tender throats. Unwisely, she allowed herself to picture a host of radiant faces, including one that might, in a happier world, have belonged to Edward and herself. She imagined a chorus of sweet, true voices. She saw herself at the piano. She began to feel ill.

"No," she said aloud. "No, no, no."

She couldn't do it, she wouldn't and, what was more, she did not intend to sit around for the rest of the day being made to feel guilty about it. No. She must confront Kate right now, utter a firm refusal and stick to it. Then she could come home and possibly calm down enough to salvage what remained of the afternoon. Last year she had been weak; this year the worm would turn.

But she must act now, while the spirit of revolution burned strong. Pausing only to pat her hair and take a deep breath, she retraced her steps through the kitchen, passed through the screen door with a flourish, returned to the kitchen again (revolutionaries do not announce their independence wearing aprons and pom-pom slippers) and finally set off across the Wilsons' cluttered backyard, where she found Dog enjoying to the full the rich pleasure of dining out in style. He removed his head from the garbage can as she passed by, but put it back immediately when greeted with nothing worse than a halfhearted "Shoo!"

Under normal circumstances, Harriet would no more have allowed Dog's act of vandalism to continue than she would have allowed herself to cross someone else's backyard uninvited. But, having just done both, she threw all further niceties to the wind and, instead of walking around the skeleton of Kate's unfinished fence to make a formal entrance through the opening where the gate would one day swing, she ducked under the horizontal top rail and headed toward the porch steps above which Veronica still presented a charming picture of relaxed feline innocence.

Harriet harbored a soft spot for Veronica who, unlike many of her species, possessed sufficient delicacy of feeling to remain outdoors when people afflicted with certain allergies came to call.

"Hello, Sweet Pussy," she said, arriving at the landing at the top of the steps with a beating heart and a failing sense of purpose. "Watch out for the big bad doggie."

Sweet Pussy rewarded this civility with a sleepy blink, then returned to battle alert. The turned worm, with no further excuse for delay, took another deep breath and knocked at the robin's door.

6

With her bold rat-a-tat still vibrating through the Taggert house, Harriet took a step back on the wooden landing and savored an exhilarating mixture of apprehension and nervous excitement. She felt like a general about to lead her troops toward a long-overdue victory; and, like any good general, she approached the hour of battle with a plan. She was, after all, wife of the mine manager and, ipso facto, social leader of Crow River society. It was not her fault that Crow River offered no society worth leading, even if her health had allowed her to do so. A queen remained a queen, even in exile. Too long had she deferred to one who, in a fairer world, would have known her place as a loyal subject and been content to occupy it. But no more. Harriet squared her shoulders and set her jaw. In the past she had been too soft, too accommodating. Today she would pull rank.

Harriet's plan had the classic virtue of extreme simplicity, falling naturally into four parts in which she would: (1) unsettle her adversary by refusing to enter the house; (2) state immediately in a firm, imperious voice that she would not be available to play for any form of public entertainment, now or ever, and that this was her last word on the subject; (3) conclude with a lofty farewell; and (4) make a fast getaway before she could be lured inside and played like a violin.

Unfortunately, the plan contained a fatal flaw in that it failed to allow for the effect of a disorganized opposing force. Kate came to the door, rosy and out of breath and, before Harriet could so much as open her mouth, launched into an incomprehensible tale involving Glassy Jack, cassoulet and a project to rearrange her bedroom furniture. Still talking, she headed into the living room, giving Harriet no choice but to scurry along behind. She then plumped her thoroughly unsettled guest into a comfortable, chintz-covered easy chair, disregarded a refusal to take tea and rushed off to make it, all the while flitting in and out with cups and plates and a cake without ever settling in one spot long enough to be spoken to.

Harriet therefore perched on the very edge of the treacherous chair, possessed herself in patience and waited for her moment to arrive. She felt relieved, at least, to have been spared an encounter with the notorious Jack McCallister and pained, as usual, by her hostess's taste in interior decoration, which ran to plain, unpatterned rugs, a cedar chest used as a coffee table, striped roll-down awnings instead of proper curtains at the windows and, worst of all, a peculiar piece of built-in furniture that transformed two upholstered single beds into an L-shaped corner sofa. Even the paintings on the wall smacked of bohemianism. She particularly disliked a disturbing print of rampant sunflowers executed by some decadent European who, in Harriet's humble opinion, had far to go before his work could be mentioned in the same breath as *Pinky* or *The Blue Boy*. Turning slightly to put the offending object behind her, she continued to take small sips of tea and even smaller bites of cake so as to be ready to pounce when the first conversational opportunity presented itself. Even then, she found it difficult to introduce her subject.

"Delicious," she began, setting down her plate. "Now, there's something I've been meaning—"

"I know what it is." Kate beamed at her. "You recognize it, don't you?"

Harriet's mind went blank. "Recognize?"

Kate laughed. "The cake. From the recipe you gave me. But I can't get it to taste as good as yours."

Baking was a subject that Harriet never ceased to find inexhaustibly fascinating. She risked sliding a little farther back in the chair and observed that she had noticed the same phenomenon after obtaining the recipe from its originator, her great-aunt Jean, whom she suspected at the time of withholding an item or two from the list of ingredients.

"You know," she added, giving Kate a significant look over the tops of her spectacles, "there *are* people who do that kind of thing, and right in the last issue of our own *Crow River Gazette,* too! But I should have known better than to think it of Great-aunt Jean, who wasn't that sort of woman at all, God rest her soul. Because ever since then I've noticed that every recipe seems to come out a little different when someone else tries it. Haven't you—good heavens, what's that?"

Kate paused in the middle of refilling their teacups. "Some poor dog must have got into the backyard," she said. "Sam gets very possessive about it."

Harriet frowned as the jumble of growls, snarls and yaps increased in volume. "I saw the animal before I came in—a vicious-looking Indian dog. Oh, dear." She paused in the middle of reaching for her cup. "Your dear little pussycat was out there. I do hope she won't come to any harm."

"I don't think—" Kate broke off as the sound of canine battle ceased abruptly, to be replaced by a thin, blood-curdling wail that seemed to be approaching the front of the house at top speed.

As if propelled by spring action, the two ladies shot to their feet and hurried over to the row of windows at the end of the room. Kate, having less distance to cover, managed to catch a brief glimpse of Dog, bearing a triumphant Veronica on his back, careening around the corner of the house. Harriet received only a confused impression of yellow eyes—one pair glazed with panic, the other lit up in a blaze of victory—before mount and rider streaked down the front path and vanished into a tangle of thick bushes, leaving behind only an echo of Veronica's wild war cry.

When it became clear that no further excitement could be expected, Harriet left the window and returned to her chair. "I never would have believed it if I hadn't seen it," she informed Kate in a slightly dazed voice. "The poor frightened thing!"

Kate's graceful admission that Dog had certainly been ill used caused Harriet's eyes to widen into full circles behind the rimless lenses of her spectacles.

"I meant your sweet kitty-cat," she said severely. "Heaven

knows what that brute of a dog must have done to provoke her into such a rash act. You must be sick with worry."

Guiltily downing a last bite of cake, Kate did her best to look concerned while observing that Veronica knew how to take care of herself.

Harriet nodded owlishly. "I suppose she's a fierce mouser."

"Well . . ."

"And you have your dog for protection." Harriet sighed. "I must admit that sometimes I get to feeling very nervous when Edward works late at the office. Particularly with all those displaced persons they've got working underground nowadays."

"Jerry says they're perfectly nice men. Just confused and homesick. Canada's a long way from Latvia—and Crow River's a long way from anywhere."

Harriet sniffed. "Did you see them down at the dock this summer? Nice men don't wear bathing suits like that, even in Latvia."

"Evil minds in skimpy trunks?"

"You know what I mean. And someday you may be glad to have a good watchdog in the house."

Kate laughed. "Not Sam. He'd lead a burglar to the family silver and want to carry it home for him. Of the two, I think I'd feel safer with Veronica." A thought struck her. "And there's something so reassuring about a soft, warm cat in your lap."

"I'm sure." The same thought had occurred to Harriet, whose personal warning system could spot a cat owner with kittens in the offing at the drop of a hint. "But when one has allergies . . ."

"Oh, naturally. But allergies are funny things. They come and go."

"Not mine," said Harriet quickly. "I have certificates. Which reminds me why I came over in the first place. I just wanted to make it perfectly clear that—oh, look. There she is!"

Harriet broke off as Veronica strolled daintily into the room with her tail in the air.

"You bully." Kate stretched out an inviting hand. "What did you do with that poor dog?"

Choosing to ignore both the hand and the question, Veronica walked over to Harriet and jumped into her lap.

"Oh, Veronica!" Kate got up. "I'll put her outside."

"It's all right," said Harriet in a brave, breathless voice. "She probably won't want to stay long." She tentatively ran her fingertips over the plush fur between Veronica's ears, then beamed at her hostess. "Listen—she's purring."

Kate mentally crossed her fingers. "And she's usually so shy with visitors."

The beam on Harriet's face took on a slightly lopsided quality. "I really should be going, but she seems so comfortable. I hate to disturb her."

"Oh, you can't do that. Let's have some fresh tea."

Harriet's alarm bells sounded again, but in vain. She had just discovered how to launch Veronica on the road to ecstasy by scratching her under the chin.

"What do you give her to eat?" she asked. "Puss, puss, puss."

Kate paused on her way out of the room. "Tinned cat food, mostly, but she adores parboiled liver when I can face the smell of it cooking. Actually, she may get some tonight."

"And you know, Jerry," she told her husband later, "she stayed on Harriet's lap for almost an hour without a single sneeze. And Harriet agreed to play for the concert after all, *and* she's going to take one of the kittens. What do you think of that?"

"Just what I've said all along." Jerry bent down and kissed his wife. "You're a terrible woman. What's that awful smell in the kitchen?"

7

On the first weekend in October, as if responding to some deep-seated primal urge, every married man in Crow River stripped the fly screens from his house and replaced them with glazed storm windows. This rite marked the true beginning of autumn. The season then fell obediently into place so that, almost overnight as it seemed, children began leaving footprints in hoarfrost on their way to school, wet clothes stiffened on the line, and the last patches of green on the birch and poplar trees across the river turned brilliant yellow. Evenings arrived early, smelling of burning leaves, and even Harriet Reese, who set off for the Friday night film before anyone else in order to take possession of a particular aisle seat, suddenly discovered a dark world waiting for her when she emerged from the house.

"Like a big, gray moth," remarked Kate on the second Friday in the month, as she happened to witness this occurrence from the living room window, "leading us on to the bright lights. Hurry up, Tilly, or we'll miss the newsreel."

The bright lights of Crow River added up to a total of two, one mounted on the edge of the recreation hall roof, the other on a nearby telephone pole. Both directed most of their output down onto a broad flight of stairs leading from street level to the main entrance porch. But enough secondary light escaped to illuminate the entire front of the building, which sent out a warm glow of its own through two rows of windows serving a long promenade-lounge outside the auditorium on the upper floor and a two-lane bowling alley in the semibasement below.

In contrast to the open arms and smiling face with which it welcomed visitors from the street, the recreation hall normally turned a cold, dark back on the river. But on autumn nights such as the one that found Harriet, Kate and Tilly hurrying in to town, light from the front of the building mingled with a lingering haze of leaf smoke in the air to halo the bulky two-story silhouette with a luminous aura. In turn, this borrowed brightness sent a pale simulation of moonlight washing down toward the river, growing fainter and fainter as it trickled over the yellowed plumes of uncut grass until it finally expired altogether at the water's edge, unable to penetrate the thick darkness that hung over the river and the swimming dock.

Directly across the river, however, a single square of light shone out bravely from the crest of the ridge. Glassy Jack McCallister had left a kerosene lamp burning in the front window of his log cabin. And farther downstream, beyond a wooded bend in the river, several weaker lights blinked on and off behind a curtain of waving treetops. These issued from the Taggert living room, accompanied by howls of despair from Sam, intent on informing the entire town that an innocent, faithful animal had been abandoned by his unfeeling family who were doubtless taking a delightful W-A-L-K (as Sam had learned to think of it) and even now sniffing tree trunks, finding sticks to carry, wading in fragrant river ooze and generally enjoying themselves to the hilt without him. The very thought brought on a heartrending howl ending in a dying yodel, one of the performer's particular specialties. But after a quarter of an hour devoted to this exercise, Sam felt the need of a restorative nap, and quiet descended on the river.

Peace at last. He moved under the high diving tower and leaned back against one of its cool steel uprights. The light in the window still regarded him with an insolent stare, so he shut it out by closing his eyes and fixing his thoughts on the almost unnatural silence that now made him feel as if he had been enveloped in a cocoon of cotton batting. He breathed a sigh of relief. This was what he had come for, to abandon what his senses could tell him and, instead, feel what he could neither see nor hear.

Pulling back from himself, he allowed his mind to drift upward, sending it higher and higher through the wind in the treetops and the low-lying layer of clouds hanging over the river until it emerged into a glittering night sky. Then, looking down, he conjured up the same vision reflected in the smooth, black water so that the dock and the solitary figure at its far end seemed to float on a background composed of stars and planets in which even the tiniest speck in the Milky Way gleamed with a diamond brilliance.

He smiled. Such a pretty picture and such a lie. On the surface, a glittering veil of stars. But underneath, oh, underneath—still the same stinking river where torpid jackfish drifted through rotting weeds, spotted leeches undulated with the current in search of prey, and crawfish scuttled over the disgusting black riverbed where swollen dead things decomposed.

It was the same everywhere. Rot and corruption hidden just beneath the pretty veil. One had only to lift a corner and look. Like the boys who sprinkled salt on leeches scooped from the river and then crowded around to watch as each clenched living entity dissolved into a puddle of gray slime. Or the handsome young degenerate in tonight's movie, holding on to his youth and beauty while his painted image became more and more hideous with each new crime.

And what about me? he wondered. If I get careless, will someone scoop me up and let out the putrid ooze? Do I exist somewhere in an old snapshot, slowing turning into a monster? And if I wanted to, could I turn it back? Could I stop my thoughts and sweat out the nights and bury myself in this godforsaken town with nothing to do and nowhere to hide and no one to understand and somehow turn everything back? Without waiting for a reply, he pushed himself away from the steel upright, left the dock and headed away from the water.

He came to a halt in a shadowy area to one side of Number Three bunkhouse. Located directly across the street from the recreation hall, this building sat astride the boxed-in insulated pipeline that carried steam heating to most of Crow River's public buildings and some of its newer houses, linking them in a giant connect-the-dot pattern laid out over the face of the town. In winter the pipeline provided a raised path through heavy snowdrifts, and in summer it became a convenient, if splintery, source of outdoor seating. He therefore made a careful inspection of its surface before sitting down to light his pipe and watch the illuminated parade of filmgoers as they climbed the recreation hall stairs.

Harriet led the field, as expected, narrowly beating out a small group of like-minded Friday night regulars who also had designs on particular seats. Others showed up at random, willing to take their chances on finding a place neither too close to the front rows favored by the schoolchildren nor to the back, where the Ojibwa-speaking members of the audience sat in serene isolation amid an overpowering scent composed primarily of fish, dog and smoked moosehide. Several of his friends passed by, but failed to notice him; and although the occasional person paused to wave before continuing up the stairs, no one walked over to disturb him as he lapsed back into thought.

His little irregularities couldn't go on forever, of course. Especially in a small place like this. Strange how it had seemed such a good choice at the start. Plenty of potential for the long haul. But he had reckoned without the effect of his days of plenty. Easy access had made him greedy, and that was dangerous. He mustn't make the mistake of expecting the locals to remain dense forever. The best he could hope for now would be another one or two episodes, three at the most, and only if he rationed them carefully, like chocolate during the war. He smiled. Coupons, anyone? But it wasn't funny. Abstinence, once so natural, had become a torture now that he knew just exactly what he liked, what he needed, what made everything else in life seem merely like playing for time. This was what drug addicts must go through, he told himself. No wonder they can't stop. In the end, though, they had no choice. Give up or die. It was something to think about.

The plank beneath him began throbbing to a heavy, measured tread as Ray Witkowski, a miner from Number Two bunkhouse, came strolling along the pipeline. They exchanged greetings.

"Kinda cold to be sitting out." Ray hopped off the pipeline. "Going to the show?"

He shook his head. "No rest for the wicked."

"My roommate went this afternoon. Said there's a picture in it scared the sh—, the hell outta him."

"I'd be the same. Nightmares for a week."

Ray laughed. "That's a good one. Hey, Mac! Look who's scared to go to the show." Jerking a thumb backward to indicate the object of his teasing, he jogged off to join a friend. Their bantering voices died away as they headed toward the recreation hall.

At the same time, Kate and Tilly came hurrying down the street. He waved when they glanced in his direction, but they appeared not to see him. Without breaking stride, they followed the miners up the stairs, Kate taking the steps two at a time and Tilly scrambling behind at a run. There was something touching about that. He liked the eagerness in her step and the way her dark blond braids bounced up and down on the back of her coat. Very sweet and eager and just the right age. Odd that he hadn't thought about her before. But part of their charm was the way they ripened overnight, if one had the patience to wait.

Fortunately, he had never needed to wait. The war doled them out on a plate. At the start, a chocolate bar or a couple of cigarettes could get you anything you wanted and no complaints afterward, or nothing another stick of chewing gum couldn't fix. They practically asked for it. Later on, there were the orphaned ones with gaunt faces and huge sad eyes, haunting the ruins like little gray ghosts. Perfect timing. Starved for affection as much as for food, they'd follow anyone who gave them a kind look. And nobody missed them when they failed to return. So easy when you had a nice smile, and he flattered himself he had a very nice smile indeed. What he needed now was another war. Or anything at all to ease the painful tension that had been coiling up inside him over the last few days.

Shivering, he dropped his spent pipe into the pocket of his red and black mackinaw jacket and stood up with a wince as his lower joints unbent at their own reluctant speed. Ray had been right. It was getting colder. He took a few tentative steps to work the stiffness out of his legs, then stopped. So many delights to choose from. Rec hall or beer parlor? Just putting it into words made his heart sink. He sighed and shook his head. Even when you wanted to be a good boy, they made it so difficult.

Which would it be, then? The beer parlor, located half a mile away on the Springfield road, guaranteed enough noise and boisterous company to overwhelm even the most persistent of unwelcome thoughts. The recreation hall, on the other hand, would probably be almost empty downstairs and therefore dangerous. But its central heating would be on, and he needed warming up. Shivering again, he crossed the deserted street and walked around to the left-hand side of the building, where a small porch at the bottom of an inclined path admitted him to a blissfully overheated vestibule on the lower floor. Tantalizing fragments of newsreel commentary floated down a flight of stairs to his right, but he resisted their invitation to eavesdrop in the upper lobby and, instead, turned left through a pair of swinging doors into a combined lunchroom and lending library.

One look around the room erased any lingering hope that he might find a congenial spirit with whom he might strike up a conversation. At the very least he had expected to find Ernie Johnson, who ran the snack bar, and possibly Rita Griswald, who dispensed books from the library on a random timetable of her own devising. But the library shelves were locked. And Ernie, nowhere to be seen, had probably run upstairs to catch the newsreel and cartoon. This was just as well since, on second thought, he had no wish to sit through another of Ernie's marathon monologues on the dire state of the peacetime world, even if bribed with a free Coke. Nor did he recognize either of the two miners leafing through magazines at separate tables, apparently quite oblivious to the continous musical selections broadcast by a massive multicolored jukebox located in the corner of the room farthest from Mrs. Griswald's literary domain.

Although Crow River had to wait a full two years or more for new movies to trickle down through the North American circuit, no such problem existed with records. Shipped in by air direct from the distributor, these landed in the jukebox with their shellac barely dry and their hit parade ratings still on the rise. Crow River, of course, had a hit parade of its own. After a few preliminary clicks, the machine began to dispense the current favorite.

"*I wonder who's kissing her now*," crooned Perry Como in mellow tones.

"*Wonder who's showing her how . . .*"

The song caught his attention. He had heard it first as a child.

"*Wonder who's looking into her eyes*
Breathing sighs, telling lies . . ."

At a party, it was, or perhaps an organ grinder on the street.

"I wonder who's buying the wine

For lips that I used to call mine . . ."

Other people's problems! He had enough of his own. Skirting the snack bar, he made his way into the adjacent pool room.

"Wonder if she ever tells him of me . . ."

That, of course, was a different matter. He set up a table and sent the balls flying. Sooner or later, one of them might talk out of turn. But who would believe her? Choosing a ball at random, he tapped it into a corner pocket. Even if she had the remotest idea who he was or the words to make herself understood. Which, of course, he always made sure she never did. Another ball followed the first. And so far they had always threatened first. One—such a satisfying word—one could always tell when they were bluffing and when they actually meant it. He lined up a difficult shot. And then one took appropriate action. Two balls disappeared into two different pockets. Perfect. A new record dropped down in the jukebox. Now if he just tapped the blue . . .

"A small café, Mam'selle . . ."

Why did all these songs sound alike?

"Our rendezvous, Mam'selle."

The ball slowed to a stop, missing its objective by a bare millimeter. Stupid game. He dropped his cue on the table, then left the pool room by another door, crossing a hallway into the bowling alley. The sound of the jukebox followed.

"The violins were warm and sweet and so were you, Mam'selle . . ."

And why did they all have to sing about the same thing? Finding one of the alleys set up for tenpins, he chose a ball from the return channel, took careful aim and launched it onto the polished wood. But the ball rolled off into the side gutter. Not his game. And his hands were sweaty.

"There's just one place for me, near you . . ."

Francis Craig had taken over from Art Lund.

"It's like heaven to be near you . . ."

He should have gone to the beer parlor after all. In the hallway again, he started to walk toward the far end of the building, stopping to look into the men's room. He washed his hands, dried them, then rubbed the damp paper towel over his face. Better. Just as he returned to the hall, a new record began.

"*Across the alley from the Alamo . . .*"

He smiled. He liked the Mills Brothers and this was one of his favorites, a bright nonsense jingle about a pinto pony, a Navajo Indian and their unfortunate encounter with a railway train.

"*One day, they went a-walkin', along the railroad track . . .*"

A door sat open at the end of the corridor, where the building manager, Bert Nichols, had his office. Inside the office would be a telephone, a rare commodity found only in official mine buildings and the houses of staff members.

"*Toot! toot! they never came back.*"

He should go. He should go right now. He looked in at the doorway. Yes, there was the telephone. His hands felt wet again. He rubbed them down his pant legs. Bert would be upstairs in the projection booth. And the feature had probably not even begun yet. If he took the car, he still had a good two hours. But it really was too soon after the last time. And he was finding it harder and harder to hold back.

"*Toot! toot! they never came back.*"

Although no harm would be done if he kept it short. Just for a little. Not to do anything. He reached for the telephone. Or nothing much.

He dialed the three-digit number and listened as the connection clicked through and began to ring at the other end. And ring.

"Come on," he said. "Answer the phone."

Maybe it was a sign. Maybe he should hang up.

And ring.

All right. Three more rings and he'd hang up.

"*There's just one place for me . . .*"

Two more times.

And ring.

"Answer the phone, you bloody little—"

"Hello?"

Her voice sounded small and sleepy and far away. Also a little afraid. Excellent. He looked back down the corridor. Still empty. He swung the door shut with his foot.

"Who's there?"

In an instant all his tension had drained away, to be replaced by a soothing sense of warmth and affection and anticipation. Some of the warmth settled into his throat, making it easy to hit the deep tones.

"Ho, ho, ho!" For once he really felt like laughing. "Guess who's flown all the way from the North Pole, just to see his little Margie?"

"Well!" exclaimed Harriet on meeting Kate and Tilly on the porch stairs after the film. "I never dreamed it was going to be *that* kind of a picture. I should have stayed home." She glanced severely downward. "Like a certain Someone Else I could mention."

"I liked it," said Tilly.

Kate threw an apologetic look in Harriet's direction. "I didn't think the picture would be quite so awful."

Harriet shivered. "I shall have nightmares all night."

"I won't," said Tilly. "I shut my eyes. Why was Dorian Gray supposed to be so bad?"

"Ah . . ." said Harriet, who had not quite fathomed that point herself. "Oh, look!" She pointed at a shiny black Ford sedan parked on the opposite side of the road. "Edward's brought the car to take us home. Edward," she said, trotting happily toward the chubby, pink-cheeked occupant of the driver's seat, "you are naughty. You promised you were going to keep me company and I saved you a seat."

Her husband gave them all a welcoming wave from the window while tapping the ashes out of his pipe. "Sorry, pet. Something came up at the office."

"Something always comes up at the office," sniffed Harriet as she walked around to the other side of the car. "You might just as well be back overseas."

"Well, you know what they say." Edward twinkled over the tops of his round rimless glasses. "No rest for the wicked." He twisted about to look over his shoulder. "What are you doing back there, Tilly? I know you like the front. Come sit up here with Uncle Ted."

8

"Where ya going?"

The question, delivered in rasping basso tones, seemed to materialize out of thin air, stopping Margaret Wilson in her tracks. Coatless, hatless, coffee mug in hand, she had planned to outrun the effects of a chill autumn day by sprinting over to the Taggert house next door. Instead, she came to an abrupt halt and turned back to face her eldest son.

The budding ventriloquist, down on all fours, appeared to be intent on navigating a large tin dump truck around the perimeter of his brother's sandbox. But on receiving no immediate reply, he brought the truck to a halt, looked up through a thick fringe of brown hair and repeated his question.

Not for the first time, Joey Wilson reminded his mother of a grubby but amiable sheepdog. Hugging herself against the bite of a sharp, gusting wind, she gave him a smile.

"You need a haircut."

"Don't like haircuts. You going to the Taggerts?"

Margaret combined a nod with a shiver as a particularly strong gust set the hem of her flowered housedress flapping against her legs. It also carried a snatch of "The First Noel" from the house next door where Harriet, having bowed to the inevitable, had begun a stiff rehearsal schedule designed to last over the next ten weeks.

The seasonal music briefly jolted Margaret's thoughts into another channel—surely it wasn't that time already?—then released her to continue the conversation. Clutching her cup in both hands, she took a sip of coffee and reassured her son.

"I won't be long. How's His Majesty?"

They both transferred their attention to Davy Wilson, busily engaged in reconfiguring the sandbox interior with the help of his favorite toy, a yellow bulldozer executed in realistic detail down to black rubber treads and a bright orange blade. Indifferent to the fact that he had become an object of general interest, Davy continued shoring up his mound of sand, occasionally supplying a low "rrrm, rrrm" to help the machine on its way.

Joey sighed. "He's a pain. He won't even let me in there with him." By way of illustration, he assumed a bright, ingratiating manner and hailed his brother. "Hey, Davy! Why don't I bring my dump truck in with your dozer?"

"No." Davy pushed another load of sand into place.

"You could fill up my truck and then we could dump it."

"No."

"See?" Joey turned back to his mother, who had begun to hop up and down in an effort to keep warm. "That's all he ever says. I might's well not even be here." He added a nonchalant air to his voice. "I wouldn't go into that sandbox anyway. Sam Taggert piddles in it."

"No!" Davy looked up at last, eyes round with alarm.

"All the time. I seen him."

"No!"

"Joey, stop that!"

An ominous puckering around the bulldozer operator's mouth gave warning of imminent tears. Margaret knelt down beside the sandbox. "Don't pay any attention to Joey, darling. He's just teasing you." Davy's mouth remained screwed up. The moment had arrived for a carefully phrased question. "Do you want to come inside with Mommy?"

"No." Davy returned to his pile of sand.

Margaret stood up, feeling pleased with herself. Her book on child care couldn't have handled the situation better. But it had been a near thing. She frowned at Joey.

"Stop teasing your brother. You know what he's like."

Joey made a face and attempted to strangle himself.

Margaret's frown melted. "Just hold on a few more months. He'll be better when he's three." Another blast of wind suddenly framed her face with flying strands of shoulder-length brown hair. "I've got to get inside or I'll freeze. Be an angel and look after Davy for another half-hour." She set off again toward where the pickets ended on the Taggert fence. "And don't get him upset!" she called back.

"That's the only time he's any fun!"

"Joey!"

A drawn-out sigh floated after her on the wind, accompanied by a few notes of "Adeste Fideles."

Margaret let herself into the kitchen through the back porch, announced her presence with a loud "Whoo-hoo!" and walked through into the living room. Here she found most of the Taggert family disposed in various attitudes about the L-shaped sofa unit. Pulling up the chintz-covered easy chair, she sat down and nodded pleasantly at Tilly, who lay sprawled out on the right-hand sofa beside a large wine-colored *Book of Knowledge* and a visibly pregnant Veronica. Of her hostess, she could see only a pair of legs stretching horizontally from the other sofa to the edge of the cedar-chest coffee table. The rest of Kate remained hidden behind Sam, seated happily but precariously in her lap. Margaret therefore addressed her opening remark to the sandal-shod feet facing her across the cedar chest, pointing out that anyone who persisted in wearing shoes with holes in them would sooner or later suffer for it.

"I know." Kate's voice arrived from behind Sam's shaggy bulk in a slightly muffled condition. "But they're so comfortable." The endangered feet began to rock to and fro. "Come on, Sam. My legs are asleep."

Sam cast a fond glance over his right shoulder and thumped his tail on the sofa.

"Sam, get up."

Having only recently deposed Veronica from his present perch, Sam saw no reason to abandon it so soon. He therefore resumed his former position and stared out of the window in a placid, thoughtful fashion.

"Sam." Margaret patted her hands together in an enticing fashion. "Sammy. Come see me."

"Sam." Kate's voice took on a strained edge. "Off!"

Helped on his way by a firm shove from behind, Sam plopped sideways onto the floor, revealing a somewhat flushed and disheveled Kate clutching a green pencil in one hand and a pad of lined yellow paper in the other. He ambled over to Margaret and presented his head for attention.

"So," said Margaret, absently running her hand over the plush black fur. "How's the Great Christmas Pageant coming?"

Kate exhibited the pad, full of insertions, arrows and erasures. "Eugene O'Neill has nothing to worry about," she announced ruefully, then tapped a leather-bound book lying beside her on the sofa. "Why didn't someone warn me there's almost no conversation in the Christmas story?"

Margaret considered for a moment. "Doesn't Herod say something?"

"Not much."

"The Wise Men?"

"Just a couple of sentences."

"What about the angels?"

"Oh, the angels never shut up."

"There you are." Margaret spread both arms in a broad gesture of acceptance. "When in doubt, bring on an angel."

Kate looked unconvinced. "Most of what they say isn't very suitable for tiny ears. Speaking of which"—she turned to address her daughter—"don't you think it's time you went outside for a while?"

Tilly looked up from her book. "I'm just getting to a good bit."

"You can't concentrate with us talking."

"Yes, I can. I just shut my ears."

Kate smiled. "You said that about your eyes at the movies last Friday and you're still having nightmares."

"That was different. They showed the picture before I could get them closed."

"Well, it wouldn't hurt to get some fresh air. You could go to the store and pick up a can of corn for dinner. And take you-know-who." Kate wiggled her eyebrows in the direction of Sam, who was preparing to sit down on Margaret's lap.

Tilly closed her book with reluctance and managed to slide off the sofa without disturbing Veronica's slumbers.

"Take a dollar from my purse," added Kate. "And wear a sweater under your jacket."

"Okay." The word emerged as a semigroan. Then, more cheerfully, "Are you coming to my party, Mrs. Wilson?"

Margaret assumed an expression of bright interest. "Will it be a drunken binge with an orgy after?"

"No," Tilly giggled. "What's an orgy?"

"We've got everything planned," Kate put in hastily. "We're going to decorate the room and put out all of Tilly's games and have hot dogs and beans or corn, and then everybody goes out to trick-or-treat."

"That sounds good too." Margaret lowered her eyelids and adopted a thick accent. "I veel cawm as Geepsy Magda and tell vvvonderfull saxy forrrtune for aaaverybody."

Kate opened her mouth.

"Suitably modified for tiny ears," added Gypsy Magda quickly. "How many will there be?"

"Well, we haven't decided." Kate turned to Tilly. "You've got to make up your mind—either the whole school or just your own grade. One or the other."

Tilly gave a writhe of indecision. "I want everybody except Mona Meade."

"You can't do that. Everybody or just grade three. Say which. Halloween's only two weeks off."

"Okay." The answer came packaged in a sigh, punctuated by a kick into the carpet. "Everybody."

"Fine. But remember—when you give a party, you have to ask everybody nicely, make them feel welcome and see that they have a good time, Mona Meade included. Promise?"

"All right."

"Smile when you say that."

Tilly bared her teeth in a ghastly grimace. "All right."

"That's my brave little hostess. Don't forget the corn."

"If I meet Mona on the way she'll beat me up. Do I have to go?"

"Yes," said Kate impatiently. "Unless you intend to spend the rest of your life hiding out on this side of the river. Now, have a nice walk and don't be silly. If you meet Mona, try smiling at her, and if you can't do that, just leave her alone. I'm fed up with this Mona Meade business," she went on after Tilly and Sam had taken themselves off. "She's turning into an awful bully."

"The minister's daughter . . ." Margaret shrugged eloquently.

"I suppose." Kate made a few idle scribbles on her pad. "Tilly's been after me to talk with her father, but I think that would make things worse. Maybe the party will help."

Presented with an ideal opening for the purpose of her visit, Margaret sat up and became animated. "You missed a good party last night. Why weren't you there?"

"Oh, Jerry had to drive over to Springford, and I didn't feel like going by myself."

"Silly. You could have come with Dan and me, or later on when Jerry got back. The Allens missed dinner altogether because Margie made a terrible scene about being left alone, so they had to wait until she fell asleep and then sneak out. And Doug Barlow didn't make it until after eleven. Minus dear Pamela, of course." Margaret put her head on one side and became thoughtful. "Do you think Doug's cute?"

"Well . . ."

"Oh, I know he's not Jerry. But if I were Pam, I'd spend a lot more time at home with my husband and a lot less chasing around with those staff-house boys. Some day the word's going to get out that it's open season on Dr. Doug and then it'll be every girl to her guns." Margaret twirled a finger on the padded arm of her chair. "I wouldn't mind having a shot myself."

Kate made a face. "You've had a shot. You got Dan."

Margaret shrugged. "Of course, I wouldn't stand a chance. That's what I came over to tell you about." She began to smile. "You know what the McCreas' parties are like—more booze than food—which meant that later on in the evening nature called me off to the bathroom. And I'd just settled down on the throne when the door opened and in came Dr. Doug looking a million miles away and—I don't care what you say—*cute*."

Here Margaret allowed Kate a moment to picture this interesting scene in full.

"Well," she continued, "doctors know all about calls of nature, so I sat there and waited for him to notice me, but he just walked over to the sink and started washing his hands, leaving the door wide open and me on full display to anyone going in or out of the kitchen! No, wait"—Kate had begun to laugh—"it gets better. He kept on scrubbing up and staring at himself in the mirror and I kept on sitting and expecting to have to wave at someone passing by outside until at last I had to say *something*, so I said, very sweetly, 'Dougie, dear, do shut the door—it's getting drafty over here.' "

"And did he?" asked Kate obligingly.

"No!" Margaret widened her eyes. "He just turned and stared at me. And then Mike Reynolds came past from the kitchen and he *did* wave, so of course I waved back and Doug stood there with his mouth open and his hands dripping until I said, 'Well, if you don't want to go, why don't you *lock* the door?"

"Margaret!"

"Just to see what would happen."

"And?"

"He turned as red as a beet and ran like a rabbit." Margaret wiped her eyes and cleared her throat. "So I didn't make a conquest—and I had to get up and close the door myself!"

"Served you right—respectable wife and mother of two."

"I know." Margaret fluffed her hair back over her shoulders. "But sometimes it's fun to forget it. Don't you ever feel like that?"

A loud wail penetrated the room from the yard outside.

"Oh, damn," said Margaret.

Kate laughed. "His Majesty calls."

"Baw!"

"God save the king." Margaret collected her coffee mug and got up wearily. "I guess I'll have to go and see what the little bastard wants."

"Margaret!"

"What?"

"Baw!"

"Don't call him that."

Margaret grinned. "Who should know better than his mother? Next month he may be Little Lord Fauntleroy, but right now he's a bloody little Bee. Good luck with the play." And draining the last of her coffee, she let herself out the front door and ran off to make peace at home.

Kate listened as her friend's steps died away in the distance, then returned to her yellow pad. Exposing a fresh page, she took a deep breath and began to write in a large, purposeful hand:

"Scene One. The—"

She stopped. What did houses in Nazareth look like in the year zero? Did they have bedrooms? Living rooms? Did it matter?

"A room in the house of Mary and Joseph. Mary is—"

Another pause. Reading? Making bread? Doing a little dance? She bit her lip.

"Mary is weaving."

Too elaborate.

"Mary is sewing. Enter Joseph."

Hello, dear, what's for lunch? No. She drew a line through the last sentence and tried again.

"Enter a neighbor."

What on earth for? Stop wasting time, she told herself. Make the audience sit up and pay attention. She drew another line. What had Margaret said? When in doubt . . .

Ah, yes.

"Enter an angel."

And then . . . Congratulations, you're pregnant? No. A little on the abrupt side for an angel, although it had sounded just fine earlier this morning in the doctor's office when Doug strode in with a big grin on his face and delivered those very words. Of course, Kate reminded herself happily, she had been almost certain what he was going to say, so the situations were hardly comparable. And there would be no problem about telling Jerry when they finally got a moment alone, so that wouldn't produce any useful dialogue either. She frowned and nibbled the top of her pencil. The angel definitely had a tricky assignment. But, come to think of it, this might be an occasion where she could make a direct quote.

Relieved, she reached for the leather-bound book.

9

When Tilly emerged from her bedroom, suitably bundled up in a padded blue jacket topped off by a red woolen tam-o'-shanter, she discovered Sam waiting for her in an anxious frame of mind. Fearful that a plot might be afoot to slip out of the house without him, he had taken the precaution of planting himself directly in front of the door leading to the porch under the pretense of making a close study of its dull brass knob and keyhole. Tilly gave him a withering look.

"Oh, Sam," she said.

Sam waved his tail slightly and continued to inspect the doorknob.

"I won't leave you behind. Move over."

Without taking his eyes off the knob, Sam shifted a grudging fraction of an inch to the right.

"Sam!" Resigned to following an inflexible sequence of steps choreographed over a period of years, Tilly leaned against Sam's massive left shoulder and rocked with her full weight until she had succeeded in jostling him far enough to one side so that she could reach the knob and pull the door ajar. She then withdrew her hand and jumped nimbly backward as Sam, having immediately pressed his nose into the narrow opening, surged ahead to occupy a new position half in and half out of the kitchen, where he paused to await Tilly's next move. This involved squeezing sideways into the porch and following the same general sequence of steps to open the outer door after which, by way of a grand finale, both parties burst through the screen door beyond, scampered together down the outside steps and set off at a run toward the neighboring yard where the Wilson brothers continued to operate their heavy equipment.

"Tilly, Tilly." The first to spot their visitor as she ducked through the bare fence framework, Davy paused in his earth moving to beam and wave. "Play with me, Tilly!"

"Hello, Davy. Hi, Joey."

"Play with me!"

Tilly seated herself on a corner of the sandbox and accepted a small gardening trowel, once enameled red but now worn down to bright metal. Off in the distance, Harriet Reese began work on some preliminary chords to "Away in a Manger."

"Dig!"

With the tip of the trowel, Tilly cautiously extracted a few grains of sand from an area located as far as possible from the main excavation site. On meeting no objection, she began work on a small hole while her host, satisfied that the modest nature of this new enterprise offered no threat to his own project, resumed bulldozing to the accompaniment of a favorite tune, hummed under his breath.

"*Tilly-illy-illy,*" he sang.

"He won't let *me* do that."

This observation, delivered in a mournful growl, floated out of the air somewhere above Tilly's right shoulder. Joey had decided to make a remark, although without looking up from his dump truck.

"And I'm his brother," he added bitterly.

Tilly quietly filled in her dig and began again. "It isn't really me he likes," she said. "It's my name."

"Til-ly." Davy savored the word softly to himself.

"He'll probably get tired of it and start singing 'Joey.' "

"No!" Positively, from the sandbox.

"I don't care." Joey looked up with a sly grin. "Anyway, I can sing something, too."

"No!"

"*Jingle bells, jingle bells . . .*"

"Jingle, jingle, jingle, jingle!"

"He likes that one," Joey explained. "I been telling him about Christmas and Santa Claus and presents. He wants a tractor."

Tilly looked into the sandbox. "You've got a tractor, Davy."

"No, not like that! Davy, tell Tilly what you want for Christmas."

"Twactor."

"What kind of a tractor?"

"Big."

"How big?"

Davy made a gesture. "Big!"

Joey rolled back, laughing. "He wants a real tractor!"

"Don't tease him." At the age of three, Tilly had made the mistake of asking for the dappled milk-delivery horse that stopped outside her grandparents' home in Toronto, unaware that her adorable words ("Me want Spottie for Twistmas") would survive as a piece of family lore that never failed to bring a blush to its heroine's cheeks and tears to her grandmother's eyes.

"What do *you* want?" she asked, to change the subject.

But she already knew. For the past two winters, she and Joey had bumped themselves black and blue on the large metal eyelets used to secure the safety ropes around the edges of their toboggans. This year they intended to ask for new toboggans with soft leather loops instead of hard steel.

Replying as expected, Joey went on to augment his main choice with several smaller items culled from the expanded toy sections that made Eaton's and Simpson's winter catalogs required reading for every child in town.

". . . and a doctor's set with candy pills and one of those mirrors you wear on your head and a real penlight," he concluded. "What about you?"

"Oh, I don't know." Tilly reached out to pat Sam as he settled down beside her. "Margie Allen is getting a big bride doll with a veil and everything."

Joey reacted to this news with a quick glance from under his eyelashes.

"Thought you didn't like Margie."

Tilly shrugged. "She's different this year. She's . . ." Not having planned to say more, she paused, then continued in a rush. "She wants me to spend the night at her house."

Joey whistled. "What'd yer mom say?"

"Nothing."

"D'ja tell her?"

"No."

"Why not?"

Tilly shrugged again. "I guess I don't want to spend the night." Putting down her trowel, she stood up and brushed off her skirt. Sam got up too, panting hopefully.

"Where ya going?"

"The store."

Joey looked wistful. "Like to go too," he said.

"Well . . ." Tilly began.

"Gotta look after *him*."

They turned to look at Davy, now in the midst of burying his tractor with Tilly's discarded trowel. Next door, warming to her task, the put-upon pianist began harmonizing a descant to the basic "Away in a Manger" melody.

"All day?" asked Tilly, grateful once again for her status as an only child.

"Just till Mom comes back from your place. But"—Joey heaved a gloomy sigh—"you know what it's like when my mom and your mom get together."

Tilly nodded. Meals had been known to suffer and bedtimes come and go without a story. She prepared to set off on her errand.

"Except maybe . . ."

"What?"

Joey hesitated. "Well, it might work or I might get a licking. Anyway," he brightened, "at least I'll get away from *him*. Watch this. Davy . . ."

Attracted by a new note in his brother's voice, Davy looked up. Joey thereupon cast his eyes toward heaven and began to sing in a clear, steady soprano.

"There'll be bluebirds over the white cliffs of Dover
Tomorrow, just you wait and see . . ."

Davy set down his trowel. "No!" he announced in a loud, positive tone.

"There'll be love and laughter and peace ever after
Tomorrow, when the world is free."

"No!"

"The shepherd will tend his sheep,
The valley will bloom again,
And Davy will go to sleeeep—"

"Baw!"

"In his own little bed again."

"Baw!"

"There'll be bluebirds over the white cliffs of Dover . . ."

"Baw!"

"Tomorrow, just you wait—"

He broke off as his mother came striding around the front of the Taggert house. At the same time, the Christmas music from next door halted in midnote and a glint of rimless spectacles twinkled through the kitchen window.

"All right," said Margaret, panting a little as she scooped up her moist and tearful youngest. "What's wrong now?"

Joey regard her with wide innocent eyes. "Nothing. You know what *he's* like."

"No bed," howled Davy.

"Joey, you've been singing at him."

"Well . . ."

"About the white cliffs of you-know-what."

"Just a little. Tilly asked me to."

"I never!"

"Baw!"

"Oh, Davy, dear, do shut up." Margaret planted a kiss on the weeper's forehead and turned to Joey. "You know what I said about teasing your brother. I think you ought to go straight to your room."

"I wasn't—"

"Please, Mrs. Wilson." Having dissociated herself from the situation, Tilly felt free to step in with a plea for clemency. "If you make Joey go in, I won't have anyone to play with. Couldn't he come to the store with me?"

Back at her piano, Harriet attacked a Mendelssohn scherzo with resolute cheerfulness.

"How about it, Mom? Can I go?"

"Well . . ." Margaret gave Davy a little toss in the air to improve his mood and prevent her arm from going to sleep. "I suppose you're better out of the house than making trouble in it."

"Thanks, Mom."

"If you're going to the store, you could get me—"

"Bye, Mom."

"Joey!"

But Joey had already pelted off at full speed, closely followed by Tilly and Sam.

Freed from the role of stern parent, Margaret allowed a smile to turn up the corners of her mouth as she watched the last of Sam's tail vanish around the corner of the Taggert house. She then transferred her attention to Davy, whose face required some touching up with a wad of Kleenex kept handy at all times for just such a purpose.

"All right, my love. Time to go in."

Davy voiced his usual negative, but without conviction.

"And we'll open a can of applesauce, mmm."

Davy showed signs of interest.

"And we'll eat it all up," whispered Margaret in her most confidential manner. "Mmm. And we won't give any to anyone else."

"Mmm."

"Mmm." Margaret laughed and hoisted her son a little higher up on her right shoulder so that his arm came to rest naturally around her neck. At the same time, she experienced a shock of surprise as she found herself gazing into a pair of round trusting eyes that seemed to float like blue stars over a smile of angelic radiance.

Well! she thought, as this vision warped and blurred behind a film of sudden tears.

"Maybe I was wrong," she said to the glowing angel. "Maybe you're not such a little Bee after all. How's about a big kiss for Mommy?"

Davy made a face. "No!"

"On the other hand . . ."

Pulling her thoughts back to the subject of the applesauce, Margaret set off briskly for home.

10

Tilly soon fell behind in the dash for freedom that followed Joey's long-sought release. From time to time she caught a glimpse of Sam's white tail-tip beckoning on ahead, but for the most part she found it necessary to keep her eyes on the ground as she pelted through a barrier of bare, whiplike branches thrown into her way by the overgrown bushes on each side of the narrow path. An unfortunate encounter with a sharp twig reminded her that she was not having quite the pleasant recreational walk envisaged by her mother. And, as the sound of heartbeat grew louder in her ears and her breath began to come in gasps, she began to consider stopping in her tracks and turning back, because enough was enough and the sooner she braved the excursion into town and accomplished her errand at the store, the sooner she could return to her book. Just at that moment, however, she turned a corner and discovered Joey sitting on a large log at the top of a broad clearing in the bush where, within a few weeks, every child in town would be lining up with a toboggan or sled for a fast, bumpy ride downhill to the frozen river.

Glad of a rest, Tilly sat down on a natural depression in the log, polished to satin smoothness by many previous occupants and warmed by the last faint heat to be squeezed out of a pale, autumn sun. This comfortable spot offered a fine view across the river where, amid a grove of dark spruce trees, the recently rebuilt fire hall gleamed like a white cardboard box on the charred site of its predecessor. Overhead, two ravens on their way back to the garbage dump showed off by executing a perfect imitation of the double-barreled hoist signal while, deep in the bush on the other side of the path, Sam crashed about in search of a suitable object to carry until such time as something worthwhile, such as a wrapped loaf of bread or a parcel from the butcher, came his way. The noise brought an uneasy thought into Tilly's head.

"We've come in the wrong direction," she pointed out to her silent companion on the other end of the log. "We've got to go to the store."

Joey continued to squint across the pale blue river. "Lots of time," he said. "Let's go look at the old mine shaft."

A thrill of horror broke out at the base of Tilly's scalp and traveled down the back of her neck like a woolly caterpillar. She shook her head. "We're not supposed to go there."

"Who's gonna know?"

"And you can't see anything now they've fixed the door."

Joey heaved a weary sigh. "Didn't mean go *in*. Just outside."

"Anyhow, I don't want to."

"Why not?"

"I just don't."

"You're scared."

"I am not."

In the pause that followed, Joey regarded his companion with a quick sideways glance, then fixed his gaze on an innocent-looking drop in level halfway down the hill where, come winter, all those unfortunates still using toboggans with metal eyelets would sooner or later suffer major bruising.

"Heard that Ellie Hayes fell right down to the bottom," he observed.

The caterpillar on Tilly's neck rapidly worked its way down to her spine.

"An' when they found her, there was just bones."

This was too much. Tilly had not lived in the same house as a hunting cat for nothing.

"That's silly," she said. "She was gone on Friday and they found her Tuesday. Bones take way longer."

"Unless something ate her. Like rats or bats or—what's wrong with you?"

Two large tears overflowed down Tilly's cheeks. "I don't want to talk about it anymore," she announced. "And I don't want to go to that place." She stood up. "I'm going back to the store."

But Joey, too, had learned a few things at home. "I know what," he cried in the bright voice he generally reserved for dealing with Davy at his most tedious. "Let's go look at your mom's pictures on Mr. McCallister's house. Come on!" And without waiting for reply, he jumped off the log and raced away down the path.

As suddenly as it had come, the sadness released its grip on Tilly's heart, leaving her in a state of giddy happiness. With a call to Sam, who had just wrestled the skeleton of a six-foot pine tree out of the bushes, she put her head down and raced after Joey, pausing for neither twig nor branch until, quite without warning, a pair of heavy rubber boots appeared on the path directly in front of her. Two stout legs encased in heavy corduroy trousers rose out of the boots and eventually disappeared into the bulk of a heavy woolen mackinaw above which beamed a round, ruddy, cheerful face.

"And where are you going, my pretty maid?" asked Edward Reese, twinkling down at her through the same type of rimless glasses as those favored by his wife. "The correct answer is 'I'm going a-milking, sir,' " he added while the pretty maid tried to put out of her mind an unpleasant notion of what might have been said if she and Joey had been caught at the forbidden mine shaft by the mine manager himself.

"I'm going to look at Mr. McCallister's house," replied Tilly when her hammering heart allowed her to speak.

"You could start building one of your own," remarked Edward as Sam arrived with his tree. "But I don't think you should spend too much time around Mr. McCallister. He's not always—quite himself."

"I won't," said Tilly, thinking how unfair it was that she should be in this uncomfortable position while its perpetrator roamed free and undetected. "I just wanted to see Mom's pictures."

Edward's face softened again. "Ah, the Dramatic Club backdrops. A painted history of my acting career." He stepped back a pace and pointed an accusing finger at Tilly. " 'Too long have I kept silent. The truth will out. *You* are the daughter of Silas Twigg!'

I don't suppose you remember me in *Lucy of the Lighthouse?*" he asked hopefully.

"Not *very* well," said Tilly, who had been six years old at the time. "When Daddy tells about it, you say, '*I* am the daughter of Silas Twigg!' "

"Only on the first night," replied Edward in a wounded tone. "A perfectly natural slip of the tongue."

Tilly suspected that amends should be made. "I remember you in *The Mikado*," she offered. "Everyone laughed a lot."

Edward brightened. " 'Another insult,' " he intoned, weighing an imaginary bribe in his outstretched hand. " 'And, I think, a light one!' Yes. Not bad at all. Pity your mother isn't doing an operetta this year. How's she coming with the pageant?"

"She says she's sorry she started."

This news elicited a somber nod from Edward. "And life at our house is one continuous Christmas carol. We should have done *The Pirates of Penzance*." The thought inspired him to sing a few bars of "Oh, better far to live and die." Then, turning suddenly red, he announced that he had to be on his way.

"Don't go too near the McCallister place," he cautioned. "Or the river." And, with a pat on the head for Sam, he stumped off in silence down the path. After a few steps, however, he began to hum, and by the time he had turned the first corner Tilly could hear his rich baritone informing any passing chipmunk or rabbit that he was a Pirate King, hurrah! His voice continued to drift back even after the bold red and black checks on his jacket had disappeared behind the screen of gray branches, where a few tenacious leaves still provided a light sprinkling of yellow polka dots.

"Thought you'd got lost," remarked Joey from his seat on a mossy outcrop at the edge of a clearing in the wood.

"I met Mr. Reese," Tilly informed him. "He must have been over at the old mine shaft checking the lock on the door. We could've been caught if we'd gone."

Joey shrugged, unimpressed, and moved over a little so that Tilly could join him on a flat part of the outcrop in which golden-flecked veins of white quartz alternated with bands of gray stone to produce a design similar to the layered cream-cheese sandwiches currently in favor at Crow River afternoon bridge parties. Under ordinary circumstances, Tilly would have spent a pleasant quarter of an hour inspecting this rich treasure. But today the charms of geology paled to comparative insignificance beside those of architecture, as represented by the strange building in the middle of the clearing.

Constructed along opportunistic lines, using whatever materials came easily and cheaply to hand, Jack McCallister's home had begun life as a conventional log cabin, positioned to take advantage of a fine river view. It still presented this appearance to townspeople on the opposite shore, few of whom realized that, at the back of the house, Jack had assembled an exotic tentlike extension to his premises using stolen pieces of two-by-four lumber and cast-off backdrops painted by Kate for past Dramatic Club presentations. The sum of these disparate parts possessed a picturesque charm all its own. At the same time, the colorful conglomeration seemed so oddly out of place among the silent pine trees and barren bushes that, after making a close study of Jack's east wall—a rocky maritime landscape with a white lighthouse in the distance—Tilly began to experience the same mixture of fascination and doubt that Hansel and Gretel must have felt at their first view of the gingerbread house.

"Come on," cried Joey, jumping off the rock. "Let's see the pictures on the other side."

Tilly hung back. "We shouldn't go snooping outside other people's houses," she said.

Her remark gave rise to an exasperated sigh. "There's nobody in," said Joey in a voice of weary patience. "And we're not snooping. Come on."

Accordingly, he strode off in a counterclockwise direction, bypassing the lighthouse wall and the Japanese willow end flaps of the extension until he came to a halt opposite its west wall, painted to represent the library of a stately home, complete with wood paneling, bookshelves, a brocade bell-pull and, sketched in above the mantel of a massive fireplace, the portrait of a stern-faced ancestor in an ornate gilded frame. As on previous visits, the sight produced in Joey a deep sense of aesthetic satisfaction.

"Now that's real pretty," he informed Tilly.

"Damn right, sonny."

Startled by the high nasal voice from behind, the two trespassers spun about in their tracks to find themselves standing opposite a short, stocky man who seemed to have appeared by magic in the center of a nearby ring of birch trees. A shaggy mop of gray hair and a matching beard concealed most of his features; but gaps in the upper fringe revealed a well-polished snub nose, apparently carved from brown mahogany, and two black shoe-button eyes that never failed to remind Tilly of her much loved Raggedy Andy doll. Indeed, the newcomer might very well have been a stuffed doll, for his tall moosehide moccasins, baggy trousers and thick fur-trimmed parka all seemed to have been inflated to bursting point by countless layers of clothing in a manner calculated to confirm the popular suspicion that Glassy Jack McCallister carried his entire wardrobe on his person at all times. He also carried a soiled canvas knapsack, which he now swung over one shoulder as he set off in the direction of his house.

"Damn right," he repeated, tramping noiselessly across a bed of dried leaves and twigs. "That there is Art, and don't let nobody tell you different. And if you think it looks good from here, you just wait till you see it from inside. Well, come on," he called over his shoulder as Tilly and Joey showed signs of lingering on the path. "You come to see somethin', so come on and look."

And with that, he vanished into the lean-to through its willow-patterned flaps.

"Are you going to go in?" Tilly whispered as Joey took a step in the direction of the house.

"Sure. Why not?"

"Mr. Reese said not to. And we have to go to the store."

Joey spread his arms. "We'll *go* to the store. After we see inside. Anyhow," he added quickly as Tilly opened her mouth to protest further, "we've been invited."

This was true and unanswerable. Tilly knew that one always accepted a social invitation unless one could furnish an excellent reason for not doing so. She therefore followed Joey through the light fabric flaps of the lean-to, taking comfort from the fact that Sam, having set down his tree by the side of the path, had decided to attach himself to the party.

They found Jack waiting for them in the center of the enclosed space, apparently designed partly as a shelter for his ancient rusty Ford sedan and partly as a work area for curing skins. A shaft of sunshine entering through the open flaps revealed a number of these stretched taut in wooden frames and propped up against the log walls on each side of Jack's front door. Warmed by the incoming sun, the skins gave off an acrid smoky scent which, when blended with the stronger, sharper odor of Jack's moccasins, filled the room with a thick, heavy perfume of a unique and suffocating nature. Sam immediately began to investigate this intriguing new scent. Tilly, however, preferred to position herself in line with an incoming draft of fresh air until Jack cut off this resource and her hopes of a speedy escape by unfastening the entrance flaps and allowing them to drop shut.

Tilly's heart executed a palpable thump at the sudden change in light level, but leapt again as her eyes adjusted to the startling transformation in the room. She caught her breath and, in the same instant, heard a similar gasp from Joey.

"Yep," said their host. "Pretty, eh?"

Tilly moved her mouth, but could not reply. An inner voice, however, uttered a fervent Yes as the reeking lean-to, now lit from behind like a giant transparency, threw off its worldly disguise and stood revealed as a palace of wondrous possibilities where each luminous wall seemed to have become an enchanted doorway inviting her to step through the cloth into a different world. For although the thickness of the material and some of the overpainting produced opaque areas here and there, they more than compensated for this by bringing to each scene new qualities of depth and mystery.

The library now glowed with a rich, solid air, evoked by flashes of polished wood, leather and brass; while, on the adjacent wall, strange purple shadows twined around the delicate blue willow fronds that hung down from the slanted ceiling to frame a distant view of strange globular trees, pagodas and an odd little arched bridge suspended like a chunky crescent moon above a winding stream. In contrast to the delicate rendering of this exotic locale, the boulders along the base of the maritime scene took on mass and weight, the clouds popped out of the sky like fluffy cotton balls, and the sea glowed in deeper, more inviting shades of blue. Only the distant lighthouse suffered from this new perspective, for it appeared to have severed its connection with the land and become a fat firecracker ready to shatter the reverent hush that hung over the room until, at last, Jack cleared his throat, brushed away a sentimental tear and announced that if someone didn't get that effing dog's nose out of his knapsack he was going to kick it.

Joey instantly pulled Sam back by the collar while Tilly announced their immediate departure, explaining to anyone who might be interested that they had to go to the store. But her words went unheeded. Jack had already placed a cupped hand behind one ear and assumed an expression of intense concentration.

"Shh," he whispered.

Silence reigned once more, except for a light, rapid scrabbling sound on the cloth roof. Jack put a finger to his lips and bent down to the ear level of his guests.

"It's one of them damned ravens," he breathed. "Stay here."

And as silently as he had moved through the woods, he glided over to the log wall of his house, reached in behind a pile of stretched skins and returned with a double-barreled shotgun in one hand and a smooth stone the size of a tennis ball in the other.

"Okay," he whispered, pressing the stone into Joey's hand. "Can you hit the top of the roof with this? Good. Now when I say 'Go,' you count to three and then throw this here rock just as hard as you can. Ready? Go!"

Almost before he had uttered the last word, Jack hared out of the lean-to at a speed amazing for one his age. Tilly followed, reaching the canvas flaps just in time to hear the flat thump of Joey's stone against the fabric roof and see her host discharge both barrels of his gun at a target some distance above her head. The sound of the double explosion blended with a melancholy "gonk" that faded away in the direction of the river.

"Missed," said Jack, returning in a state of exhilaration with a glossy black feather tucked behind his right ear. "But I sure gave that flying poop-factory something to think about. Come on in."

He vanished into the house, with Joey and Sam at his heels.

Conscious of being abandoned by those who should have lingered to find out what *she* wanted to do, Tilly considered making them all sorry by setting off for the store at once and alone. But reason whispered in her ear that they might not be as sorry as she would wish. At the same time, caution stepped in to remind her that she might be grateful for Joey's company in the event of an encounter with Mona Meade, while curiosity demanded in an incredulous manner if she really intended to pass up a look inside the gingerbread house.

Thus advised, she threw proper pride to the winds, swallowed once and marched bravely through the door.

11

Tilly knew as well as anyone else in the third grade that reality seldom lives up to the promise of an active imagination. She was therefore delighted to discover, on entering Jack McCallister's house, that she had chosen well in assigning it a fairy tale counterpart.

To begin with, there to the right of the doorway loomed a massive cast-iron stove with an oven quite large enough to accommodate even the most substantial witch. A bin on the floor contained sufficient cut wood for hours of slow baking; water stood ready to hand in two large enameled pails; and a galvanized steel tub hung on a nearby spike in the wall. As for the other items of furniture—the narrow bed, the small square table and three chairs under the window in the far wall, the work counter near the stove, even the closet with the canvas curtain behind which Jack had temporarily disappeared—all sprang from the hand of one who, while lacking a convenient supply of gingerbread, cake and icing, had managed equally well with hewn logs, stripped tree trunks and whatever he could pick up in the way of finished lumber during late-night scavenging trips to the sawmill and building sites about town. Pictures and advertisements cut from magazines added color to the brown creosote-stained walls, as did three plank shelves bearing small wood carvings, several miniature birchbark canoes, a set of coffee tins labeled Pins, Thread and Buttons, two unmarked cardboard boxes and a basket overflowing with woolen socks to be darned. Dog-eared copies of *Time, Life* and *The Saturday Evening Post* lay in stacks on the floor. Otherwise, in accordance with the housekeeping standards set by children's literature for every respectable cottage in the woods, the room was as clean and neat as a new pin.

As always when this phrase popped into her head, Tilly began to wonder why a new pin should be particularly neat; but before she could come up with a fresh speculation or even a clear mental image of what a really messy old pin might look like, her host emerged from behind the cupboard curtain carrying a corked stoneware jug in one hand and, in the other, three small Coca-Cola glasses suspiciously similar to those used in the recreation hall lunchroom.

"Yep," he began after directing Tilly to take off her hat and sit down at the table, where Joey and Sam had already claimed places, "if there's one thing I can't stand, it's a raven. Messy bird. Tastes bad, sounds worse and got no respect for Art." Here he occupied the last remaining chair, set down the three glasses and, with painful concentration, manipulated the jug to pour an inch of bright red liquid into each. "That's why I rescued your ma's paintings from the dump," he continued, when this operation had been accomplished without mishap. "Got to thinkin' nights about all that there Art and beauty rottin' away with all them scraggy sons-a-bitches scratchin' and peckin' at it, so I just took a trip across the river and brought it back here. Cheers."

The glass and its luminous contents rose toward the horizontal slot in his beard, but sank down untouched when a high, thin note of anguish began to quiver in the air over the table. Jack took a quick backward look over each shoulder. On seeing nothing, he gave the right side of his head several thumps with the heel of his hand.

"What the hell *is* that?" he demanded when this remedy failed to result in the expected silence.

Tilly turned pink. "It's Sam," she said. "He thinks he's being left out. Sam, stop that."

Jack stared at his uninvited guest with distaste. "Don't suppose he will, though," he observed, "if he's one of them spoiled house pets that never does a lick of work."

Truth compelled Tilly to admit that Sam neither toiled nor spun.

Jack nodded slowly, in the manner of one who had expected no better. Then, heaving a sigh, he got up and disappeared once more behind the cupboard curtain. He returned bearing, on a cracked plate, four brownish-gray strips of some substance that, although clearly intended to be eaten, appeared to embody very few of the qualities Tilly normally associated with food. Casting about for an idea as to what it might be, she could come up with nothing better than pounded leather. Her heart went out to the eager, unsuspecting Sam, drooling by her side in pleasant anticipation.

"Oh, I don't think he could eat all that," she said in a small voice.

"Ain't all for him." Jack set the plate down on the table with a flourish. "One piece for the mutt, one for you, one for me and one for your pal here who don't talk."

"Not hungry."

This brief statement, delivered in a firm, deep voice from the hitherto silent end of the table, effectively drowned out Tilly's fainter protest. She aimed an accusing stare at Joey, but failed to catch his eye. Jack took a more direct approach.

"Don't give me none of that crap," he said jovially, helping himself to a leather strip and then shoving the plate toward the reluctant diner. "Kids is always hungry. Dig in."

Helpless in the face of a direct challenge, Joey dug in with all the enthusiasm of a Florentine upstart forced to share a meal with several smiling Borgias. Sam accepted his share of the feast in a similar manner and wandered outside holding it gingerly between the tips of his front teeth, like a cigar.

I bet he buries it, thought Tilly enviously as she gathered her courage and reached for the last morsel on the plate. Slowly she raised the unlovely object to her lips and bit off as small a piece as might be consistent with the rules for party behavior so often set forth by her mother. Cautiously she moved the piece back on her tongue and, unable to postpone the evil moment any longer, reluctantly chewed.

Neither as hard nor as tough as it looked, the mysterious food broke down easily in her mouth, releasing an odd combination of flavors in which a bland smoky background took on sometimes a fat gamy quality, sometimes a tart fruity sweetness enlivened by tiny granules that popped between her teeth. Tilly took another bite and smiled at her host.

"This is good," she said. "What's in it?"

Jack, who had a habit of casting his eyes up to a corner of the ceiling when thinking, cast them now while considering how best to summarize his recipe. "Bear, mostly," he said at last, wiping the back of his hand across his mustache. "And blueberries. Indian squaw taught me, but mine tastes better'n hers because I got a secret ingredient." He glanced over his shoulder to check for eavesdroppers before continuing in a confidential tone. "Add a slug of rye when I'm poundin' it up like my ma used to do with her Christmas pud. Helps stick the stuff together and keeps it good while it's dryin' out in the sun." He leered. "And it don't hurt the taste none either, eh?" Struck by a thought, he took another quick look at the ceiling, then reached over to one of the shelves on the wall and grasped a tall brown bottle. "I'd offer you a slug," he said as he added a generous tot of rye to the liquid already in his glass, "but yer mas wouldn't like it. Well, here's mud in yer eye."

Once more Jack raised his glass, inviting Tilly to do the same. Made bold by one successful venture into the unknown, she readily embarked upon another and drank without a qualm.

Summer exploded in her head at the first sip. For, at the same time as its intense sweetness cloyed on her tongue, the thick, viscous liquid released an almost overpowering fragrance that transported Tilly back to jam-making sessions in the kitchen and afternoons spent in secret parts of the woods where hot air shimmered, warblers sang in every bush, and heavily laden raspberry canes leaned forward to drop plump, warm berries into her empty lard pail almost of their own accord. Enchanted, she closed her eyes, raised the glass to her nose and inhaled the concentrated raspberry vapor until her head swam.

When at last, with a little shiver, she opened her eyes and returned to the present, she saw her dreamy mood reflected in Joey's face across the table. Jack, too, appeared to be similarly affected, but a closer look revealed that he was staring with misty eyes at a colored advertisement for canned soup hanging on the wall behind her left shoulder. The art work featured a pair of chubby toddlers, a boy and a girl, both with cannonball heads, pink dimpled faces, laughing eyes and auburn pixie curls falling down over their foreheads. Sighing, Jack drained his glass, bit a piece off the edge and, after a few alarming crunches, addressed Tilly.

"That little gal up there allus reminds me of yer ma," he confided, turning to stare out the window as his guests followed the progress of his snack with wide eyes and open mouths. "Specially like she was in *Lucy of the Lighthouse.*" He crunched a little more glass in a thoughtful way, then sighed again. "Oh, yeah," he continued between crunches, "she was supposed to act all cold and haughty-like, but you could see she wasn't that kind at all. And with her short hair and button nose and got up in that there white sailor dress, she mighta been a kid herself. Never seen nothin' like it. Pretty as any of that Art out there."

After a pause to sniff away a sentimental droplet at the end of his nose and make a quick exploration with his tongue somewhere in the region of his back teeth, Jack swallowed and addressed Tilly directly. "You'd look more like her if yer hair was short, but you'll do. And I'm gonna tell you somethin'." Bending down to a level directly opposite Tilly, he lowered his voice to a slow, hoarse whisper. "Sometimes I drink a bit too much here 'n' there. And sometimes I ain't so sure afterward if what I remember is real or not. But I remember some bad things. And if I was a little girl like you and my folks left me alone in the house at night"—he leaned closer into Tilly's face—"I'd make pretty damn sure all the doors was locked."

With this message off his chest, he straightened up, set the remains of his glass down on the table, and took a firm grip on the bottle of rye. "Well, thanks for droppin' by. I got some serious business to attend to now, so unless any of you wants some more to eat . . ."

They blurted out hasty farewells and fled.

"That was fun," said Joey as they stood outside the house considering what to do next. "Specially when he shot his gun and ate the glass."

Tilly nodded. "I'm glad he didn't hit the raven, though." She kicked at a pebble. "I wonder what he had in that big canvas bag he didn't want Sam to sniff at."

"Just a old red jacket."

"How do you know?"

"Took a look."

"When?"

Joey grinned. "When he run outside to get the raven."

Tilly grinned back, impressed by this show of initiative. At the same time, her eye came to rest on a stretch of river below Jack's house where a squat square-ended rowboat and its occupant were just about to drift past the small dock where Jack moored his canoe, fished and filled his water buckets. Tilly pointed at the familiar red and black mackinaw.

"Look," she said. "It's Mr. Reese again." A thrill of excitement jumped into her voice. "Oh, no it isn't. It's Dr. Barlow. Maybe he'll row us across the river!"

And, ready to face the worst that Mona Meade could offer if heaven would only grant a blissful quarter of an hour with Dr. Barlow, Tilly pulled off her tam, waved it in the air and began to run downhill toward the dock.

12

Unaware that she had just become one of the principals in a bargain with heaven, Mona Meade took a deep breath, clenched the tip of her tongue firmly between her teeth and, with the toe of her shoe, pressed down very gently on the sewing machine control button. Instantly the machine gave out a subdued roar and hurtled into action, churning material past the pressure foot at an alarming speed. Total loss of control seemed only a second away. However, by keeping a fast hold on her courage and concentration, Mona managed to produce a seam that, despite a few wavering departures from the straight and narrow, could pass all but the most critical inspection.

Not that anyone was going to inspect it, Mona told herself by way of encouragement, or even notice if the skirt turned out all crooked. That was one of the advantages of having no friends: it didn't matter how you looked or what you wore, any more than it mattered if you were pretty like Miss Walter and Margie Allen or plain like, well, like someone she would see if she crouched down under the sloping attic roof and risked a look into the faded mirror at the back of her small dressing table. It would be sad, though, if she had ruined a perfectly good dress. The very thought allowed a creeping chill to penetrate the thick woolen bathrobe she always wore when spending any time in her bedroom. Perhaps it might be a good idea to put everything aside and look at it again tomorrow. But, after all, she would only spend the next twenty-four hours worrying about it. Better to know the worst at once.

With a shiver, she stepped out of her robe and slipped the dress over her head. Even after two years in the closet, it still gave off a hint of the light floral scent that somehow remained a stronger part of her mother's memory than the more precise details of voice and appearance. But as soon as she pressed her face into the soft, fine wool and took a deep breath in an attempt to recapture a more solid sense of the past, the elusive fragrance pulled away from her like a mirage, became fainter and vanished altogether.

There was nothing for it but to let the dress fall into place and fasten it up, a process that turned out to require a surprising amount of athletic agility. At last, after a good deal of twisting and writhing, she managed to get a grip on the zipper in the back, work it gradually upward and complete the closure at the neckline by fitting a tiny metal hook into an even tinier metal eye. These contortions left a generally satisfactory impression as to the matter of fit without telling her anything at all about how she looked. She needed a mirror.

Certainly the one on the dressing table would not do. It enveloped its subjects in a thick mist and, in any case, could display a standing figure only in progressive sections, a few inches at a time. She must therefore make an excursion downstairs to her father's bedroom where, once upon a time, her mother had caused a fine walnut-framed pier glass to be hung behind the door.

Skillfully avoiding those floorboards with a tendency to creak and then, when the boards came to an end, stepping lightly across the exposed wooden joists, Mona managed to gain the top of the stairs without producing any jarring sounds likely to travel downward and disturb her father, presently at work in the little room off the kitchen that had once been hers before the pressure of his accumulating books and papers had pushed her upstairs. A tiptoed descent brought her into a small square hallway giving access either straight through into the living room, right into the bathroom or left into the kitchen, beyond which she could hear her father intoning a trial passage from tomorrow's sermon. Reassured that she could count on some time alone, Mona moved quickly through the living room into the main bedroom where, without a pause, she switched on the light, closed the door and presented herself for judgment to the cold, impartial glass.

She would have given a good deal to have it lie outrageously. Any truly charitable mirror, she felt, faced with such an unpromising beanpole, would have cast a kindly spell and carried out a little tactful remodeling. If she could be just six inches shorter, with an invisible neck, legs that didn't look like two drinking straws, and hands and feet of a size to match the rest of her body, then she could bear everything else. The lank blond hair that Bob Dwyer the barber kept trimmed to chin level and pulled off to one side with a celluloid bow clip, the long pale face with its angular cheekbones and huge gray eyes apparently devoid of lashes or brows, the full lips and wide mouth so unlike Margie Allen's adorable rosebud, all these she would suffer without complaint if only some kind fairy would wave a wand and transform her into just another unexceptionable thirteen-year-old, of average height, with no distinguishing features to set her apart from the other unexceptionable thirteen-year-olds occupying the row of desks given over to the eighth grade. But since she had asked this in her prayers every night for the last three years to no avail, it seemed unlikely that any minor supernatural power would step in where God had refused to act. With a heavy heart, she turned her attention back to the remodeled dress.

It was the last garment her mother had bought before her final illness, but she had worn it a good deal that winter and Mona could still put together a hazy image of how lovely she looked just before donning her coat on the way out to a bridge party or afternoon tea. Dark green had always been her color, thanks to the red highlights in her hair, and the style typified her mother in that it combined the sobriety expected of the minister's wife, as expressed by the modestly draped neckline, with just a dash of something more daring in the form of a dropped waist gathered into a silk bow at the right hip. Worn with a hat like an inverted plate, sheer stockings, smart little open-toed shoes and perhaps a discreet spray of icebox flowers for special occasions, it never failed to take Mona's breath away and bring forth a compliment from her father, just as it never failed to make certain Crow River ladies remark to others that young Mrs. Meade seemed, well, just a little frivolous for her position in the community, don't you think, dear?

People could be very severe in their judgments. Mona set her mouth and prepared to do likewise with regard to herself. Well, at least the hem was all right. They couldn't laugh at that. And the material was good. Her mother had always believed in quality. A belt would take care of the excess inches at the waist, the silk bow could be removed, and she had no objection to the way the soft folds of the neckline concealed that part of her chest where, if heaven smiled, she might one day develop something to conceal. True, the dark green color brought out the sallow tone in her face, and her only accessories—pink or blue barrettes, thick cotton stockings and heavy shoes—seemed at odds with the general style of the garment. But it might all have been very much worse, if only it weren't for . . . if only it hadn't . . .

As always, the main trouble lay in the shoulder padding, which grafted onto her thin frame an imposing breadth more appropriate to planning a career in sports rather than simply hoping to get through the day without comment *(Hey, look! Mona's wearing her hockey pads!)*. She knew from a previous experiment that removing the pads would do no good. The dress had simply sagged and died like a partially deflated balloon from which every reminder of the previous wearer had fled. And Mona, faced with a choice between providing merriment for the rabble *(Got your stick in there, too, Mona?)* and giving up the comforting sense of her mother's presence, had put back the pads and prepared for the worst.

For, really, it hardly mattered what she did. If they didn't laugh, she knew they whispered behind her back. It hadn't been like that when her mother was alive. Turning away from the mirror Mona wandered over to the bed and flopped down on her back. Life had been so easy, back in that golden age. Even when her father had left to go overseas, things had gone on much as usual. Without her even having to think of it, meals appeared at mealtimes, presents at birthdays, and new clothes in larger sizes just when she needed them. Reason and certain Sunday school teachings told her that she ought to be grateful for past happiness, however short. Still, when everyone she knew continued to lead a regulation life in conjunction with the standard number of parents, she couldn't help but suspect that, somewhere along the way, she had been shortchanged.

It wasn't that her father didn't love her. She knew he did. But he had always been helpless in domestic matters, so it was only natural that she should have taken over the running of the house. And how could he spend more time with her when he had so many important things to worry about? Things like the starving children of Europe, to take just one example. Since the end of the war, part of Mona's room had been home to several large cardboard boxes full of cast-off clothing, tirelessly collected by her father for the relief of those unfortunates. And for as long as she could remember, his weekdays had been taken up with study and writing, and his nights with vestry meetings, choir meetings, Ladies' Church Committee meetings, Sunday school meetings—the list of meetings never ended. In bygone days, her mother had always claimed Friday nights as belonging to the family, but now he often spent that night out as well, leaving Mona to go to the movies by herself.

So it was not surprising that he failed to notice when her clothes became too small or wore out, any more than he noticed or complained about what she fed him or how she ironed his shirts. He had never been up to her room in the attic, so how could he know that the remodeling work, initiated just before her mother's illness, had never been completed or that she had outgrown her bed? If she asked, of course, he would give her anything. But she already asked for so much—shoes, stockings, outerwear, gloves, money for haircuts, money for the movies, money for the store, the butcher, the bakery. The demands on his resources seemed enormous.

At least—here her sagging spirits lifted a little—at least she didn't have to trouble him about the things she could make for herself. From the moment she had obtained access to the long white muslin bags hanging on her mother's side of the closet and, by a painful process of trial and error, taught herself to use the sewing machine stored just beneath them, that had been her pride. Despite the laughs and whispers *(hockey, hockey)*, despite the resulting battles and her growing reputation as a bully (but who cared?), despite the frequent temptations to raid the cardboard boxes in her room and appropriate for her own use just one dress from the abundance destined for the backs of those chic little orphans in war-ravaged Europe, she managed to take comfort from the quiet sense that in some small way she was lightening her father's burden at a time when he must be feeling (although he never spoke of it) as lonely and sad as she.

Still, thought Mona, as she tipped herself off the bed, it *would* be nice to be like everyone else and wear plain, ordinary dresses, like the ones in the beautiful colored pictures in Eaton's and Simpson's catalogs. There was one especially, a pale blue check with a little lace collar . . .

But she had better things to do than mope about dreaming of a dress she was not going to get. Giving herself a little shake, Mona returned to the mirror. Soon it would be time to start dinner and there were still a few things she could do with the dress she had. She might try cutting down the shoulder pads just a little, and resetting—

"Mona! Mona dear!" The tentative voice arrived in a muffled state from some distance away. "Are you up there?"

Mona opened the door and discovered her father standing in the little hallway at the far end of the living room, preparing to call upstairs once again.

"Mona!"

"I'm here, Daddy."

The Reverend Augustus Meade executed a slight leap in the air, turned around and blinked at his daughter through large horn-rimmed spectacles. Never a dapper man, even when dressed under strict supervision, he appeared to have spent the night in his clothes. His voluminous gray trousers sagged over the tops of his scuffed slippers, his gray woolen cardigan showed signs of following a similar route to his knees, and the knot of his stained tie lay twisted under the limp collar of his flannel shirt. To match this air of disarray, his long graying hair, instead of sweeping back from his face in its normal Sunday attitude, had slipped its side moorings and collapsed over his ears. These signs, together with a faintly dazed expression in her father's eyes, informed Mona that tomorrow's sermon had not yet come together on the page.

"You're still wearing your old shirt," she said. "What happened to the nice clean one I left out on your bed?"

"Ah." Mr. Meade pulled a fold of the offending shirt from under his cardigan and stared at it blankly. "Ah," he said again, brightening. "The object on my bed. I thought you had had a mishap in the wash with my nightshirt. Chilly knees all night."

"Oh, Daddy."

"No matter, no matter." Mr. Meade waved an airy hand. "I shall put it to its correct use tomorrow. Today I have more important matters on my mind. That unfortunate scene after last Sunday's service . . ."

Mona nodded. Everyone in town knew about Alec Barrie's staunch Protestant reaction to the two quite small candles placed on each side of the altar by Mr. Meade. Having turned a variety of colors over the course of the service, from pink to a rich shade of purple, Alec had barely waited for the final notes of the organ to die away before expressing his outrage at the introduction of insidious Anglican accouterments into what was supposed to be an interdenominational church, all in language equally unsuited to his surroundings, his standing as store manager, and the delicate sensibilities of those slower-moving members of the congregation still on their way out of the building. Several ladies, including Harriet Reese, took the precaution of covering their ears. Nevertheless, enough was heard to enliven many a Sunday lunch and prompt some speculation that the Crow River All People's church might require reconsecration.

"I am attempting a slight rebuttal in tomorrow's sermon," continued Mr. Meade, "based on Matthew 5:15. 'Neither do men light a candle, and put it under a bushel.' But it is not turning out the way I would wish." He blinked again. "It occurred to me that a cup of tea might improve matters. Will you make it, or shall I?"

"I'll make it, Daddy."

"Thank you, dear. And after that, if you have nothing else to do, perhaps you could take this letter up to the mine office for me."

"Well . . ."

"It's to the bishop, and I want to make sure it gets out on Monday's plane."

"All right."

"There's my good girl. Don't go to any fuss with the tea. Just a plain cup, with perhaps one or two of your delicious cookies on a plate. 'Neither do men light a—' " Preparing to depart on a quotation, Mr. Meade stopped abruptly and looked again at his daughter. "Isn't that one of your mother's dresses?" he asked.

Mona blushed. "I've shortened it for school. Is it all right?"

"Very nice." Her father put his head on one side. "Of course I know little of these things, but don't you think perhaps . . ."

(Hockey, hockey.)

"I'm taking the bow off."

"Ah. The bow. Yes." Mr. Meade nodded vaguely. "That would do it. You're sure you have time for my letter?"

Mona sighed. "Yes, Daddy."

13

Tilly, Joey and Sam stood in a row at the end of Glassy Jack's dock and waited patiently for Dr. Barlow to bring his boat alongside, a complicated maneuver that appeared to require a good deal of spinning about on the spot, rescuing of oars and mumbling under the breath. Eventually, however, the river itself took charge and swung the boat into a controlled collision with one of the supporting piles, after which the doctor removed his gray felt hat, wiped his brow and informed his audience that displays of rowing such as they had just witnessed were not to be seen on the river every day of the week.

"What are you all doing here?" he asked, mopping his forehead once again before replacing the hat at a rakish angle on the back of his head.

"Going for a walk," Joey replied quickly, before Tilly could reveal any specific details that might not meet with adult approval.

Tilly, however, had no wish to speak. She felt quite content to stand and enjoy the pleasant sight of dark eyes twinkling under even darker brows, strong white teeth shining in a bold jawline, and sun highlights gleaming in the tousle of light brown hair pushed forward by the doctor's battered hat. At the same time, she knew that she must say something to further the conversation. She mentioned her errand in town.

Douglas Barlow's face fell. "And I thought I was called over to display my brilliant wit and delightful conversation, when all you wanted was a ride to the other side. Right?"

Tilly and Joey grew bashful, but managed to beam and nod.

The doctor sighed. "Well, get in. But don't be surprised if I begin at the end of the alphabet when it comes time for the next round of inoculations. You can sit at the back there. Do we have to take the dog? What a silly question," he said, clinging hard to the side of the rocking boat as Sam stumbled past him on his way to the prow. "Now is everyone quite settled? Nobody wants *my* seat? Then here we go."

"I hope you realize this is very kind of me," he remarked when they had safely negotiated the delicate process of pushing off. "Here I am running a ferry service, just when the fish are biting."

Joey inspected the back of the boat and under the seats for signs of a catch. "Don't see no fish."

The doctor's eyebrows rose. "What do you call that?" he asked, jerking his head toward the bottom of the boat.

Joey followed his gaze. "Water."

"*Now* it's water. But what do you think it was before?"

"Water."

"I can't believe my ears." The doctor appealed to Tilly. "Lived up here all his life and doesn't know a melted ice-fish when he sees one."

Tilly, who loved being teased, giggled. "That's not a fish."

"You too! What grade are you in? Third? I don't know what Miss Walter teaches you all year long. When I was your age, my Uncle Max used to take me out every—" Astonishment robbed the doctor of his words. He looked back and forth from one delighted passenger to the other. "You've neither of you heard about ice-fish?"

They grinned and shook their heads.

"Well! It's clear that this meeting was planned by Fate." Changing to a light oar stroke, the doctor halted the boat in midriver. "You've seen the photograph of Uncle Max in my office?"

Both remembered the picture. Uncle Max, very young in a leather jacket and helmet with goggles, stood proudly by the wing of a flimsy biplane that looked as if it had been put together with string and glue from a kit of parts. He had fought and died in the First

World War and had been given a medal. They stopped grinning and nodded solemnly.

"Very well." Having managed to produce a pipe from his jacket pocket and light it, Dr. Barlow withdrew the stem from his mouth and pointed it at his young audience. "What my Uncle Max told me from his bottomless well of wisdom, I will now pass on to you." He took another puff. "Know, then, that the *piscis frigidus*, or ice-fish, is related to the tasty pickerel with which it shares these waters. Know, too, that it resembles its cousin in almost every respect except for one major difference: it is made of ice. Scales, skin, eyes, bones, teeth, insides—all made of ice."

"What does it eat?" asked Joey.

"Ice," said the doctor. "And, being clear as crystal, it is absolutely invisible in the water. Which is why you never see one when you're in swimming."

It was Tilly's turn to ask a question. "But there isn't any ice in the summer. Wouldn't it melt?"

"Of course it would." The doctor gave her an approving nod. "I was wondering if you'd think of that. Summer is the ice-fish's worst enemy. So before the water begins to get warm, every sensible fish digs a hole in the river bank and fills it full of ice—just like Mr. Barrie does in the icehouse behind the store. Then, when summer comes, the ice-fish packs himself away in his burrow and hibernates until it's winter again. Like a bear, except the other way round."

"How does it know when it's winter again?"

The doctor released a stream of smoke into the sharp river wind. "When it burrows into the ice, it goes backward so that just the tip of its nose sticks out. The nose has a little bump on the end, and this bump senses when the water is cold enough for the fish to wake up and start swimming again. Very clever, really."

Joey considered this information carefully. "If they're all asleep now, how'd you catch one?"

Tilly's heart beat a little faster as the doctor treated them to a broad smile. "I thought you'd never ask. Well, just as a bear wakes up now and again during the winter, so does an ice-fish when the water is beginning to turn cold. And the trick is to have a big empty hook hanging in front of his burrow when he opens his eyes, because when he sees that big empty hook, of course he thinks there's a piece of invisible ice on it. Then it takes a big bite and you've caught an ice-fish."

"So how many did you catch today?"

The doctor inspected the small puddle of water at his feet. "Two," he announced. "Not counting the whopper that got away. Five pounds if he weighed an ounce."

Joey frowned. "Don't believe you."

"Well, maybe four pounds."

"You made all this up."

"Would Uncle Max lie?" The doctor tapped his pipe on the side of the boat, replaced it in his pocket and began rowing toward the swimming dock. "And me a man of science with no imagination at all! Just for that, I won't ask Miss Walter to let me come and address the school on the subject of natural history, and you'll go out into the world ignorant of countless marvels not discussed in even the most up-to-date *Book of Knowledge*. No, no! It's too late to beg. My feelings are wounded and my mind made up. Well, here we are." They thumped sharply into the upstream side of the dock, allowing Tilly and Joey to pull themselves up and over the edge. "How's His Lordship going—?"

But before he could finish his question, Sam moved forward, struck a delicate pose with all four feet bunched together on the front edge of the boat, and plunged into the water.

"Nice doggy," said the doctor when he had dried his face and wrung himself out. "And stop laughing. I'm very uncomfortable."

"Looks like you've caught some more ice-fish," said Tilly, pointing down at the bottom of the boat, now thoroughly awash.

"I'll probably catch a cold." The doctor sniffed. "Which even I cannot cure. Or pneumonia. Next time you can all walk. Goodbye."

He rowed off, sneezing pathetically.

"Like to see one of those old ice-fish," remarked Joey after they had left the dock and headed in thoughtful silence across the yellow grass toward the recreation hall.

"I thought you didn't believe in it," said Tilly.

"Well." Joey took a moment to think the matter through more carefully. "Maybe I don't, but I'd still like to see one."

Another silence ensued. At last Joey spoke again.

"Maybe when it gets colder we could go to that hole Mr.

McCallister cuts in the ice to get water and I could lower you down on a rope with a flashlight. You'd prob'ly see a whole bunch of ice-fish."

"Dr. Barlow says you can't see them in the water."

"Then you could take a net down with you and swish it about and catch one."

"It'd be too cold and you wouldn't be able to pull me out. You're the one who wants to see them. You go."

They passed the recreation hall and made a right-hand turn onto the main road.

"I know!" Joey came to a halt. "We could get Davy to do it! Then we could both hold onto the rope and pull him up when he ran out of air."

"How would we know when that was?"

"We'd have to test him." Joey's face became radiant. "We could fill up the bathtub with cold water and put in a lot of ice cubes and get a watch—"

"I don't think he'd like that."

"Well, we wouldn't *tell* him about it till we did it."

"Your mom wouldn't like it either."

Joey kicked a stone in disgust. "I guess," he said. "But I sure would like to see one of those ice-fish."

They walked on, following the road as it curved to the left around a small log building, lifted itself over the boxed-in pipeline, and came down again at a point where, had they felt in need of a longer walk, they could have entered the residential part of town, which stretched away to the right of the road, or proceeded straight ahead past the school, the All People's church, the Roman Catholic church, the hotel and the hydropower plant until, if their legs held up for another seven miles, they reached neighboring Springford Mines. Having already spent an eventful afternoon, however, they turned their backs on the town and headed toward the store.

A short distance farther up the road, picked out in sunlight against the white wall of the school, two girls of about Tilly's age solemnly turned a long length of skipping rope for a third, while several others waited in line to take their turn at jumping in. The sound of their high, clear voices came wafting across a tangle of bare willow bushes, dried grass and dead fireweed.

"*On yonder hill there stands a lady,*" they sang,

"*Who she is I do not know*
All she wants is gold and silver
All she wants is a fine new beau
So send in my dear Mar-GEE
My Dear Mar-GEE
My Dear Mar-GEE
So send in my dear Mar-GEE
While I go out to play."

At the last note, the incumbent deftly skipped out on a downward stroke of the rope as another girl skipped in, pleated skirt flying and glossy brown ringlets abounce. Joey stopped and pointed.

"That's Margie," he observed.

"Yes," said Tilly.

"You gonna tell 'er you're not spending the night?"

"I guess . . ."

"*So send in my dear Shir*-LEE
My dear Shir-LEE
My dear Shir-LEE"

"Wanta tell 'er now?"

"*So send in my dear Shir*-LEE . . ."

"No." Tilly started up the steps that led to the broad entrance platform in front of the store, famous as the site where onlookers had finally managed to part Sam and Brandy, the Wisnickis' massive St. Bernard, after their epic battle through the vegetable and canned-goods sections. "Let's go in."

They found Alec Barrie alone behind the cash counter where he kept guard over such pocketable items as cigarettes, chocolate bars and any flavorings or hair tonics with an alcoholic content high enough to interest the likes of Glassy Jack in search of a quick pick-me-up. He greeted Tilly and Joey with wary cordiality.

"Hello, Mr. Barrie," said Tilly in her most ingratiating manner. "Can Sam come in too?"

Alec, who wore severe steel-rimmed spectacles and fought daily battles against a head of thick wavy hair in the vain hope of adding years and a measure of authority to his otherwise pink and boyish face, regarded Tilly with what he hoped was a withering look. In case the look failed to wither, he mouthed a silent "No."

"He gets lonely outside."

Alec shook his head.

"Yours is a heart of massive rock, Mr. Barrie," said Tilly, seizing on an appropriate quote from one of Edward Reese's Gilbert and Sullivan recordings, "unmoved by sentimental shock."

"You bet," Alec agreed, ignoring a peremptory bark from outside the door. "What can I get for you?"

"I can find it." Tilly swung around on one foot and wandered off behind the tall display island that ran down the center of the room.

"Nice red hat," Alec called after her. "Where'd you get it?"

"My grandmother knitted it," replied Tilly. "For my birthday. She thinks it's cold here all year round."

With Joey in tow, she made a slow progress between stacks of cans, bottles, packets and boxes until she came to the rear of the store, home to hanging clusters of rubber boots and racks filled with blue denim overalls, heavy gray socks, tan and olive cotton pants, a few matching shirts and a generous supply of red and black mackinaw jackets. These, however, held no fascination for either of our shoppers, both of whom responded to the call of a long illuminated glass counter set across the front of the clothing section. Elbow to elbow, they draped themselves over the edge and, breathing intently, stared down through thin veils of mist that came and went on the glass.

If the contents of the counter seldom varied, neither did their charm. At one end, bright hunting knives with handles of black Bakelite and carved wood nestled beside stitched leather holsters, flashing fish hooks, lead sinkers, wire leaders, spools of fishing line and glossy multiplier reels. These gave way, by midcase, to a pleasing jumble of beadwork bookmarks and coin purses, dainty figurines that tasted of salt when licked, an assortment of small Celluloid mascot dolls, sunglasses with green or blue lenses and, in the stationery section, fountain pens, automatic pencils and a costly new type of writing instrument guaranteed to perform its function even under water.

"We could give Davy one of those to draw us a ice-fish," murmured Joey. " 'Cept he only draws tractors."

Tilly failed to respond adequately to this interesting suggestion. Instead, she moved farther along the counter to her ultimate destination: an illuminated compartment lined with mirrors and filled with a veritable treasure-trove of gem-encrusted costume jewelry. Several pins already occupied a place in her heart, especially a solemn owl with emerald-green eyes, a silver lady in a dimpled crinoline skirt, and a bouquet of flowers that could hardly have sparkled more alluringly had they been made of real rubies and sapphires. But, like every other girl in her age group, she lingered longest in front of a satin-lined pink velvet box, hinged open like a clam to reveal a heart-shaped silver locket. On the hinged cover of the locket, picked out in delicate engraving, a hummingbird with a long curved bill hovered over a tiny pearl.

"Ellie Hayes was going to get one like that," she said softly.

Joey edged over to follow the direction indicated by her finger. "She never! Look at how much!"

And indeed, a discreet black tab on the satin lining carried the figure "$18.99" in gold letters.

"She told me."

"Never told me."

"She—" Tilly tore her eyes from the locket and turned her back to the counter. "It was a secret."

While they had been poring over the novelties, a third customer had entered the store. Small and slim, with an oval face, wide gray eyes and dark shoulder-length hair, she wore a wine-colored woolen jacket fashionably flared at the back, a bright paisley scarf, a plaid skirt and comfortable crepe-soled walking shoes. One of these shoes rotated idly in the air while its owner leaned across the counter to chat with Alec, but returned rapidly to earth when Joey and Tilly approached.

"Hello, you two," said the newcomer as Tilly deposited a can of corn and her dollar bill on the counter. "What a nice red tam."

"My grandmother made it," replied Tilly, who always felt a little tongue-tied on the rare occasions when she encountered her teacher outside the schoolroom.

Fortunately, Diana Walter had no such problem. "How's your mother getting along with the Christmas pageant?" she asked.

"She's working hard."

"Yeah," Joey agreed. "Sometimes I can hear her from the yard."

Diana laughed. "Well, as soon as she decides which Christmas carols she wants to use, maybe you could let me know so we can start learning them. I think Mrs. Reese is a bit anxious about that. And any time she wants to start rehearsing *Santa's Magic Toy Shop* is fine by me. Are you going to be Santa again, Alec?"

"Well . . ." Alec adjusted the set of his spotted bow tie and coughed. "I thought I'd give someone else a chance this year so I could . . . I mean, I don't want to be stuck in a Santa suit for the dance afterward."

Diana flushed a becoming shade of pink. "That's all right. We can find someone else. But you'll have to turn in the suit."

"Turn in?" Alec looked puzzled. "Haven't you got it?"

"Me?"

"Yes. I hung it up in the dressing room with the other costumes when I went home."

"And I thought you'd given it back." Diana hesitated as an idea occurred. "It belonged to the Taggerts. Maybe Kate—oh, that is . . ." She darted a glance at Tilly and tailed off in confusion.

"That's all right," Tilly assured her. "Daddy used to pretend to be Santa Claus when I was little, but he stopped last year. Mommy said she didn't want it back."

"So someone walked off with it." Alec shook his head. "I should have hidden it away."

Diana shrugged. "We can make another. But it's too bad all the same. Please tell your mother I'm sorry," she added, as Tilly and Joey prepared to depart.

"Don't forget your corn." Alec handed a brown bag and some change across the counter. "And here." He produced a round sandwich cookie with jam in the middle. "For Sam. It's a bit stale, but he won't mind."

"Thank you," said Tilly, who had a better knowledge of Sam's epicurean tastes. She paused at the door. "I'll tell him you're sorry you couldn't let him in."

"Only if you want a lie on your conscience."

Tilly smiled and let the door swing shut behind her. The only lie she expected to tell in the foreseeable future was something quite harmless—more of a fib, really—to avoid spending the night at Margie Allen's house. She hoped to put off the evil moment for as long as possible but, when she glanced up the street, the first thing that met her eye was Margie marching toward her in a purposeful manner.

Quailing within, Tilly offered Sam his cookie and braced herself for perjury.

14

"Hello, Tilly."

Margie came upon Tilly and Joey at the top of the store steps while Sam sniffed suspiciously at his cookie.

"Hi, Margie," said Tilly. "Make up your mind, Sam."

"Hi, Margie," said Joey.

Margie tossed her glossy brown ringlets and continued to address Tilly. "I was just coming to ask Mr. Barrie if I could use the store phone to call you."

At this point, Sam opened his mouth a fraction of an inch and allowed Tilly to post the cookie.

"I've been out a lot," she said as Sam demolished his morsel in three crunches and a gulp.

"That's okay." Margie put on her best smile. "Are you going home now? I can walk you as far as the cookery."

"Well . . ." Tilly glanced uneasily at Joey.

"There's some kids starting a baseball game," said Joey. "Let's go play."

Margie acknowledged the presence of a third person with a cold look. "You go," she said, seizing Tilly's hand in a firm grip. "I want to talk to Tilly."

Joey stood his ground. "Wanta play, Tilly?"

Tilly opened her mouth to accept, only to be interrupted by a sharp tug on her hand and a peremptory "Come *on*" from Margie.

"I guess not just now," she said, averting her eyes from the reproachful look on Joey's face. "See you later," she called back over her shoulder as Margie drew her away toward the road.

But Joey had already raced out of earshot.

"I hate boys," Margie announced in a conversational manner when she deemed it safe to release Tilly's hand.

"Why?" asked Tilly, who had never given the matter any thought.

"They're so . . ." Unable to find an exact adjective, Margie finally settled for "Ugh!"

"Joey's nice."

"Maybe. Anyway, that isn't what I wanted to talk to you about." Margie set her ringlets bounding with a hop and a skip. "Mommy said why don't you come back with me after school on Friday and stay to dinner. Then you won't have that long walk to your place and back again in the dark and we won't have to go to bed right away. Won't that be fun?"

The time had come for a lie, but the hoped-for inspiration failed to strike. Tilly's brain began to race. What would happen if she said no? She would be telling the truth, no one could blame her, and she wouldn't have to go. Margie might be a bit hurt, but then she would withdraw the invitation and everything would work out for the best. Why do I have to lie, anyway? thought Tilly pathetically. Why do I have to feel like this? I don't even like her and I thought she didn't like me. I should just say no.

But instead she said, "I haven't asked my mother yet. Maybe she won't let me."

"Sure she will," said Margie. "She lets you do anything."

This statement contained just enough truth to pass without argument.

"And I kind of wanted to go to the movie."

"But it's a scary one. You said they give you nightmares."

The recreation hall appeared on their left. Tilly crossed her fingers and wished fervently for a change in the motion picture lineup; but when they came abreast of the main entrance, a sinister poster on the notice board at the bottom of the stairs proclaimed *Gaslight* as the next attraction.

"Well, sometimes," she admitted. "But I still like them. Won't your parents ever take you to a movie?"

Margie shook her head. "They always play bridge on Friday."

"You could come with us."

Another shake. "They think movies are bad for children. Except *Snow White.* They let me see that."

They walked on for a little in silence. Then: "Wouldn't you love to be Snow White?" Margie asked suddenly.

Although somewhat taken aback by the question, Tilly had no trouble in framing an immediate answer. "No," she said. "The Queen hated her, and then someone tried to kill her and chased her into the forest, and then there was the Witch and the apple . . ."

"Oh, yes." Margie dismissed the objection. "But everything turned out all right in the end and she went off to that lovely castle and lived happily ever after. That's what I want," she continued with fervor. "I wouldn't care what happened to me if only I knew it would stop and be all right. It's when it won't—when you know it'll just go on forever and ever and—oh, Tilly, please come and stay with me on Friday. We can play with my cutouts and I'll show you my books and my dolls. I'll give you one, if you want. I've got a lovely one in a pink dress. She closes her eyes and says 'Ma-ma, Ma-m-m—' "

And, much to Tilly's horror, Margie began to sob.

"Don't. Don't, Margie." Tilly felt her own eyes welling up. "Please don't cry. What's the matter? Please . . ." Brushing away a few stray tears with her knuckles, she caught sight of a tall figure just rounding a bend farther up the road. "Oh, *no,*" she wailed.

Margie looked up from mopping her nose with a wad of Kleenex and said, "What?"

Tilly pointed. Despite the distance, there could be no mistaking the pale face, the straight blond hair and the eccentric wardrobe.

"It's just Mona Meade," said Margie, dabbing at her eyes. "In that ugly coat of her mother's. And look at her feet!" She managed a giggle. "She's wearing rubber boots when it isn't even wet!"

Tilly saw nothing amusing about the situation. An encounter with Mona on this stretch of road, with no chance of a detour and no adult visible in any direction, could have only one possible outcome.

"She'll beat us up," she managed to whisper, fighting down a tendency for each word to break apart in the back of her throat.

"No, she won't," said Margie briskly. "There's two of us and she's only one. We'll just walk by and pretend we don't even see her."

"And not say anything."

These words expressed Tilly's last coherent thought before panic spun her brain into a jumble of emotional fragments. In any case, the time for further discussion had passed, for they were now coming within earshot of the advancing Mona.

Staring straight ahead at nothing in particular in a manner calculated to convey bland, yet inoffensive indifference, Tilly endeavored to mold her mind into a perfect blank. But the harder she fought to keep down unwelcome thoughts, the more easily they seemed to slip through her guard, like bubbles rising to the surface of an otherwise placid pond, each a potential depth charge capable of calling down disaster with a loud pop. For every dangerous thought increased the tension building up within her, and every increase in tension brought her nearer to the brink of a nervous giggle.

And whatever she did, she must not laugh. No matter how many times she had succumbed in the past—set off in school by a well-timed snigger when called upon to read aloud a dangerous word like "bean" or "bottom"—however many times she had exploded into nervous titters, she must be strong now, for (none knew better than she) a titter to Mona was as a red flag to a bull. It was hard, though, particularly when she thought of Margie walking along beside her wearing the same poker face, perhaps fighting down the same urge to explode, perhaps even planning some way to make *her* laugh.

Because it wouldn't take much. It never did. And with her set face aching and her mouth twitching and Mona now only ten feet away (nine feet, eight feet) and her heart beating and her breathing reduced to shallow gasps (six feet, five feet) and her legs weak (four feet, three feet) and a sudden nudge in her side—

"Hockey puck," said Margie, very distinctly.

And Tilly laughed.

"What happened then?" asked Kate a short time later, staring gravely across a much depleted yellow pad at her red-faced and indignant daughter.

"I ran and she chased me."

"And?"

"She sat on me and made me chew on my tam."

"Oh, dear." The corners of Kate's mouth quivered, but managed to remain firm. "What was Margie doing all this time?"

Tilly plumped down on the sofa beside her mother. "She ran after us and yelled at Mona to leave me alone. But Sam was barking so much you couldn't really hear her. He thought we were playing," she concluded, aiming a hurt look at Sam, who had fallen asleep on the other sofa.

"Of course, you *did* laugh," Kate pointed out. "Couldn't you have explained and said you were sorry?"

Tilly transferred the wounded expression to her mother. "I had my mouth full," she said.

This time Kate laughed.

"It wasn't funny!"

"Of course it wasn't." Kate composed her face and gave Tilly a comfortable hug. "I'm sorry you had a bad afternoon."

"And there's something else," Tilly sighed. "I told Margie I'd sleep over at her house on Friday."

Kate experienced a small sharp twinge just to the left of her heart. Well, here it is, she thought, her first time away from me.

"That'll be fun," she said.

"I don't want to."

"Then why did you say you would?"

"I don't know." Tilly wriggled her shoulders under Kate's arm. "She stuck up for me when Mona had me down . . ."

"She also got you there in the first place."

"Yes, but . . ."

"What?"

"Nothing." Tilly brightened. "Couldn't you call Mrs. Allen and say I can't go?"

"No." Kate leaned back a little so that she could look into her daughter's eyes. "But I'll call and say you'd rather not spend a whole night away from home."

"Oh . . ." Tilly began banging her heels against the wooden front of the sofa. "I guess I'll go." She thought for a moment. "Could you call Mr. Meade and get him to make Mona leave me alone?"

"Stop kicking my carpentry."
"But will you?"
"I'll see," said Kate.

"And are you going to call him?" asked Jerry, planting a kiss on the base of her neck.

They lay curled up in bed, talking in soft murmurs and listening to the sound of their own breathing, augmented now and then by a thin whistle from below, where John Henry had settled in for the night. Richly content, Kate pulled the satin-covered eiderdown closer to her chin and pressed herself more snugly into the warm body behind her.

"I can't," she said. "It's not a good situation, but if I go complaining to Mona's father, she'll just take it out on Tilly and everything will get worse. Maybe it's just a phase she'll get over all by herself."

"Mm." Jerry brushed a midnight-shadowed chin lightly over the back of her shoulder. "But in the meantime?"

"There must be something—"

"Shh."

"What?"

"Listen . . ."

Faintly in the distance, several hundred Canada geese gave notice of their coming in a continuous fanfare of raucous cries. As they approached, their calls grew louder and louder, like a shrill pack of bronchial hounds hot on the scent of some aerial prey. Their presence filled the room, and at its climax the heady magic of their song seemed to sweep away the ceiling, conjuring up a familiar vision of sleek winged bodies grouped into a long airborne wedge that undulated, shifted and regrouped but never strayed far from its perfect streamlined shape as it appeared over the ragged horizon, sailed across the moon and finally lost itself among the distant stars.

"Time to go a-hunting," murmured Jerry when the last note had faded into the distance and only John Henry's small whistles remained to puncture the resulting silence.

Kate stretched and nuzzled into her pillow. "I thought you'd forgotten about that."

"Certainly not." Jerry clasped his hands behind his head and lay back. “And I’m all prepared. I’ve got Ted Reese’s rubber waders and Doug Barlow’s rifle—”

“Doug doesn’t hunt.”

“It belonged to his uncle.”

“Jerry!” Amid a thrashing of bedclothes, Kate rolled over onto her elbow and glared down at him. “Uncle Max died in 1918. That rifle must be almost thirty years old.”

“They don’t make ’em like that anymore.”

“It’ll blow up in your face.”

“It’s in perfect condition. I’ve checked.”

“And don’t you need a shotgun for birds?”

“I only want *one*,” said Jerry in his most reasonable voice. “And with a whole lake full of geese, I don’t see how I can miss.”

“I do,” said Kate, who hated it when Jerry became reasonable. “Why don’t I just stay home and you can tell me all about it?”

“It wouldn’t be the same. This is supposed to be a family outing. Something that’ll bring us all closer together.”

“You said that last year when you marched us off in snow up to our waists to get a Christmas tree. We hardly spoke for days after.”

“Only because you don’t know when to give up. I expected to cut down one basic tree, not half the forest.”

“That’s because the short ones looked so skinny when the snow fell off.”

“All over me.”

“I told you to bring a saw.”

“Yes, well—”

“And if you’d just cut down a really *tall* tree . . .”

“Okay, okay.”

“And taken just the top eight feet . . .”

“Kate.”

“Because the tops are always—”

“Kate!”

“All right. You brought it up.”

“No, I didn’t.” Jerry compensated for being reasonable by reaching up and stroking his wife’s hair. “This will be different, you’ll see. This year you’ll have a wonderful time.”

Kate smiled and took his hand as she slid down onto her pillow. "Last year wasn't so bad," she conceded. "After all, you're the one who came home with snow down his neck. When do you want to go?"

"How about this Saturday?"

"Can't. Tilly's spending Friday night with Margie Allen. And next Friday's Halloween, so she'll be tired the day after."

"Hmm." Jerry began to ponder. "And we can't go off shooting on a Sunday. And it could snow any time after Halloween. We'd better make it this week on Tuesday or Wednesday. Lift your head a second."

Kate lifted her head and settled it back against Jerry's shoulder. "We can't take Tilly out of school."

"All in the interests of a rounded education."

"Try telling that to Miss Walter."

"It'll be a day to remember."

Kate made a sound halfway between a laugh and a sigh. "That's what I'm afraid of," she said.

She laughed. "What are you doing now?"

"Jerry," she said.

"Listen," she whispered, some time later. "We've scared off John Henry."

She fell asleep while listening to the silent room, but woke again with a start, full of an uneasy feeling that she had forgotten something.

"What else was there to tell you?" she wondered aloud. "Oh, yes—panic's over. We now have a Christmas pageant. I finished it when you went out after dinner. It's going to be called *The First Nowell.* And—"

She yawned.

"And I had an idea about Mona Meade," she continued drowsily. "She needs friends, but there aren't any girls her age in town." She interrupted herself with another yawn. "Which means she must be alone a lot. So I thought maybe . . ."

But her thought slipped off into a dream.

Jerry, already dreaming, slogged forward once again on that long final march, waiting in helpless anguish for the explosion and the bloody aftermath that would jolt him wide awake, shaking with panic and drenched in sweat. When it happened, he took a moment to gather his courage before he looked over at the pillow next to his. But Kate slept on, undisturbed, which meant that he had held himself together without crying or thrashing about. For this, he was grateful. Things had been going so well.

15

Early Monday morning, Kate commandeered Jerry's office and began pounding out a final version of *The First Nowell* on his ancient Remington typewriter, much to the annoyance of Veronica, who, having turned up her nose at a towel-lined cardboard box behind the bathtub, preferred to spend the last days of her confinement in the bottom drawer of the filing cabinet behind his desk. The slow process of hunt and peck consumed a good part of the day. But by midafternoon Kate had a stack of twenty-one neat stencils ready to be cranked off on the much sought-after copying machine used to produce *The Crow River Gazette*. Having accomplished this task and dropped off a suitable number of stapled copies at the school, she walked over to a house on the western edge of town where she now hesitated, trying to decide whether to follow convention and knock at the kitchen door or make a more formal approach through the living room.

Of course, it might not matter, she told herself. He might be out and I can go away and do this some other time.

But since Augustus Meade seldom walked when he could ride and since his mud-spattered black coupe sat parked by the side of the road, any hopes of finding that gentleman not at home seemed likely to be dashed. Kate therefore took a stern grip on herself, marched up the front steps and knocked on the edge of the screen door.

She had just raised her hand to knock again when the inside door swung open to reveal an ashen face hovering like a moth on the other side of the wire netting.

Good heavens, thought Kate, the poor thing looks petrified.

"Hello, Mona," she said brightly. "Is your father in?"

After a brief hesitation, Mona stammered an affirmative answer and stood aside from the door.

"How smart you look," said Kate as she passed through into the living room. "Where did you get those beautiful slacks?"

Mona replied in a whisper that they had belonged to her mother.

Kate shook her head ruefully. "And she left you her long legs too. Have you grown into all her clothes?"

"No," said Mona. "I—I have to take them in a bit."

"You mean you altered these yourself?" Kate bent closer and inspected a seam. "That's splendid. I always end up with puckers. You're a real seamstress."

Mona turned pink with pleasure. "I'll just tell Daddy you're here," she said, and fled.

Left to entertain herself, Kate made a quick survey of the somber twilit room, in which an amazing quantity of polished wood, cut glass, knickknacks, figurines, wine-colored plush upholstery, basket-pleated satin cushions and starched white antimacassars managed to coexist cheek by jowl within a still atmosphere redolent of furniture polish and floor wax. The poor kid must spend her life keeping this clean, she mused, averting her gaze from the contents of a wall-mounted whatnot and allowing it to rest briefly on a flight of plaster ducks poised to collide with a large pink painting of snow-clad mountains. Unless they never come in here, she thought, as she turned her back firmly on the ducks and wandered over to a window in the opposite wall.

Recently washed and hung with fresh net curtains, the window overlooked a plot of low bush and beyond that, on the other side of a dirt turnaround, the final three houses in a row that ran west to east downhill toward the store. All appeared deserted, except for the house directly opposite Kate. There, in the last backyard before civilization gave way to bush, Margie Allen skipped rope while her mother pulled in a line of laundry through the small window in the black tarpaper-covered porch.

Kate found the sight disturbing. She knew Mary and Tom Allen only slightly and had never been inside their home. Nevertheless, she could imagine the room where Tilly would be sleeping on Friday night just as clearly as if the expanse of white wall to the right of the porch had slid away to reveal the pretty coverlet on Margie's bed, the matching curtains at her window, the framed animal pictures on her wall and the lush collection of dolls and toys disposed about her charming suite of child-size furniture.

For it was common knowledge that the Allens spent money on their daughter. Kate, on the other hand, never bought when she could make and enjoyed the challenge of improvising with whatever happened to be available. She had always taken it for granted that the rest of her family thought along similar lines. Now, standing at the window, half hidden by the sheer curtains, she experienced a twinge of uncertainty. How would Tilly regard her old bed, darned quilt and faded curtains when she came back to her own room on Saturday morning? How would she feel about the movie posters tacked to her wall, the home-made braided rug and the ragtag collection of furniture?

It isn't as if it weren't a good quilt, Kate told herself. It's real eiderdown. Try and find real eiderdown nowadays. After all, who said that everything had to be new? She'd never find anything like those curtains again either, with their funny plump chenille flowers along the bottom. Tilly had always loved those flowers, just the way she loved the pink and blue dancing pigs Kate had painted for her on the abandoned table and chair they had discovered in the basement on first moving in.

Or at least I think she does, thought Kate unhappily, as she watched the last of Margie's flounced dresses disappearing off the clothesline across the road. At any rate, she wouldn't let me paint over them. She won't even let me take down her old movie posters and put up new ones. But maybe that's because she doesn't know any better. I wonder if her friends feel sorry for her when they come to visit. I wonder if our friends feel sorry for Jerry because he has to live in a shabby house. Maybe I've been selfish and silly. Maybe I should be out there spending money on chesterfield suites and coffee tables and doilies and fussy little outfits for Tilly and—

"Mrs. Taggert."

The rich pear-shaped tones of Augustus Meade halted Kate's train of thought in midreproach. Turning from the window, she discovered the reverend gentleman himself framed in the hallway at the far end of the room.

"What a pleasant surprise," continued Augustus, who, with pale myopic eyes and rumpled clothing, had the air of one just roused from bed. "I apologize for my tardiness in greeting you, but I was in the middle of a telephone conversation with Mrs. Rydell."

Joyce Rydell ran the church Sunday school.

"An excellent woman," Augustus pronounced, clasping his large sensitive hands against the top button on his cardigan. "But several parents have questioned her choice of singing matter as being just a little, well, extreme. I wonder if you and Mr. Taggert . . . ?

"Not at all," said Kate. "Children like a good rousing song. Tilly sings 'Washed in the Blood of Jesus' every time she gets into the bathtub."

"Ah." Augustus sounded unconvinced. "Well, I suppose that would . . . it's just that I sometimes wonder if Mrs. Rydell misrepresented her religious affiliations when she began the school. Her attitude seems most un-Anglican. But, of course, there's no one else willing to take the class, unless—"

"I think Joyce does a marvelous job," Kate cut in quickly. She waved a copy of *The First Nowell* in a vaguely introductory manner. "Actually, I came about something else altogether."

"Yes?" Augustus gave his head a shake and began to look a little more alert. "Yes, of course. What am I thinking of? Come into my study. We don't use this room often." (Aha! thought Kate.) "So if you would just walk this way . . ."

Kate obediently walked into the kitchen, where she found Mona, wrapped in a capacious polka-dot apron, cautiously edging a round of pastry onto the top of a well-filled apple pie. Two potatoes sat near the sink ready for peeling, and from under the lid of a heavy cast-iron pot on the stove came the rich scent of beef and vegetables.

"Something smells good," remarked Kate as she began a U-turn around the stove. But Mona, intent on the fragile pastry, merely ducked her head down closer to the pie and said nothing. Only a delicate pink flush on the back of her neck indicated that she had heard.

"Now!" said Augustus in an encouraging voice when he had settled himself behind a worn oak office desk and waved Kate toward an equally worn upholstered chair in a book-lined corner just to the right of the window.

Kate closed the study door behind her, cautiously occupied the chair and mentioned that she had a slight problem.

Augustus glowed and rubbed his hands. "Exactly what I'm here for! And of course you may be assured that anything you wish to say . . ."

"Oh, it isn't anything like that," said Kate, blushing. (It must be catching, she thought.) "It's very simple, really." She waved *The First Nowell* again before letting it drop on the floor. "I've finally finished the Christmas pageant and started making sketches for the scenery. Nothing elaborate." She leaned forward and drew a few airy diagrams in the air. "Just an overhead platform for the angels, and under that a curtain with lots of fir boughs sewn on it. And then at the end, the curtains will draw back to reveal the Nativity scene with a painted backdrop showing the little town of Bethlehem. The problem is," she concluded, settling back again into the chair, "that I haven't the foggiest notion of what Bethlehem looks like, especially back then, and I wondered if you might have a picture of it anywhere."

"A picture, a picture . . ." Having recovered from a mild attack of chagrin at not being consulted on a more serious matter, Augustus pulled his spectacles down on his nose and began to glow again. "Yes, I do have a picture. In fact, if you could just turn to your left and pull out that book with the green spine on the second shelf—yes, that one—and turn to the frontispiece . . ."

The picture, executed in pastel watercolors, showed a hill covered with white adobe buildings and lush palm trees.

"Oh, yes!" Kate beamed at Augustus, who had produced a well-aged meerschaum pipe from the pocket of his cardigan and begun to fill it with tobacco. "This is lovely. Perfect. And how wonderful of you to have just what I need."

Augustus beamed modestly back at her. "On the subject of my library, I admit to the sin of pride. Of course the volume is slanted toward a popular audience and consequently rather romanticized, but for theatrical purposes . . ."

"Perfect," Kate repeated. "I am grateful. Could I just make a quick sketch?"

"Borrow it. Do." Augustus made an expansive gesture that sent him creaking backward in his chair. "I shall be charmed to see the illustration reproduced onstage." He selected a match from a small ceramic barrel on the corner of his desk. "May I?"

"Of course. And thank you." Kate set the book down beside her script and prepared for the difficult part of her visit. "Now I have another favor to ask."

Augustus's chair creaked forward again in the wake of a thick cloud of smoke.

"It's about Mona."

Augustus pulled his spectacles still farther down his nose and peered over their top edges.

Kate cleared her throat, which had picked this inconvenient time to dry up. "You see," she said, "I want to use all the small children as angels—you know, the heavenly host—but I need someone older to say the lines and look after the young ones so they all get on and off at the right times. And I wondered if you would mind if I asked Mona to be Head Angel."

"Head Angel?" Augustus looked blank.

Slightly unnerved, Kate rattled on.

"I know it sounds a bit unbiblical, but I had to give a name to the angel who has that nice speech about good tidings of great joy. And Head Angel sounded better than Second Angel. Because, of course," she added, as her tongue began to run on of its own accord, "there's an Annunciation Angel at the beginning. But it doesn't matter *how* I designate her in the script because nobody actually *calls* her anything onstage, so it's really just a convenience for learning lines and rehearsing, although there *is* the cast list in the program and if you don't like Head Angel . . ."

She petered out. Augustus continued to look dazed.

"Mona? Head Angel?"

Kate's attack of nerves vanished as quickly as it had come. Damn it, she thought, what's wrong with him? Any other parent would be thrilled. Sensing that her lips had compressed themselves into a tight line, she made an effort to relax them into a smile.

"Yes," she said pleasantly. "I think Mona would make an excellent Head Angel. Don't you?"

Augustus put down his pipe, which had gone out, and pressed his fingertips together in a thoughtful manner.

"Mona's a dear girl," he said. "A very dear girl. But to put her on a stage, in a prominent part . . ." He flexed his fingers and shook his head. "Might that not be inviting . . . ? I mean, with her . . ." He waved his hand vaguely. "Surely someone a little more . . . comely . . . ?"

Dizzied by a rush of blood to her head, Kate gripped the arms of her chair with both hands and remained silent while Augustus tapped the end of his pipe against a silver frame sitting on one side of his desk. The frame contained a tinted studio photograph of a young lady with tight blond curls, large eyes, high cheekbones and sharp, pretty features set in a perfect oval face.

"You are perhaps shocked," he said, "because I am not one of those parents who exists in a cloud-cuckoo land of his own delusions. Mona's mother was lovely. Mona, alas, is not. But what of that? Beauty is not everything. There are many paths to self-fulfillment. Mona has a sweet, good, uncomplaining nature. She has selflessly taken up the burden of running the manse, enabling me to devote my days to writing and study and many of my nights to seeking out those lonely, unhappy men who frequent the beer parlor and that, ahem, infamous place on the Springford Road."

Augustus hesitated slightly at this daring reference to Mary Hogan's discreetly run establishment and its ever-changing brood of young ladies, but quickly returned to his solemn Sunday style.

"Many of these men are from foreign lands," he continued, "and many have, like myself, served their country abroad in the recent war." He paused for a smile of sad remembrance. "To these I offer what poor solace and counsel I can," he said humbly, "in an attempt to bring them back to the ways of temperance and self-control, even at the price of spending more time away from my daughter than I would otherwise wish. But she is content. And I flatter myself that our joint sacrifices have not been in vain. I therefore wonder if it would not be wiser to leave our little lives undisturbed by the spurious glamour of the theater and, as I suggested, choose another young lady of a—how shall I say?—more worldly nature. But then"—he spread his arms in a gesture of resignation—"I may be wrong. I may lack perspective. Have I perhaps failed as a parent? I leave it to you. What do you think? Speak frankly." He relit his pipe.

Although strongly tempted to take Augustus up on his invitation, Kate had already mastered her temper and formed a plan, in the interests of which she intended to smile and be ruthless. Nevertheless, being a little unsure of her ability to inject the required smile into her voice, she essayed a trial "Well" and then, having settled on what she hoped was a pleasantly modulated tone, she began her speech.

"First of all," she said, "I suggest you take a good hard look at your daughter. Next, I would like to apologize on behalf of all the churchgoers in this town. We've been standing by while you carried out two very difficult jobs all by yourself, with no help at all, and I think this should change. You can't be at your best as a minister or a father when you have to worry about the added burden of running a household. Now about the housework . . ."

She proceeded to outline her plan.

"So there it is," she said to Mona twenty minutes later as they stood once again at the front door, wrapped in a warm scent of apple, cinnamon and cloves drifting through from the kitchen. "Mrs. Donner who cleans for Mrs. Reese will come here one day a week. She won't do as good a job as you, but that can't be helped. There are more important things in life than a spotless floor. The Ladies' Church Committee will take it on a rota basis to drop off a casserole or something once a week, and I'm going to teach your father some of my best fast meals so you can share the rest of the cooking between you."

She paused to look intently into Mona's face, which had lost its last trace of color. Mona stared back with her father's round dazed eyes.

"This should give you a bit more spare time," Kate went on, trying to estimate in the back of her mind how she might break Mona's fall in the event of a sudden faint. "So if you think you could tackle the Head Angel and mind the smaller angels—you know, as a big sister—I'd be very grateful. And perhaps you might like to help a little with the costumes. Mrs. Holzer is wonderful with the sewing machine—you might get some helpful tips from her."

She paused again, hoping for a response. Mona said nothing. Kate began to feel guilty.

"Of course, I realize that I'm interfering terribly," she said. "And if you'd rather not do any of this, then please just—"

"Yes," said Mona.

A weight lifted.

"The angel?" asked Kate.

"Yes."

"And the costumes?"

"Yes."

"And the big sis—"

"Oh, yes."

"Well, that's wonderful," said Kate happily. "I'll call Miss Walter and Mrs. Holzer and then we'll—"

But before she could say anything more, Mona rushed out of the room and fled upstairs, leaving Kate to see herself out the door.

"Did you see Mr. Meade yesterday?" asked Tilly, when she came home on Tuesday to find her mother at the kitchen table, brushing up on the recipe for her special one-dish macaroni dinner.

"Yes, I did." Kate made a note on a piece of yellow ruled paper.

"Did you tell him about Mona and me?"

"No, I didn't."

Tilly sat down at the table. "Because Mona was so nice to me today. She didn't sit on me or anything."

"Maybe she was just going through a phase. She's probably quite a nice girl."

"She's going to be Head Angel in the pageant. I thought 'Ugh!' when Miss Walter told us, but I didn't say it."

"Good for you." Still intent on her book, Kate reached across the table and lifted the top off a white pottery crock. "Have a cookie."

"Thank you very much. What's for dinner?"

"Macaroni and meat sauce."

"Mmm. What's for dessert?"

"Vanilla pudding with oranges and bananas."

"Yum."

Kate looked up. "May I take it that Madame will be dining in tonight?"

Tilly grinned. "I guess so. Are you sure you didn't tell Mr. Meade about Mona being a bully?"

"Not a word."

Tilly kicked her heels against the bottom chair rung. "Well, will wonders ever cease?" she said.

"No," replied her mother. "Or you wouldn't see me getting up at five in the morning tomorrow to chase a wild goose."

And, shutting her book with a thump, Kate seized a knife and went off to chop onions.

16

"Isn't this fun?" asked Jerry, teetering precariously on the edge of a crumbling stump. "Isn't this a great moment? Our whole little family out together on an adventure. Doesn't it make you feel good? Aren't you glad you came? Don't all answer at once."

They had been tramping in semidarkness for over an hour and were now following Sam's lead across a patch of shallow muskeg, trying their best to keep dry by leaping from one fallen tree trunk to another. Occasionally they managed to move easily across a patch of ice, but more often they found themselves wading through a soupy mixture of sphagnum moss and standing water that, so far, had remained at a level below the tops of their rubber boots. Kate and Jerry wore the knapsacks they had acquired for last summer's camping holiday, unfortunately cut short owing to rain and insects. Jerry also carried a gleaming lever-action rifle slung over his shoulder. Tilly, bundled up against the cold but otherwise unburdened, kept her head down and concentrated on keeping up. Sam splashed happily on ahead.

"Well, I feel good," Jerry went on in a defensive tone. "And look, we're coming to a hill. We'll be out of this soon."

This was true. As the sky ahead lightened to a dim gray glow, there appeared before them a smooth rise of land topped by a stand of tall, thin pine trees. And by the time the glow had taken on a faint tinge of blue, they were tramping across a sprung floor of dry pine needles on their way through a silent maze of slim brown tree trunks that sprang up from the ground like tent posts only to vanish again into an overhead canopy of gently waving boughs.

At length the hunting party emerged onto a broad circular expanse of lead-colored rock, quite bare except for patches of moss and a few low shrubs rooted into some of the larger fissures. Behind them, the forest closed in on itself and vanished almost immediately into darkness; but ahead, vertical slashes of pale light could be seen shining through a sparse screen of thin trees, as if a section of sky had slipped its moorings and settled across the earth. This was Beaver Lake. They had arrived within sight of their destination.

Kate took a deep breath of sharp, fragrant air and set down her knapsack.

"Who's hungry?" she asked.

Within two minutes, blankets had been spread and toasted bacon-and-egg sandwiches produced, together with slabs of chocolate cake and two thermos bottles of hot cocoa. Everyone pulled off gloves, loosened scarves and sat down, ravenous.

"I wonder where Sam is," said Tilly, who took it for granted that all meals would be taken under the watchful eye of a large animal.

A loud crashing in the bush answered her question. Moments later Sam broke through into the clearing proudly bearing a large, smooth stick of just the right size and weight to be thrown and retrieved. At the sight of food, however, he abandoned his prize and sat down by one of the blankets to stake a claim to whatever good things happened to be on the menu.

"I hate to move," said Kate, when they had finished eating and packed away the debris, "but shouldn't we be getting over to the lake?"

A flock of geese passed high over their heads, a long oblique line of pinpoints in the sky.

Jerry looked up. "Jack McCallister says they won't land until after sunrise, and that won't be for a little while yet. I'm going to try a few practice shots." He selected a brown paper bag from Kate's knapsack and crumpled it into a ball. "Tilly—see that cracked tree over there at the edge of the clearing? Put this on the stump for me and we'll find out what Uncle Max's rifle can do."

"That's it," he said when Tilly came racing back with her errand accomplished and Sam at her heels. "Now we'll just load up"—he reached into the pocket of his jacket for bullets and slipped them into the Winchester 94—"one, two, three, then cock it"—the lever hinged down and back with a satisfying click—"and then . . ."

He aimed and fired.

A small white gash appeared on the left-hand edge of the stump.

Jerry frowned. "It's pulling a little." Adjusting his aim, he tried again.

The crumpled bag vanished.

"Not bad. Let's see. That branch behind the stump . . ."

The branch leapt and shuddered.

Jerry grinned at Kate. "Pretty good, eh? Want to try?"

Kate shook her head.

"Let me, Daddy. Let me try." Tilly began jumping up and down.

Jerry cast another quick glance in Kate's direction. "This is an old rifle," he said dubiously. "There's quite a kick."

"That's okay. I've got lots of padding in my parka. Just once."

"Kate . . . ?"

Kate made a face. "If you think it's all right."

"Well . . ." Jerry bounced the rifle in this hands, then smiled down at his eager, pink-faced daughter. "Go put the bag back."

"Okay," he said when she came running back. "I've cocked it and it's ready to fire. That means it's dangerous and you have to be very careful. Are you ready?"

Tilly nodded, too excited to speak.

"Now you know how to hold it." Jerry stood behind her and lowered the rifle into her hands. "Is it too heavy?"

Tilly shook her head.

"Fine. Look along the barrel. See the little bit of metal at the tip? Get that right in the middle of the bag. Got it? Now, move it just a little up and to the right. Yes. And hold it very steady. And—"

Tilly fired and fell back into Jerry's arms, where she lay staring up into her hat, the rifle clutched across her chest.

"Tilly!" Kate addressed the red tam anxiously. "Are you all right?"

Tilly emerged from beneath her pom-pom radiant with joy.

"Did you see?" she cried. "I hit it!" She stood up and appealed to her parents. "Didn't you see me hit it?"

Everyone looked at the stump, still topped by the crumpled bag.
"I saw the bag move! Doesn't that mean I hit it?"
Jerry repossessed the Winchester and studied the stump again.
"Well," he said slowly, "it doesn't seem to be right in the center anymore. If you didn't hit it, you certainly fanned it." He dropped Tilly's tam back on her head. "That was a very good first shot. You'll make a hunter yet. Now let's go and get us a goose."
Tilly's heart swelled.
"Going to get a goose, going to get a goose," she sang as they made their way across the clearing and through the band of trees to the lake.

Although set in a circle of dark trees and partially hidden by a generous stubble of reeds, Beaver Lake now matched the brightening sky with a clear blue color of its own.
Tilly stood ankle-deep in the still, clear water and tried for an echo by calling out "goose, goose, goose." But she received no answer beyond a faint "plop" from the far side of the lake.
"Do you think the beavers are still living here?" she asked.
"I don't know," said Kate, whose knowledge of natural history had its limitations. "Maybe we'll see one while we're waiting." She turned to Jerry. "Where are we supposed to lurk?"
The hide consisted of a shallow trench, fronted on the lake side by a low mound of earth and concealed from above by an almost flat latticed roof strewn with branches, dead leaves and moss. Tilly crawled in first.
Kate inspected the shadowy depths with deep suspicion. "I've changed my mind," she announced. "I am not glad I came."
"What's wrong?" Jerry squatted down next to her.
"You didn't say we'd be stretched out in a hole. It's probably full of snakes and toads."
"It's too late for snakes and toads. By now they're either dead or hibernating."
"I don't care what they're doing. I'm not getting in there with them."
During this conversation, the sky had been amusing itself by trying on a number of gaudy colors. It now cast aside the obvious charms of violet, pink and orange and donned a more intense shade of its original blue. At the same time, narrow shafts of yellow began

to shoot through the ragged trees on the eastern side of the lake. Jerry scanned the sky nervously.

"Kate, darling. You can't stay outside. You'll scare the geese."

"I'm sorry, but I'm scared too."

"It's all right, Mommy. There's nothing down here."

"See? Tilly says it's all right. Get in."

"Oh . . . I can't."

"Tilly, call Sam."

"Here, Sam. Here, Sam."

"Look, darling. Sam's gone down. If anything had been there, he'd have chased it off. Now, please . . ."

During the tense pause that followed, the tip of the sun burst over the treetops in a theatrical gesture worthy of a trumpet fanfare. Instead, it coincided with a much fainter sound from the north, far beyond the lake.

"My God," Jerry whispered. "It's the geese. Kate, get in there."

"Oh, Jerry . . ."

"Kate, I'm begging. I'm on my knees . . ."

And indeed, Jerry had collapsed on all fours, ready to make a dive into the trench. The sound of the geese grew louder.

"Mommy . . ."

"Kate . . ."

"Oh, all *right*!"

And before she could think better of it, Kate tumbled into the trench beside Sam, who now lay safely wedged between Tilly and herself.

Meanwhile, Jerry had crawled along the edge of the trench and taken up a position to the left of Tilly. With a shaking hand, he slipped three more bullets into the rifle, cocked the lever and took aim over the raised mound of earth. He then concentrated on regaining his calm and steadying his hand, glad that none of his youthful hunting friends could see him out after goose with a deer rifle.

At the other end of the trench, suffused in the sharp scent of wet fur and decomposing leaves, Kate cast her thoughts wistfully back to Veronica, no doubt still fast asleep in her warm drawer. Next to her, Sam pricked up his ears and stared fixedly at a spot just above the treetops at the far end of the lake. Tilly, pressed against his other side for warmth, ran through a list of names suitable for a pet goose and indulged in a happy daydream of what life would be like when Gilbert (or perhaps Gregory), fully recovered from his superficial flesh wound, moved in as a full-fledged member of the Taggert family.

But as her eye continued to scan the lake, it picked out several dark shapes hiding in the reeds on the far left-hand side. She leaned over toward her father and pointed.

"Geese," she whispered.

Jerry shook his head. "Decoys," he whispered back. "Mr. McCallister made them."

"Why isn't he out today?" asked Kate, without taking her eyes off the sky.

"Because I paid him five dollars to stay home." Jerry reached into the breast pocket of his jacket and produced a bulbous wooden object shaped along the lines of a sweet potato. "And I bought this."

"What on earth is it?"

"Shh."

Three scouting geese had appeared above the treetops and were now heading across the lake just to the left of the hide. Jerry lifted the sweet potato to his lips and blew. The resulting honk, plangent but penetrating, received a faint answer, much to the surprise of everyone in the hide. Just then, the main body of geese passed high over the lake, sending Jerry into a paroxysm of honking.

"Jack said they need a lot of encouragement from the ground," he explained between gasps, after the last bird had disappeared.

"But they've gone," said Tilly in a small, sad voice.

Jerry continued to stare across the lake.

"There's a breeze coming from behind us," he said. "If they decided to land, they'll come around and head into it. Let's stay put."

They waited, hardly daring to breathe or move. Tilly, straining to catch the slightest sound, could bring in only Sam's heavy breathing on one side of her and the ticking of her father's watch on the other. She began to despair. But the very act of shifting her thoughts seemed to sharpen her hearing. And she could hear something. At first she feared that it might be only imagination, but soon there could be no mistake.

The geese were returning.

Almost as if a radio had been turned abruptly from soft to loud, the sound of their voices rose to a deafening level. And just when the uproar reached a peak beyond which any increase in volume seemed impossible, it managed somehow to become even louder as, with a great rush and flap, the flock swooped into view from behind the hide, soaring around the side of the lake in a great arc that brought them back over the distant treetops.

For one heart-stopping moment, it seemed as if the great solid mass of birds might hold together and continue on its way. But then a single goose broke from its position in the vanguard and dropped toward the lake, followed by the other members of the vast flock who, slipping, sliding and diving, skillfully maneuvered through a thousand potential traffic jams and collisions until, with webbed feet thrust well forward, wings outstretched and tails depressed, they all flopped, fluttered and splashed down among the reeds like a ragged team of water skiers coming off a ramp.

There followed a scene of joyous flapping and splashing as the geese celebrated the successful completion of yet another lap on their long voyage south. Soon, however, they settled down to the serious business of feeding, which they accomplished by scooping their long black necks down into the shallow water or by tipping forward so that only their tails could be seen pointing straight up at the sky. A contented gabbling replaced the cacophonous din of their flight song.

Lying with one arm thrown across Sam's neck and the rest of her body stiff with tension, Tilly stared at the magnificent scene as if hypnotized. The sheer number of living things set down before her somehow blended together into a single physical presence of almost miraculous splendor. She fell in love with it on the spot, she wanted to laugh and cry, and she wanted the particular moment of time in which she found herself to go on forever. She also wanted to ask an urgent question. Leaning a little to her left, she whispered it to her father.

Jerry, who had also been staring in a dazed fashion at the solid wall of birds stretched out across his line of fire, now turned and stared blankly at his daughter. Tilly repeated her question.

"When we get the goose home," she hissed, "can he live in the house with us?"

A new look came into Jerry's eyes. And as he continued to stare at her in the manner of one faced with a sudden case of gibbering lunacy, Tilly began to suspect that their plans for Gregory (or Gilbert) might turn out to be mutually incompatible. The suspicion became certainty when, turning forward again, Jerry lifted the rifle to his shoulder.

At that moment, Tilly knew that she could live without a pet goose just as surely as she knew she could never eat one. It was enough to look, and all she wanted was to continue doing so for as long as possible. But her father had already taken aim. If she intended to act, it had to be now.

Leaning forward again, she whispered a single pleading "No."

Or at least she intended to whisper.

Somehow, though, through nervous excitement or the effects of a dry throat, her voice cracked and the single syllable emerged unabated, at full conversational level.

In the ensuing silence, a twig could be heard falling in the forest and the ticking of Jerry's watch once again became the loudest sound in Tilly's ear. Nothing stirred. Every bird had raised its long neck and frozen in the same alert attitude so that, for the duration of a heartbeat, it seemed to Tilly as if a new growth of dark reeds had suddenly shot up to cover the surface of the lake.

Then, with a great flurry of wings and warning cries, the geese bounded off the water and into the air as Jerry, recovering from the shock of this unexpected turn of events, let off a volley of shots into their midst.

"Shit!" he wailed when the rifle failed to fire after the fourth pumping of the lever.

Tilly, who had never in her life heard a parent swear, stood by in horror as her father repeated the dreadful word while searching in his pocket for more ammunition and then added a "God damn it" when his fingers fumbled the bullets clumsily into the loading chamber.

"Take that, you honking bastards!" he yelled, firing after the last dwindling dot on the horizon, "And that! And—oh, hell."

With nothing left to aim at, Jerry lowered the rifle and allowed his shoulders to sag.

"I can't understand it," he mourned. "All those birds spread out in front of me. How could I have missed?"

"I'm sorry, Daddy."

Jerry shook his head. "It's not your fault, baby. I waited too long." Removing his peaked cap, he wiped his forehead with a crumpled blue handkerchief. "It was a stupid idea anyway. You can't get a goose with a deer gun. I should have—"

"Jerry, listen." Having followed Sam to the edge of the lake, Kate stood with her head craned forward, doing her best to see past a thick stand of tall, yellowing bulrushes.

They listened, but heard nothing.

Kate pointed to the left. "It came from over there."

They listened again. Sam, now on the alert, began to move along the edge of the water in the direction Kate had indicated.

This time they heard it, a soft flutter and splash, followed by silence.

"By God," Jerry whispered. "There's something there. Maybe I didn't . . ."

Setting down the rifle and grabbing his knapsack, he set off after Sam at a run, leaving Kate and Tilly to catch up at their own speed.

Beyond the rushes lay a miniature bay of clear water bounded by low reeds on its farther side. And there, about twenty feet from shore, partly hidden in the sparse vegetation, sat a large Canada goose, looking very much like one of Jack McCallister's decoys. When they lined up and stared at it from the water's edge, it appeared to stare back. And when Sam barked, it raised one wing and hissed. Otherwise, it made no effort to escape.

Jerry raised his cap again and rubbed the top of his head. "It must be hit," he said. "It wouldn't just sit there if it could get away."

As if reading his thoughts, the goose craned forward and flapped its good wing, then folded it up again and resumed its impersonation of a decoy. Jerry knelt down to open his knapsack.

"What are you going to do?" asked Tilly.

"I can't leave the poor thing out there with a bullet in it." Jerry produced Edward Reese's black rubber waders and began kicking off his own rubber boots prior to donning them. "I'm going after it."

"Sam, *you* get the goose." Kate waved a hand and made agitated body movements in the direction of the wounded bird.

Sam sat down, cocked his head and gave her his full attention.

"Go on, Sam. Go get the goose. Get the goose!"

"Get the goose, Sam." Tilly joined her mother in dancing up to the water's edge and then retiring. "Please, Sam. Rescue the goose."

Still with his head on one side, Sam looked back and forth from one mad person to the other. Jerry meanwhile had finished fastening himself into the waders, which encased his body up to a point just beneath his arms.

"Well," he said, pulling on his gloves and lowering one cautious foot into the soggy lake bed. "Here I go."

"Oh, Jerry. Be careful. That's an awfully big bird."

"Don't hurt it, Daddy."

"Don't go out too deep."

Jerry took another step forward. "I can't go out too deep. The whole lake is nothing more than a big wide puddle. Just keep calm and I'll be back in a minute."

And with that he set off, striding in slow motion through water that, as promised, rose no deeper than his knees. Kate and Tilly watched nervously from the shore, while the goose kept an impassive lookout from its place in the reeds. Only when Jerry crossed an imaginary barrier, approximately eight feet from the bird, did it pull back its sleek black and white head and emit a harsh, vicious hiss.

Jerry retreated an involuntary step, then pressed forward again. As he drew near, the goose arched its good wing in a defensive posture and flopped backward to the edge of the reeds. Jerry followed, only to find himself entering water that, contrary to expectations, began to rise toward his waist. He took another cautious step forward, whereupon the goose abandoned its threatening posture and paddled rapidly back into the thickest part of the reeds, leaving Jerry with no alternative but to press on into still deeper water.

By keeping a woolen mitten clapped firmly over her mouth, Kate managed to say nothing as she watched her husband's head descend lower and lower into the reeds until it finally vanished altogether. The addition of a second mitten enabled her to remain silent even when the chase resolved itself into two centers of flurried agitation that thrashed through the reeds like miniature whirlwinds, while an alarming jumble of hisses, honks, flaps, curses, cracks, snaps and splashes rolled in to shore from the deepest depths of the dense vegetation. But when the reeds became still and the sounds ceased, Kate could contain herself no longer.

"Jerry," she called. "Jerry, what's happening?"

A reed snapped.

"Jerry?"

"Daddy?"

"Nothing's happening."

"Your voice sounds funny. What are you doing?"

Silence.

"Jerry, for God's sake—"

"It's all right. I'm staring at the goose."

"Why? What's it doing?"

"Staring at me."

"Maybe you should come back for your gun."

"Please, Daddy. Don't hurt it."

"Tilly, hush."

"If I could have just a little quiet"—Jerry's voice dropped into a slow, precise rhythm—"I think I've got it hypnotized. And there's a spot just below its head. And I'm just close enough. So that in just one moment. I'm going to jump. And I'm going to grab it. And I'm going to—"

His words ended in a tremendous splash. At the same time, the goose shot backward out of the reeds into a clear patch of water, where it raised its head and utter a series of mournful notes.

"*Awp, awp, awp,*" it bleated.

"Oh, Daddy . . ." wailed Tilly, pierced to the heart by each cry.

"It's okay, baby." Jerry's breathless voice emerged from deep within a storm center of waving foliage. "I'm all right."

Kate, with half a mitten thrust into her mouth, said nothing. Sam, however, advanced to the edge of the water, lowered his head and began barking.

"Oh, shut up, Sam." Hatless and weighed down by his sodden jacket, Jerry staggered out of the reeds. Spikes of wet hair hung down over his eyes, and with each step a small tidal wave of water sloshed out of the top of his waders.

Kate extracted her mitten. "Jerry, come in here right now. You're turning blue."

"I don't care if I turn tartan." Jerry turned to face his quarry, presently engaged in investigating its wounded wing. "I'm not giving up until I get my hands on that fat, feathered son of a . . ." Leaving his sentence unfinished in deference to the tender ears of his daughter, he began another slow advance in the direction of the preoccupied goose.

As before, he found himself entering deeper water that rose from his knees to his waist to a point almost halfway up his chest. The goose, however, appeared not to notice. Another step submerged Jerry almost up to his shoulders. But he now stood within eighteen inches of his objective. His moment had arrived. Slowly he raised his arms. Slowly he reached forward. He lunged. He vanished. The goose vanished. Kate and Tilly screamed. Sam barked.

In the ensuing nervous moment, the small shorebound audience of three stared silently at a bare patch of water now marked only by a series of expanding circular wavelets. Suddenly two flailing webbed feet rose up through a froth of roiling bubbles, followed by a tawny gray underside, a beating wing and, finally, a black and white head with Jerry's hand clamped around its throat. These portions of anatomy thrashed about for a moment on their own. Then, slightly off to one side, Jerry's own head broke the surface, gasped and sank again, pulling the goose down with him.

"Oh, my God," Kate wailed, clutching Tilly to her. "He's out of his depth and those rubber things are full of water. Jerry!" she shrieked, as Jerry and the goose made a return appearance. "Let go! Let go!"

"Daddy, let go!" echoed Tilly.

Jerry looked at his loved ones as if they had abandoned their senses, said "Augh!" and went down once more, leaving behind only a churning patch of water as a guide for Sam who, having waded out as far as his feet would take him, was now swimming strongly in that general direction.

"Hold on, Jerry," Kate called when Jerry and the goose made their third ascent, this time a little closer to shore. "Sam's coming. Sam, get Daddy!"

"No!"

Instead of going down again as expected, Jerry remained with his head and shoulders out of the water, rocking unsteadily on an underwater foothold made even more precarious by his waterlogged waders and the frantic actions of the furious goose still locked in his right hand.

"Made it," he gasped. "Just don't . . . don't let . . . go away, Sam. Go! Stop! Augh!"

"Sam!" cried Kate and Tilly.

But too late. Sam had already grabbed the back of Jerry's jacket collar and toppled him helplessly off balance. Jerry struggled, but Sam knew panic when he saw it. They screamed at him from shore, but he remained calm. With his master's head held firmly underwater, he proceeded with his rescue.

"Sam, let go!"

"Drop it, Sam!"

"Help!" yelled Jerry, managing to thrust his head into the air for a moment.

Kate and Tilly changed their tactics.

"Here, Sam. Good boy."

"Hurry up, Sam."

Jerry again exerted himself to surface briefly, submerging the unfortunate goose as he did so.

"Augh!"

"*Awp!*"

"Faster, Sam."

"Come on, Sam."

"Good boy," they said when Sam at last dropped his limp cargo at the edge of the lake and waded to shore. "Clever boy," they added after he had drenched them with a miniature rainstorm from his coat and presented himself for praise.

"Clever!" Lifting himself from the shallows, Jerry sloshed toward them in billowing waders with the protesting goose held a safe arm's length in front of him. "That idiotic animal almost drowned me, and you have the nerve to tell him he's clever! What's so clever? He bungled the job. Silly old Sam," he added in a voiced laced with heavy irony. "Better luck next time, old chap. That brainless, useless, fatheaded—"

"Jerry!"

"What?"

Kate gestured toward Sam, whose ears, eyes and mouth had all drooped into an expression of utter misery. "You're hurting his feelings."

"*His* feelings?" Jerry waved his arms in an expansive gesture that set off a new round of bleats from the goose. "I'll give him feelings! If I could just lift my leg, I'd give him a swift kick right up his bloody backside. What about *my* feelings? I'm soaked and frozen and I'll probably get pneumonia—oh, Lord, what now?"

Tilly had burst into tears. Instantly melted, Jerry bent down toward her.

"It's all right, baby. I just lost my temper. I won't get pneumonia and I won't kick Sam. I know it wasn't his fault—he was just trying to help. Please, sweetie. Don't cry."

Tilly bubbled out a few unintelligible words. Kate and Jerry bent closer.

"Really, baby. Everything's all right."

"What is it, dear?"

"Gilbert," squeaked Tilly, with a hiccup.

"Gilbert?"

Tilly pointed. "He's crying. Help him. Please help him. Make him better."

Kate knelt down. "Darling, we can't make him better. He's been shot. I thought you knew . . ." She looked helplessly at Jerry, then back to Tilly. "That's what we came for: to get—to shoot a goose."

"No!" Tilly's voice rose to a shriek. "You can't. You can't kill him. I want him to come home with us. Make him better. Make him better!" She dissolved back into tears.

"Oh, Tilly. Jerry . . ." And Kate began to cry as well.

Moved to sympathy, Sam sat down and howled, while the failing Gilbert produced a series of dying honks.

Jerry, totally unprepared for this turn of events, dripped and shivered in the center of a spreading patch of moisture. He tried to speak, but words failed to come. He tried to move, but could only shake his head slowly from side to side. The scene before him swam and blurred. He heard Tilly's voice say, "Look, Daddy's crying," and felt his wife's hand on his arm.

"Jerry, dear." Kate sounded very far away. "Darling, what's the matter?"

By a great effort of will, Jerry managed to stop his head from moving back and forth. He tried to smile, but succeeded only in crumpling up his features into a strange puckered grimace.

"I don't know," he said. "It's all so silly. We go out to shoot a goose for dinner and end up carrying on as if someone had died." He gave short laugh. "I mean, let's be reasonable. We don't cry for a roast beef or a fried chicken. We cry for people. If we have to cry about something, let's really do a good job of it. What about the families bombed in their homes and men shot down in planes and drowned at sea and sent out to be picked off by snipers"—his voice rose to a higher pitch—"and mown down by tanks and blown up by booby traps and left screaming and begging"—he gagged and took a gulp of air—"screaming for someone to finish . . . to finish"—his voice cracked as a sudden gush of tears overflowed down his cheeks—"until someone has to take a gun and put the poor bastard out of his—oh, hell." And, grasping the goose's neck with both hands, he gave it a violent wrench.

Having anticipated her father's move in time to shut her eyes and cover her ears, Tilly could never be quite sure, on thinking about it later, whether she imagined or actually heard the ghastly grating snap that henceforth added a new and particularly unpleasant ingredient to her worst nightmares. In any case, when she opened her eyes the goose lay on the ground in front of her father, its head bent back at an impossibly sharp angle, obviously quite dead. She gasped and turned away.

Jerry stared down at the goose for a moment longer, then brushed the back of his hand across his eyes and looked up.

"Well, there it is," he announced cheerfully. "That's how we used to do it on the farm. I'm sorry I messed up the shot and I'm sorry that everything had to end this way, but at least I didn't leave poor old Gilbert to suffer, and"—he paused for a sneeze—"and since I've certainly paid the penalty for my stupid idea, maybe one of you kind people would stop looking at me like I was some kind of murderer and hand me a blanket so that we can go home and forget this ever happened. Veronica will think we're all lost."

In fact, Veronica thought nothing of the kind, having passed the entire morning asleep in her bottom drawer thinking of nothing at all. Only when Jerry banged into the office and rammed his rifle back into its hiding place behind the filing cabinet did she open her eyes and utter a drowsy mew. But Jerry merely threw his wet outerwear over a bentwood coatstand near the window and stamped out again without a word of apology.

So Veronica lowered her head and drifted back to sleep, lulled by the slow drip, drip of water droplets falling from the ruined mass of clotted red and black checks that had once been Jerry's favorite fall jacket.

17

"I don't know," said Jerry, plumping himself down at the kitchen table several days after normal relations had been restored in the Taggert family.

"Know what?"

Stationed in front of the stove, Kate kept a critical eye on the contents of her favorite enameled saucepan while maintaining an easy stirring action with a large wooden spoon.

Jerry leaned back and stretched out his feet. "I just had a short conversation outside with Davy Wilson in which I had to explain the basic concept of life and death using words suitable for a two-year-old. It wasn't something I felt prepared to do right off the bat."

"When in doubt, ask a policeman."

"Why couldn't he have asked his parents?"

"Maybe because we're the ones with a dead goose hanging over our back door."

"Only because you won't let me hang it in the porch."

"My spiced beef got there first." Kate lifted the saucepan off the stove, immersed it in a sink full of cold water and continued to stir. "And you don't know what might come crawling off that goose. Tell me what you said to Davy."

Jerry sighed. "I answered questions. I told him that Gilbert wasn't asleep and that he wasn't going to wake up ever. And I explained that he wasn't going to wake up because he was dead, and that he was dead because I had shot him bang with my gun, and that I shot him so we could have a goose to eat at Christmas."

"All that?"

"It's amazing what you can find out if you just keep asking 'why.' "

"And was he satisfied with your explanation?" Having stirred sufficiently, Kate presented Jerry with the wooden spoon.

"He was happy that he wouldn't have to share our Christmas treat and disappointed that I had no plans to dead anything else in the near future." Jerry popped the spoon into his mouth and withdrew it. "Good. What is it?"

"The filling for Daisy Daniel's Marguerite cake. There was a revised recipe for it in the *Gazette* last month, so I thought maybe I'd make a couple for Tilly's party if it passes the Taggert taste test."

Jerry licked around the shaft of the spoon. "So far, so good. When do we get to sample the finished article?"

"After dinner, with ice cream. And then you might let Crow River look after itself for a couple of hours while we go see *Gaslight*. What's the matter?"

For Jerry had risen to his feet and put on a hangdog expression.

"I can't," he said. "I can't even stay for dinner. They want me over at Springford for some kind of meeting on mine safety and security." He checked his watch. "For which I'm going to be late."

"Oh, Jerry."

"I'm sorry." He planted a kiss on Kate's forehead. "I'll be back as soon as I can. Enjoy the movie and don't let Tilly eat all the cake."

"Tilly won't"—began Kate—"be home," she finished. But the kitchen door had already closed behind Jerry. Moments later, the grating sound of his car engine turned into a low purr fading away into the distance.

Instantly the house felt empty, like a stage set waiting for the curtain to go up. Waiting for Tilly to come racing into the kitchen with news of her day at school and demands for food. But no. Performance canceled. Today she would be running into Mary Allen's kitchen. With a shake of her head, Kate turned to a pair of spice cake layers lying side by side on a wire rack and began spreading one of them with the thick raisin filling.

I hope they don't starve her until dinner, she thought. She always needs something to tide her over. And what if they serve a meal that she doesn't like or know how to eat? What if she's embarrassed about asking for the bathroom or can't sleep in a strange bed? What if she gets homesick or throws up? Oh, damn.

A large dollop of filling had overflowed onto the kitchen counter. Kate scooped it back into place, then began assembling the ingredients for a caramel icing. The house seemed too quiet. She considered turning on the radio, but it was still too early for clear reception. And stacking records on the gramophone changer always unnerved her. Even Sam and Veronica, familiar spirits of the kitchen, seemed to have wandered away on business of their own. Never mind, thought Kate, she'll be back tomorrow. And tonight, I can have some time to myself. Just what I'm always asking for. It will be like a little holiday. She scooped brown sugar out of a measuring cup and went in search of butter. The house grew lonelier by the minute.

He sat in the car and calculated. October the twenty-fourth. Nine weeks to Christmas. Eight weeks, say, until he could give himself his Christmas present. Eight times seven equals fifty-six days. Fifty-six times twenty-four equals . . . his capacity for mental arithmetic gave out.

He lit a cigarette, inhaled deeply and expelled the smoke through his nostrils, idly watching as the two parallel streams twined, mingled and coalesced into a single swirling cloud within which several undulating strands still managed to maintain their own fragile identities even as the cloud began to disperse. He found the effect mildly diverting and repeated it. Nothing like a smoke to stimulate the mind.

He smiled. Thank you, tobacco. With a pipe or a cigarette in my pocket, who needs mental resources? You are my family, my friends, my work, my books, my hobby, my social life, my . . .

He slumped back in the seat. The boredom would be his undoing. He must have been mad to dig himself into a hole like this. Right now in Toronto, Montreal, New York, any civilized place, people by the thousands would be sitting in cinemas and theaters, dining out in restaurants, walking on concrete under neon signs, losing themselves among strangers who neither asked questions nor made assumptions, too busy with their own grubby little doings to pry into the lives of their neighbors.

He drew in another lungful of smoke, holding the cigarette delicately between his second and third fingers. Yes, in a city one could achieve that blissful anonymity that expanded one's existence far beyond the imaginings of those gullible sleepwalking strangers. There one could live two, three, four different lives in as many different worlds, none of which need overlap if one were clever enough to close doors, move quietly, cover one's tracks, watch one's tongue, leave no clues. In a city one could become invisible.

Not that he had anything to reproach himself with here. He had made no mistakes, but even if he had it would hardly have mattered. Really, it had all been too easy. People saw what they wanted to see and dealt with any unpleasant thoughts that might arise by pushing them promptly out of their minds. In any case, they lacked the imagination to conceive of anything really unpleasant. In that respect, as in most others, he had the great advantage of being far ahead of the general public.

He rolled down the car window and flicked away the half-smoked cigarette. The street, the houses, the whole town seemed perfectly dead. Apart from those working underground, he must be one of the very few persons in Crow River not sitting on a hard chair in the recreation hall, hypnotized by the Friday movie. It was almost as if, once a week, the entire aboveground population cast aside all traces of individuality and transformed itself into a huge composite creature—a giant insect, perhaps—staring at the shallow flickering images with six hundred glazed eyes and soaking up their synthetic message with three hundred numbed brains that, even in their composite form, offered no threat to the Invisible Man in their midst.

He smiled again. He had never before looked at his situation in quite that light. Could it be that he had been too clever for his own good, more circumspect than circumstances required? Had he been too miserly, restraining himself with too tight a rein, rationing out his pleasures with too sparing a hand? The thought almost made him catch his breath. The answer set his heart racing. Because, of course, it was yes. "Yes," he said aloud, floating the word out on a long, sibilant breath. Yes, now that he thought about it, he had been his own worst enemy, policing his own actions, whispering useless caution into his own ear, holding back instead of boldly taking what and when he wanted. Eventually, of course, he must move on. But for now—what could they do to stop him? Especially with freeze-up coming and no one able to get in or out until the ice became thick enough to accept planes on skis.

Yes. The realization came flooding over him. Everything conspired in his favor. Fortune had opened a door and beckoned. And who was he to hang back? To the victor the spoils, to the brave the fair. He checked his watch. Only eight-thirty. And he had everything he needed in the car trunk. He reached forward and started the ignition, meanwhile humming a little tune.

"*Margie,*" he sang as he steered the car out toward the river road, "*I'm always thinking of you. Days are never blue.*"

His heart beat deliciously. He really was being very naughty. But—fact of life—he always opened his Christmas presents early.

Tilly lay in the dark, her eyes wide open, savoring the excitement of a strange bed made up with blankets instead of a comforter and fresh sheets that gave off a scent quite different from that imparted by the brand of soap powder favored by her mother. She felt happy and relieved because, so far at least, her visit had progressed smoothly with no mistakes, disagreements or embarrassing moments. Like a good guest, she had taken a lively interest in whatever her hostess chose to show her, admired her pretty room and fallen in with all suggestions. She had gone through Margie's entire collection of paper dolls before dinner, successfully negotiated an unfamiliar type of Yorkshire pudding that resembled a slab of solid custard rather than the crisp puffed-up balloon produced by her mother, and remembered to compliment Mrs. Allen on the meal. Then she had giggled her way through Shopping, a game of Margie's own devising that required each player in turn to close her eyes, place her finger at random on any page of Eaton's winter catalog and explain why she wished to purchase whatever article lay closest to the fingertip, be it hardware, sporting equipment or (very droll) men's underwear. And at last, after losing the game with a paltry expenditure of $580.10 as against a winning total of $2,524.65

("You've got to know where they put the record players and refrigerators," Margie explained later), she unpacked her small suitcase, changed into nightdress, slippers and robe, brushed her teeth and climbed into her allotted place in bed, midway between Margie and the wall.

"Are you asleep?" whispered Margie, thirty seconds after they had switched off the light.

"No," replied Tilly.

"There's some cookies for us on a plate in the cupboard. We could eat them in bed."

"I'm not hungry. Are you?"

"Uh-uh."

"And we'd have to brush our teeth all over again."

Margie snuggled down under the blankets and pulled them closer up under her chin. "Isn't this fun?" she asked.

"Yes," said Tilly, following suit. "I've never been in bed with anybody before except my mother. Have you?"

"Oh . . ." The answer slipped away into Margie's pillow.

"Pardon?"

"Mm-mm."

"Who?"

"Oh . . ." Margie bounced against the mattress. "I forget. Aren't you glad Mrs. Reese picked us to sing the descant in 'Away in a Manger'? Do you know it yet?"

"All but the hard bit in the last verse," said Tilly. "My father calls it the Death Chant."

Margie giggled appreciatively. "I know!" she said. "Let's try it now. I'll sing the regular tune and you sing the Death Chant. One, two, three."

They ran through the carol several times, taking turns singing the melody and failing to harmonize when it came to the hard bit. At last Margie became bored and put an end to the singing.

"Your mother's so nice," she said, by way of beginning a conversation. "I like it when she comes to school and teaches us the play. What are you getting for Christmas?"

Tilly shrugged. "I don't know. She won't tell. Maybe a toboggan."

"I'm getting a real silver locket." Margie drew a picture in the air, her hands black against the pale blue light coming in through the window opposite the bed. "A heart," she explained. "With a pearl on it and a little bird."

Tilly's heart gave a giant thump. "Like the one in the store?"

"Yes." Margie pulled her hands down under the covers and began smoothing the lower sheet. "Only it isn't from the store."

"How do you know it's the same?"

Margie continued to stroke the sheet. "I've seen it," she said archly. "I might even get it before Christmas."

"Has your mother said?"

"Not from her."

"Then how—?"

"I've earned it." Margie's voice took on a defiant note. "And it's a secret. You can't tell."

"I won't, but—"

"And maybe sometime I'll let you wear it."

Tilly's heart thumped again. In the silence that followed, the ticking of a little alarm clock on the night table by the bed began to fill the room.

"Tilly . . . ?" Her name came out of the dark in a whisper.

"Yes."

"Has anyone ever kind of . . . you know . . . touched you?"

"Touched me?"

"You know. Touched you somewhere . . ."

"Where?"

Margie's hand slid over.

Tilly jumped. "No," she said quickly.

"No," Margie echoed in a forlorn voice. "I didn't think so."

"I mean, maybe before I started having a bath by myself . . ."

"Oh, yes." Margie brushed off this remark as being too obvious for comment. "It doesn't—" Her sentence broke off in a gasp.

Tilly, who had allowed her eyes to drop shut, opened them again.

"What is it?" she asked.

"Nothing." The word emerged on a high, tremulous note.

"Was there something at the window?"

"No."

"I thought I saw something white."

"No."
"Why are we whispering?"
"Shh."
Tilly held her breath for a moment. Outside, a foot crunched on the gravel path. Her hand encountered Margie's under the covers and was instantly clutched.
"It's your mother and father," she said. "They're coming back."
"It's too early." Margie's voice shook. "They always play till eleven."
"There's somebody."
"No."
The rusty springs on the porch screen door twanged open with agonizing slowness.
"There!"
"No! There's no one!" Margie leapt up in bed and scrabbled at a switch on the wall. An unshaded bulb on the ceiling flooded the room with light.
The door springs creaked shut.
Margie looked about wildly until her glance returned to the bed. "I know!" she cried. "Let's have a pillow fight!"
Blinded by the light and taken by surprise, Tilly could only react to the sudden attack by putting up her arms and rolling back and forth on the bed. Margie, meanwhile, gasped and shrieked, swinging her pillow back and forth until at last Tilly managed to seize her own pillow and begin to fight back. Unaggressive by nature, she hardly knew how to fend off the frenzied barrage of soft, thudding blows delivered by her flushed, wide-eyed opponent. Eventually, however, she achieved a rhythm of her own and began to put up an acceptable defense. At the same time, out of the corner of her eye, she noticed a slight movement behind Margie. It seemed as if the thin edge of the bedroom door swung slightly away from the wall, then vanished back into it. Startled, she dropped her pillow and stared. Margie stopped screaming and whirled about. On seeing nothing, she turned back, her face ashen.
"What was it?" she asked.
Tilly shook her head. "I don't know. I thought I saw the door close."
The color returned to Margie's face, partially blotting out the

dark blotches under her eyes. She ran to the door and flung it open. The kitchen beyond lay in darkness. The screen door twanged and clicked shut. Margie turned around, smiling.

"You see?" she said. "It was nothing. Nothing at all."

She took a few steps into the room and dropped onto the bed. "Nothing at all," she sobbed. "Nothing, nothing, nothing."

"I'm sorry, Tilly," she said when they were once again lying quietly side by side in bed. "I shouldn't have asked you to stay. I won't do it again. Don't be mad at me."

Tilly squeezed her hand and pretended to fall asleep, trying all the while not to think of the blurred face with its white beard and mustache that had floated briefly up to the dark window while Margie wept on the bed.

Later, she woke to discover that the Shadow, on not finding her at home, had managed to track her down in Margie's bedroom.

There seemed to be no place one could hide.

18

On the following Friday, prior to setting off for school, Tilly could not resist planting herself in the middle of the living room and making one last critical survey of the paper decorations she and Kate had cut out and hung up the night before. They still looked magnificent. Fierce black cats arched against the windows, orange jack-o'-lanterns grinned wickedly from the lamp shades, black bats dangled from the ceiling on invisible threads and, in the far corner, a fat black spider hung wickedly over the record cabinet on a web of white crepe paper. Adding to the Halloween motif, orange and black streamers supported a pleated paper pumpkin over the center of the room, while a real carved jack-o'-lantern, terrifying to behold, sat atop a black paper cloth on the dining table. An ingeniously illuminated crystal ball awaited Gypsy Magda in the bedroom and a pile of games lay on the cedar-chest coffee table, ready to be set up before five o'clock, when the first guests would begin to arrive.

Satisfied that nothing further could be done to improve on this arrangement, Tilly returned to the kitchen, where she found Sam sitting with his chin on the counter, transfixed by the sight of two large layer cakes, each extravagantly iced in shades of chocolate and orange and temptingly displayed under a glass cover. The kitchen appeared otherwise unoccupied, offering an opportunity too good to be missed. Tilly drifted over to the counter, tilted back one of the covers and helped herself to a dollop of icing which, despite its violent color, gave off a light, fresh taste of grated orange rind. Sam, agitated beyond endurance, shuffled himself closer to the counter and uttered a low, deep moan.

"Shh." Tilly discovered another overflow of icing on the cake plate and transferred it to the tip of Sam's protruding tongue.

"Don't do that," said Kate, entering from the porch with a crockery pudding basin in one hand and a black metal lunch box tucked under her arm.

"It looked so good we couldn't resist."

"There'll be plenty for everyone at the party." Kate handed Tilly the lunch box. "Wear your mittens. It's chilly out."

Tilly pulled on a pair of red knitted mittens and collected her canvas book bag from the kitchen table. "I wish it was tonight already," she announced.

"I don't," said Kate. "Too much to do, too little time." Picking up a wooden spoon, she gave the glutinous contents of the pudding basin a trial stir.

"What's that?" asked Tilly suspiciously.

"Cooked rice." The words took on a hollow ring as Kate began to rummage about in one of the counter drawers.

"What for?"

"You'll see."

Tilly paused at the door. "You aren't going to do something—you know—funny, are you?"

"Whatever can you mean?" Having found what she was looking for, Kate shut the drawer and stared at her daughter with round innocent eyes.

Tilly pointed. "What are you going to do with that?"

"You mean this?" Kate held up an oversized pink rubber glove.

"Yes."

"You'll see."

"Because if you are going to do something funny, I wish you wouldn't."

Kate retrieved her wooden spoon and ladled up a generous helping of wet rice. "You're afraid I'm going to embarrass you," she said.

"Well . . ."

"Now would I do a thing like that?"

The rice hit the inside of the rubber glove with a sickening plop. Tilly's heart sank.

"Yes," she said.

A mad cackle followed her out the door.

Tilly rolled her eyes. Parents could be a trial. She cheered up, however, on being met outdoors by a hint of frost in the air and a light dusting of snow on the ground: perfect Halloween weather for one equipped with a skeleton costume that allowed for many layers of long underwear. She cheered up even more when she discovered that her father had kept his promise to transfer the late Gilbert from his home above the porch door to some less prominent resting place, presumably the meat storage locker in the cookery. At least she wouldn't have to answer any embarrassing questions about *that* parental eccentricity. Now as long as everyone showed up and played the games and didn't fight and liked the food and nothing awful happened . . .

Oh, I wish it was all over, thought Tilly as a sudden cold knot clamped itself tightly around the upper portion of her chest. But a full eight hours remained before the party even began, so she took a deep breath, switched her thoughts to the day's spelling assignment and, muttering "P-A-R-A-L-L-E-L: parallel" under her breath, set off for school.

Jerry pulled the last page of his monthly report out of the typewriter and read it over. Having worked on the report for most of the day, he read slowly, keeping a careful watch against slips of both mind and finger. But the page seemed to make passable sense and contained no obvious spelling mistakes, so he added it to a pile of similar pages on his desk and turned off the desk lamp. He then flexed his cramped shoulder muscles, locked his hands behind his head and tipped slowly backward in his revolving chair. He closed his eyes.

Away in the front half of the house, Tilly's party continued at top volume. Jerry opened his eyes and checked his watch. Six-thirty. If he intended to put in an appearance, he had better do it now. He groaned and tipped himself up onto his feet, taking care not to bang into the lower drawer of his filing cabinet, where Veronica now spent most of her time. In the corridor outside his office, he found the door to the kitchen closed. A sign, hand lettered in crayon, hung on the top panel. It read:

NO ADMITTANCE
Go To Back Door
THIS MEANS YOU!

Jerry had long ago learned the unwisdom of ignoring hand-lettered signs. He therefore obediently turned away from the forbidden passage and opened the outside door to his right. A freezing wind immediately forced him to huddle his arms tightly about his chest. Overhead, ragged clouds scudded past a three-quarter moon, and directly across the river the lights of the mine assay office winked at him through a shifting panorama of swaying evergreens and bare, rattling birches. Farther away toward town, a fluttering orange glow indicated that the older boys from school had already lit their usual bonfire in the bare grassland between the swimming dock and the recreation hall.

Making a mental note to check on the fire as soon as he started his rounds, Jerry began walking briskly in a counterclockwise direction around the south end of the house. Here a dim red light lit up the windows of the sun-room extension, now mysteriously quiet, and another printed sign, identical to the first, warned him away from the flight of stairs leading up to the front door. Beneath this sign, a thick red cardboard arrow pointed to a sloping path that took him through the fence gate on the southeast corner, under the main bedroom window, over the wooden pipeline housing and on past the window of Tilly's room until, having turned another corner, he came up against the screen door in the side of the porch.

Light bulbs usually burned both inside the porch and over the door. Tonight, however, the only illumination came from a grinning jack-o'-lantern placed on an upturned log at the end of the path. It gave off just enough light for Jerry to read a third sign pinned to the screen door and lettered as follows:

ENTER AND KNOCK

Jerry entered, pushing through a curtain of black material hung behind the screen door. He stood still for a moment to orient himself in the darkness, then moved blindly toward the inner door. Soft, light tendrils brushed past his face. He raised his hand and encountered something else, thin and threadlike. It was surely too late for spiders, and yet . . . He took another half step into a strange tangle that caught on his ears, brushed past his eyes and pulled at his hair. Most horribly, some of it seemed wet. Fighting down an irrational sense of panic, he struck out and hit the door with the side of his hand.

"Yay-uss?"

The thin cracked voice issued through a chink in the door, which had opened the merest fraction of an inch. Jerry broke into a grin and brushed aside more of the assorted debris hanging from the ceiling.

"It's me," he said.

The door opened a little wider and a beam of green light shot upward to reveal a ghastly twisted face half obscured by a long crooked nose, a mane of white hair and a pointed black hat.

"Who's 'me'?" asked the witch in a voice that might well have issued from an unoiled hinge.

Jerry identified himself.

"Oh, the local flatfoot. What do you want here?"

"Dinner would be nice," said Jerry. "But I'll settle for a hot dog and a piece of cake."

"Well, now." The witch considered. "All who wish to enter must pay a forfeit. Give us a kiss."

"Sorry, I have a jealous wife."

"All right—shake."

Jerry inspected the proffered hand with deep suspicion.

"Do I have to?"

"What's the matter, dearie? No guts?"

The hand was cold and clammy and squished in a revolting fashion when pressed.

"My God," said Jerry, wiping his own hand on his trousers. "What have you got in there?"

Kate laughed and pulled off her disguise. "Trade secret," she said. "Look." Opening the door wider, she directed the beam of her flashlight over to the far corner of the kitchen where, blocking the door into the corridor, a small white ghost in a highchair screamed "Boo!" in an amazingly loud voice.

Jerry clutched his heart and sank back against the door frame. "Help!" he called weakly. "A ghost! A terrible ghost."

The ghost cackled and screamed "Boo!" several more times.

"Shh, dear." Kate hurried across the room and lifted the exuberant Davy from his chair. "Come and listen to your mother."

"Margaret's sending the kids off with a Halloween poem," she explained, as they all moved into the darkened living room where Gypsy Magda sat before a small bedside table upon which rested an upturned glass mixing bowl lined with tissue paper and lit from below by a red Christmas tree light. In front of her on the floor a colorful band of cowboys, cowgirls, ghosts, witches, pirates, tramps, sultans, nurses, skeletons, pretty ladies and assorted royalty sat listening amidst a rubble of paper plates and cups, air pistols, suction darts, donkey tails, beanbags, a mechanical hockey game and a galvanized tub filled with water and a few bobbing apples. Obviously much in command of her audience, Magda risked a dramatic pause and launched into the end of her poem:

"The owl flies home to its blasted tree,
The bats to their clammy caves,
The goblins and ghouls to their haunted house,
The ghosts to their open graves

Where all will sleep for another year
Till again their troubled souls
Break forth on this terrible night to cavort
With bogies and beasties and trolls."

Here Gypsy Magda leaned forward over her crystal ball to sinister effect and lowered her voice to a hoarse whisper.

"And yet all of you here will go out, I know,
With never a thought or care
As to what might happen on All Souls' Eve
And what could be waiting there.

For why should you worry when everyone knows
That none of my tale is true?
And devils and demons don't really exist—"

The whisper dropped yet another notch.

"But then again—
maybe they do!
OOOOO-HA-HA-HA!"

Gypsy Magda ended her recitation with a blood-curdling laugh that brought screams from a cowgirl, a nurse and an Indian princess. Moving as one, Kate and Jerry quickly switched on several lamps.

"Well, that's it," Kate announced in her jolliest manner. "Time to trick or treat."

"Yay," yelled some of the older boys.

"Don't soap too many windows and keep your comments clean."

"Yay!"

"And Mrs. Reese says don't forget to call in at her house. She's expecting you."

Silence.

"She won't be giving out oranges this year. I saw the toffee apples myself."

"*Yay!*"

The party surged into the kitchen, where coats, boots, pillowcases and popcorn balls were collected.

"How did the party go?" asked Jerry, entering the living room with a tepid hot dog after the last guest had been ushered out and the small ghost sent home asleep in the arms of his gypsy mother.

"A mad success." Stretched out on one of the corner sofas, Kate addressed her remark to the ceiling.

Jerry sat down at the end of the sofa, lifted his wife's feet onto his lap and began massaging one with his left hand while feeding himself bites of hot dog with his right.

"Tired?"

"Not too bad. The party kind of ran itself. Oh, that's good."

"Who was the clown handing out coats at the end?"

"Mona Meade." Kate closed her eyes.

"You mean Mona the Menace, terror of the under-tens?"

"Not anymore. I put her in charge of the angels and she seems to have taken it on as a full-time job. You'd better give me back my feet, or I'll go to sleep and you'll have to do the cleaning up."

"Can't." Having finished his hot dog, Jerry went to work on both feet at once. "I have to try and keep all the private outhouses standing and make sure nobody burns anything down." He leaned forward and switched off the red light under Gypsy Magda's crystal ball. "How did the fortune-telling go?"

"Well . . ." Kate wiggled her toes. "I just looked in once. Apparently little Patsy Michaels is destined to become the most sought-after courtesan in postwar Europe, with wealthy men fighting tooth and nail for her services." She yawned. "She seemed quite pleased."

"She'll have to lose some weight first." Jerry leaned back and continued to knead for a while. A thought occurred. "Did she really eat nine corn on the cobs?"

"Who?"

"Patsy Michaels. She told me she ate nine ears of corn."

"Ten." The answer came out in a murmur.

"She'll be sick."

"She was. But it didn't seem to bother . . ." Kate's voice tailed away in an extended sigh.

Jerry sat a few minutes longer, then slipped gently off the sofa and made a systematic collection of used paper cups, plates and napkins. This left only a few plates, tubs and pots to be washed out. The decorations and games could be put away tomorrow. Taking a last look at Kate, still fast asleep on the sofa, he let himself quietly out of the house, crammed a giant bundle of rubbish into the garbage can and drove away.

19

By seven-thirty the party had broken up into groups and dispersed up and down the town's residential district, where they encountered a few sheepish older children in token costumes, some bemused toddlers shepherded by their parents, and a number of merry masked adults fresh out of the beer parlor. Each group set to work with single-minded efficiency, and within a short time growing accumulations of fruit and candy were being compared under street-lamps while shrill breathless voices traded information as to where the most desirable handouts could be found. By nine-thirty all signs pointed to a successful Halloween. A massive heap of embers popped and spat behind the recreation hall, two outhouses lay overturned in a lane dating from the first days of the mine, and several basic four-letter words marched across the schoolhouse windows in letters of soap. Pillowcases bulged, footsteps dragged, and a growing number of extinguished porch lights indicated that the inhabitants within, picked clean of sugared offerings, had shut their doors and retired to bed.

So it was that three foul fugitives from the grave, a skeleton, a ghost and a vampire, emerged from a house at the far end of town to find themselves quite alone on a silent, slumbering street lit only by a single electric bulb mounted on a distant power pole and such rare bursts of moonlight as managed to squeeze through an ever thickening layer of cloud. For a moment it seemed as if the whole town had closed down for the night, but then the sound of a slammed door followed by shouts and laughter came drifting through the thick strip of bushland on the opposite side of the street.

"They're playing Knock-out Ginger over on the post office road," said the vampire, indistinctly through fangs.

"Yeah," boomed the ghost in basso tones. "Let's go play too."

"Let's go home," said the skeleton, shifting nervously from one leg to the other.

"Come on, Tilly," said the ghost. "Just one."

"Yeah, Tilly." The vampire removed his fangs and became recognizable as Harvey Lewis from the fifth grade. "Just one, then you and Joey can go home."

Tilly kicked at some loose gravel lying under the toe of her right foot. "I'm not supposed to," she said. "Anyhow, by the time we get over there there won't be any houses left to knock out."

Harvey shrugged. "Okay, we'll do one here." He set out briskly toward the yellow lamp at the end of the street. "How about the Holtzers?"

"No," gasped Tilly, walking hard to keep up. "Mr. Holtzer gets mad sometimes. He might chase us."

"He won't." Joey's voice fell even lower in disgust at this display of naked cowardice.

"I know!" Harvey came to a halt in front of the last house on the street. "Let's knock out old man Meade. Pay him back for all those boring talks in church."

"We can't knock out a minister." Having so recently made her peace with Mona, Tilly had no wish to antagonize either father or daughter. "And there aren't any lights on."

"So what? We'll wake him up. Here . . ." Relieving Tilly and Joey of their pillowcases, Harvey darted off and deposited them, along with his own, deep in a patch of bushes on the other side of the street.

"Okay," he said, dashing back and lowering his voice to a conspiratorial whisper. "That's where we'll hide. Come on."

Without waiting for a reply, he jumped across a drainage ditch and marched bravely up to the Meade front steps, leaving an eager Joey and a reluctant Tilly to scuttle along at his heels.

"Now," he whispered, as Joey took a moment to gather up the flowing ends of his ghostly sheet and Tilly scanned the dark woods behind them for signs of a suitable hiding place. "I'll go up myself and you two can wait at the bottom, but nobody moves until I knock three times. Here goes."

Tilly whirled about with a vague thought of putting up another objection, but Harvey had already reached the top of the steps, where he executed not one but two bold triple knocks on the door. Struck motionless by a sudden panic, she had time to watch Joey billow away in a cloud of white sheeting and Harvey leap past her off the steps before she could summon up the proper coordination to make her own break for cover. Then the same panic added wings to her heels and brought her crashing through a gap in the bushes just a few feet away from the hollow where Harvey and Joey lay stretched out on the ground, trying to breathe heavily without making a sound.

"Well, that was a dud," said Harvey, after they had waited in vain for someone to come to the door. "Old man Meade must have gone out." He stood up and began flapping leaves out of his cape. "We'll have to try somebody else."

Tilly's heart fell. "You said just one."

"This one don't count," said Joey.

"Yes, it does."

"Don't count when there's nobody home."

"Yeah." Harvey began pushing out of the bush. "We gotta find somebody who's home. Look over there."

Just beyond the power pole with the yellow light, a large circle of sand marked the end of the street on which they stood and the beginning of another, running off at right angles, parallel to the river. On the far side of this new thoroughfare, several houses showed promising signs of life. Harvey pointed to the last one on the left, which appeared to be acting as a buttress against the encroaching forest.

"The Allens are home," he said. "Maybe we can give that snooty Margie a scare."

Splendidly attired in a Glinda the Good gown, as worn by Billie Burke in *The Wizard of Oz*, Margie had excited much whispered comment at Tilly's party by refusing to sit down, eat or participate in any of the games for fear of damaging her wand, crown or many layers of pink tulle.

Harvey's proposal met with instant agreement from Joey, who had not forgotten his recent snubbing at Margie's hands. Once again, Tilly found herself cast in the role of wet blanket.

"Margie can't be back yet," she pointed out, "or they'd have turned off the porch light. Come on, Joey, let's go home."

"Aw . . ."

"We'll do the Wisnickis next door," Harvey announced. "Then we can hide in the bush across the street, just like before. Come on."

But the Wisnicki house sat much farther back from the road than the manse (as Mr. Meade always referred to it), and Tilly's small store of courage dwindled alarmingly as they started down the dirt path that separated Mr. Wisnicki's vegetable garden from Mrs. Wisnicki's flower beds on its way up to the back porch. The terrain seemed far too exposed and the streetlight too near. Could she run fast enough to reach a hiding place before someone came to the door? And (here her knees began to tremble) what would happen if they let out Brandy who, though amiable by day, had a loud bark and, for all Tilly knew, a keen nose for tracking late-night pranksters? She longed to cast shame aside and flee, but lacked courage even for that. Instead, she came up with a plan.

It occurred to her that, although Harvey and Joey could run faster than she, they still might be seen while making a dash for the woods across the street or heard pushing through the bushes. All of this would provide an excellent diversion to draw attention from anyone else—herself, for instance—who might then make a quick dash through Mr. Wisnicki's patch of late potatoes and hide behind Margie's house next door. Of course, she would be all alone there, with no one to share in the blame if caught. And she would have to find a way to rejoin her companions afterward. However, on balance . . .

The time for balancing alternatives ran out. Harvey banged on the porch door, Brandy replied with a fearful howl from the kitchen, and Tilly bolted like a jackrabbit over the neatly hoed potato rows. Having reached a comparatively safe haven, pressed into the shadows behind the Allen porch, she glanced sideways just in time to see Harvey and Joey disappear into the bushes across the street.

At the same moment, she heard the Wisnicki's inner door bang open, the scrabble of Brandy's heavy feet on the kitchen linoleum and the musical whine of wire springs as someone pushed the outer screen door. She held her breath and listened harder.

"Who is it, dear?" came the faint, strained voice of Mrs. Wisnicki from inside the kitchen.

"Nobody here." Mr. Wisnicki sounded alarmingly loud and close. "Keep a hold on the dog. I'm going to look outside."

The springs sang again, a foot scuffed, and the door slammed shut. In the ensuing silence, Tilly gave herself up for lost. It seemed that her last sensations on earth would be darkness, terror and the acrid scent of creosote emanating from the tarpapered wall behind her. She prayed for the moon to remain covered and for Mr. Wisnicki to go back indoors, promising in return a lifetime of tidy rooms, high examination marks and dinner plates wiped clean of even cabbage and omelets.

The Wisnicki kitchen door opened and closed once more.

"Come on in, Mike," Mrs. Wisnicki from behind the screen door. "It's just some kids playing games."

"I'll say. And they've been playing them across my potatoes, the little bastards."

"Michael!"

"Go on in. I'm just going to have a look over here."

Footsteps crunched slowly across the potato rows. Leaves swished against trouser legs. Tilly combed through her mind desperately for a plan of action. She could run around the house, but this might lead to disaster if Mr. Wisnicki decided to walk around it in the opposite direction. Or she could make a break for the woods on the other side of the Allens' vegetable patch which, by a happy stroke of luck, had just been dug clear of any telltale plants. And once in the bush, she could move much faster than any pursuing adult.

Without wasting any more time on further debate, Tilly raced wildly across the churned-up earth, calling on all her experience from past First of July sports days to keep her head up, pump her arms and stretch her stride to the utmost. Straight ahead lay a dark opening between two clumps of bare pin cherry trees. If she could just pass through and keep up her speed across the clearing beyond, she could vanish safely into the thick bush that ran down toward the river. Gathering her last reserves of strength, she flew through the opening—and kept on flying as the ground vanished from under her feet, tumbling her headfirst into a pit of odorous, semirotten plant cuttings and leaf sweepings, otherwise known as Mrs. Allen's compost heap.

Unhurt, but too surprised to move, Tilly lay facedown on Mrs. Allen's pride and joy, grateful only that her mother had not found the time to paint a skeletal outline on the back of her black costume. For, as the sound of heavy footsteps grew louder, her only hope lay in camouflage. She pulled her hands in under her dark mask and waited.

All too soon the pin cherry branches rattled open and whipped back into place. A twig cracked on the groud nearby and Tilly had a dreadful thought. What if Mr. Wisnicki missed the edge of the pit and fell in on top of her? Would heaven show mercy and let her die on the spot? Would it help if she promised to eat liver? But before she could follow through on this rash scheme, the footsteps slowed and shuffled to a halt somewhere just above her head.

An awful silence followed. At last, Mr. Wisnicki spoke.

"My goodness," he said in an unnaturally loud voice. "This here's a real spooky spot. I wouldn't be surprised if maybe a ghost or two didn't come along on a bad night like this. Or maybe something worse."

Tilly's blood congealed and her head began to swim.

"Now I think whoever banged on my door and mussed up my potato patch is somewhere pretty close by," Mr. Wisnicki announced, "and I want to catch him real bad. But, brrr"—he shivered—"I wouldn't stay on in a place like this for anything. So I think"—his voice took on a thoughtful note—"I think what I'll do is go sit by the Allens' porch and make sure he stays in there so the ghosts can get him. And if he tries to get out"—the pin cherries rattled and the voice rose as it became more distant—"why, I'll be right here waiting to get him."

This disturbing statement ended in an odd sound, halfway between a cough and a clearing of the throat. At some happier time it might have passed as a chuckle. Tilly, however, knew better. She had heard Veronica purr while toying with a mouse. Now she was the mouse, and somewhere just beyond the edge of the woods the purring cat waited.

Mouselike, Tilly continued to lie still and silent, half stifled by the warm, pungent odor of roots, grass, leaves and, it became increasingly clear, some additional enrichment courtesy of Buck and Snowball, the two elderly mine horses who still consented to pull a cart or sleigh through town from time to time. Minutes passed in this fashion, during which Tilly had little to do but remain quiet, breathe as little as possible and wonder whether the sensation in her lower left leg derived from a spreading patch of dampness or merely nervous imagination. She also wondered how long she would have to stay in this uncomfortable position and how she would be able to tell when the coast had cleared.

And as more minutes ticked by, bringing no further sound beyond that of the wind in the trees, a dark suspicion entered Tilly's mind. Perhaps no one waited for her beyond the bushes. Perhaps Mr. Wisnicki had long ago abandoned his vigil (if, indeed, he had ever kept it) and that the butt of her Halloween prank might very well have managed to turn the tables and seize the last laugh for himself. Emboldened by this comforting thought, she decided to risk a cautious peep over the top of the pit. Just then a twig snapped. Someone was coming. She froze and waited.

Silly, she thought, when nothing further disturbed the silence. Twigs often cracked or moved all by themselves. A change of temperature could do it (and the air now contained more than a suggestion of frost) or the pressure of a recent footstep. Why did she always have to be such a coward? Get up, she thought. It's late. Get up and find—

Leaves rustled and branches whipped against cloth. The thud of nearby footsteps traveled through the compost and blended with the beating of Tilly's heart. Something large and bulky had pushed past the trees into the clearing.

Although submerged in darkness, with her eyes tightly shut, Tilly felt certain that the newcomer was not Mr. Wisnicki. The sounds and vibrations did not match, nor did the rhythm of the tense, constricted breathing that caught her ear when all else fell silent. But who else would come into the bush at this time of night and why? A cigarette lighter clicked and rasped. Tilly relaxed weakly into a delicious surge of relief. Her companion in the woods had nothing more sinister in mind than a surreptitious smoke, unseen by parents, teacher or tattling schoolmates. Tilly smiled. Little did he know. Once more she tensed herself to look over the edge of the pit, and once more a sudden sound prevented her from moving.

It came out as a sharp expulsion of breath, *Whee-oo*, not quite a whistle; and, after a short pause, it was repeated, *Whee-oo*, a little louder and with more urgency. Then, as if in answer, a second set of footsteps approached, smaller and lighter than the first, with much reluctant scuffling.

"What are you doing here?"

Tilly jumped. After straining so long to catch small telltale sounds, her highly tuned ears magnified the high, clear, familiar voice to such a degree that it seemed to come from only a few inches away. She made a conscious effort to adjust her hearing downward and in doing so almost missed the next sound: a small plop, as the discarded cigarette landed on some damp leaves not too far away.

"Oh, dear. Aren't you glad to see me?"

The deep rolling voice might have come from her grandfather or a favorite uncle. Warm and reassuring, it made the loose wisps of hair at the back of her neck stir and stiffen.

"No," came the answer. "You don't play fair. You said you'd give it to me last time, but you lied."

"Give you what, Margie?" The voice contained a chuckle. "Didn't dear old Santa give you enough?"

In the pause that followed, Tilly's head shot up, quite of its own accord. Unable to help herself, she abandoned caution and craned her neck farther until at last she could see over the dirt wall and into the clearing.

Margie stood about twenty feet away. Even with a coat thrown over her costume and part of her back turned toward Tilly, she still looked like a creation of gossamer and moonbeams just risen from the pages of a storybook. Sequins sparkled on the transparent layers of her long skirt as well as on the starry wand in her hand and the pointed tiara on her head. Fire flashed from her borrowed earrings and a shaft of light from the distant streetlamp turned her hair into a golden halo. It seemed perfectly appropriate that she should be facing, on the other side of the clearing, an equally fabulous creature dressed in the white beard, the red hat, and the red suit with brass buttons and fur trim that Tilly remembered so well from past Christmas mornings.

"You know what I mean," Margie said at last. "You didn't keep your promise. You lied."

"So did you, Margie."

Margie gasped. "I never!"

"Yes, you did. I'm very disappointed in you."

"I never!"

"Now, now. You can't fool Old Santa. Santa knows everything." The deep voice dropped even lower. "You promised never to tell about us, and you did."

"I didn't."

Santa shook his head sadly. "You told Tilly Taggert."

For the second time that evening, Tilly felt on the verge of a faint. She ducked her head and curled up into the smallest ball she could make.

"No." Margie, too, sounded weak and shaken.

"Don't tell another lie, Margie." Santa's voice suddenly lost some of its resonance and rose to a penetrating whisper. "You gave away our secret, didn't you? You couldn't wait. The minute you got someone into your bed, you started whispering and giggling and laughing and you blabbed everything, didn't you?" The whisper became almost a shout. "Didn't you?"

"No." Margie had begun to cry. "I didn't," she quavered. "I never. I wouldn't."

"That's what you say. But how can I believe you?"

"I couldn't," wailed Margie pathetically, after a shuddering sob. "You know I couldn't."

"Oh, Margie, Margie. What am I to do with you?"

Trembling in her dark hiding place, Tilly tried to imagine herself at home, safely under the covers, listening to the unseen actors on a radio program. But why, asked a small voice in the back of her mind, why did the actor playing Santa utter his harsh words almost as if he were pleased when he should be sounding angry? And who did he remind her of? Whose familiar voice did she hear there, as distorted and far away as the tiny voice one heard in a tin-can telephone at the end of a tight string? Sometimes the answer seemed to be rushing toward her, but it always flew away before she could seize it. All she could do was pay attention and try her best to follow the story.

"Can I believe you?" Santa asked when his previous question failed to elicit a response. "Should I give you another chance?"

"No!" replied Margie with passion. "I don't want another chance. Just go away and leave me alone. Please leave me alone."

"Well, since you ask so nicely." Santa's deep voice flowed out as smooth as butterscotch sauce. "We'll make a little bargain. I'll come once more. That won't be so bad, will it? And you'll get to wear this"—Tilly saw the silver heart and its pearl catch the light as clearly as if she had her eyes open—"and then, well"—Santa chuckled—"we'll think of something, won't we? And after you put it on you'll never see me again. How does that sound? Is it a bargain?"

Margie must have nodded, for Santa seemed pleased with her response.

"Good," he said. "Now why don't you run inside and jump into bed before you catch cold? And Margie—" He raised his voice to stop the light footsteps as they began to move rapidly away. "Margie, look."

Tilly heard a little gasp of surprise, or perhaps even pleasure.

"Isn't it pretty? Wouldn't you like it?" Leaves rustled as Margie began to walk slowly back toward the center of the clearing. "You can have it, Margie." The cajoling voice became even softer and more silky as Margie advanced another few steps. "Does it remind you of someone?" it asked. "Yes? Me, too. Now let me show you what happens to little girls who tell secrets."

Something snapped.

The sharp, sudden noise clicked a switch in Tilly's mind, flooding it with an image of mist and marsh and reeds and of her father's feet half hidden by a limp bundle of wet feathers lying in a spreading pool of water. At the same instant, Margie drew a sharp breath, then turned and fled away through the pin cherry arch. Santa laughed.

"Ho, ho, ho, Margie," he called after her. "You forgot your present."

An eternity passed before a small, almost weightless object landed on the leaves behind Tilly's head. And, with another laugh, Santa too left the clearing.

Thoroughly paralyzed by cold and fear, Tilly remained curled up in her hiding place until long after the sound of heavy footsteps and cracking branches had faded away into the deepest part of the woods. At last, when she heard the distant sound of an automobile start up and drive away, she opened her eyes, raised her head and cautiously got to her feet.

The clearing looked as deserted as before. Nothing remained of the scene she had just overheard except for a burnt-out cigarette butt near the edge of the compost pit and, at her feet, a small Celluloid doll similar to the ones she and Joey had seen in the store. Similar, yet somehow different because, after all, this was a little girl who told secrets. Tilly bent down. The doll smiled up at her bravely, displaying the same merry blue eyes, dimpled cheeks and pixie curl that brightened the soup advertisement on Glassy Jack's wall. Tilly picked it up. Gently she tried to induce the twisted, lolling head to sit up straight and face forward again. But when the torn neck snapped in her hand she buried the severed head and body in a makeshift grave under a pile of leaves, collected her pillowcase from its hiding place on the other side of the dusty intersection and walked home as fast as her shaking legs could carry her.

She found a light on in the porch and her mother in the kitchen, putting away a stack of pots and pans.

"Hello," said Kate. "You're home late. Did you have a good time?"

"Yes," said Tilly.

"Lots of loot?"

Tilly held up her pillowcase.

"Not bad." Kate shoved her large enameled jam kettle into a counter cupboard and shut the door. "Any adventures?"

"No," said Tilly.

"Not a one?"

"No," said Tilly.

Kate gave her daughter a shrewd look. "Are you sure?" she asked.

Before the hesitation that followed could stretch into a pause, a thin, querulous voice floated into the kitchen through the open door leading to Jerry's office.

"I been bad," it bellowed. "I done it again. The devil's in me and no mistake!"

Tilly looked down the corridor into the dark office.

"Isn't Mr. McCallister kind of early tonight?"

Kate sighed. "He just got in a few minutes ago. I tried to get there before he threw away the lockup key, but I missed. Your poor father's going to have to go rooting around behind the filing cabinet again. Which reminds me—we had a happy event while you were out."

Tilly brightened a little. "Kittens?"

Kate beamed. "They're so sweet. One's all black, and there's a tortoiseshell just like her mother, and the rest are black with white spots. Don't you want to see them?" she asked, as Tilly lingered on by the door.

"Oh, yes." Tilly twisted back and forth on one leg. "I was just wondering . . ."

"What?"

"About Santa Claus . . ."

"Santa?"

"When he used to come with the presents Christmas morning dressed in that red suit . . . it was Daddy, wasn't it?"

"Well, yes, dear."

Tilly nodded. "I thought so."

"Didn't you know that?"

"Yes." Tilly nodded again. "I just wanted to . . . you know . . . be sure."

And, summoning up a faint smile, she turned and wandered away down the corridor.

20

On the morning after Halloween, Sam called in at Jerry's office to see what Veronica had been up to overnight. Inserting his nose into the bottom drawer of the filing cabinet, he discovered the new mother reclining voluptuously beside six singularly unprepossessing infants, each barely larger than a good-sized mouse. Veronica acknowledged his presence with a languid nod. The mice turned their blind, blank faces in his direction, opened their six pink mouths and hissed at him fiercely. Sam therefore withdrew his nose and padded back to the house in the hope that, with Veronica out of the way, someone there might need a little canine companionship, preferably on a lap or a long W-A-L-K. But no one did.

This state of affairs dragged on over the next few days. Jerry, as usual, came home too tired to feel much like throwing sticks or playing tug-of-war. Kate walked to the store several times and always remembered to provide a parcel for him to carry home; but for the most part, she spent her days directing the two Christmas plays in the schoolhouse (dogs not welcome), making sketches of costumes and sets, and dyeing old sheets from the bunkhouses until the clothesline groaned under its load of multihued fabrics in colors suitable for a broad range of Middle Eastern society from virgins and shepherds to innkeepers and kings. She also spent hours on the telephone consulting with carpenters, electricians, owners of sewing machines, makers of crepe-paper flowers, and anyone else capable of contributing to the production. Veronica, of course, had no time for him at all; Harriet Reese, in a fever of nerves over her Christmas carol settings, only played louder when he scratched on her door; and even Tilly seemed moody and subdued. So Sam sighed a great deal and spent most of his time at home lying in places where someone might trip over him or at least step on his tail.

"Tilly, dear," said Kate after Sam had leapt up with a yelp for the third time in one afternoon. "You aren't getting enough fresh air. Why don't you go play with Joey or take you-know-who for a you-know-what?"

Sam's ears went up on the alert, but Tilly ignored them. "I don't feel like it," she murmured.

"You look pale. Are you coming down with something?"

"I don't think so." Tilly slid off the sofa onto her feet. "I guess I'll go visit the kittens," she said and scuffed out of the room.

The kittens, recently fed, were taking a nap. Tilly sat down beside the filing cabinet drawer, reached in and gently ran the tip of her finger over the feeble little bodies, smiling as each one woke, raised its head for a moment and then curled back into sleep. Even with their miniature needle teeth and claws, they seemed so weak and helpless, so absolutely at her mercy. Just to pet them required constant self-control. It was almost like being a friendly giant in a fairy story. But giants, of course, tended to be wicked. Given power over something weak and small, they would be more apt to do something brutal, press too hard, perhaps, or squeeze, or grasp and twist until the cruel game ended in the same dreadful snap that had put an end to both Gilbert and the Celluloid doll in the clearing.

What must it feel like to do such a thing? Tilly shivered. And to do it—the awful question forced its way into her mind once again. Could even the worst kind of giant do it just for telling a secret? Margie, after all, had told very little. Surely Santa wouldn't hurt her for that. But then, Ellie hadn't said much more and Ellie had died for it. Closing her eyes, Tilly pressed her forehead against the cool metal of the filing cabinet. No matter how hard she tried to hold them back, her thoughts always returned to Ellie and the mine shaft, asking the same questions over and over, with the cruel, inexorable rhythm of a delirious nightmare. Was she alive when she fell? Did she know what was happening? Or had those strong, efficient hands at least made sure that she knew nothing before they threw her in? Because to know would be worse than anything. To fall and fall, knowing what was to come, waiting for the moment— And what about me? wondered poor Tilly as her mouth went dry, as it always did at this point. For if Ellie and Margie had told secrets, they had told them to her and Santa knew. He had said her name. "You told Tilly Taggert," he said, in that oddly familiar voice she could never forget and yet never quite—

"Hello, honeybunch." Her father stood smiling in the doorway. "What's the matter? You look like you just saw a ghost."

"Were you asleep?" he asked, on getting no reply.

"No," said Tilly when she could trust herself to speak. "I was looking at the kittens."

Jerry walked over and knelt beside the drawer. "They're getting bigger every day," he said. "Veronica's a good mother." He reached down and tickled Veronica under the chin. "Sleepy girl. You wouldn't think she'd ever hurt a fly in her life."

Tilly looked down at the little sleeping family. "She wouldn't hurt any of her own kittens, would she?"

"Why, no," Jerry laughed. "Why should she?"

"Just like Mommy or—or you wouldn't hurt me."

"Well, we might still manage a good spanking before you get too old."

"No, I meant . . ."

"Darling, of course we wouldn't hurt you." Jerry grasped her gently by the shoulders. "You know we wouldn't."

Tilly nodded. "I know. I just . . ." She stood up.

Jerry stood up too. "I tell you what. I've got some notes to write up. Why don't you stay and keep me company? You can use the typewriter."

"I can't." Tilly backed away. "I've got some things to do." She paused in the doorway. "I've got to take Sam for a walk. Bye."

It couldn't be, she told herself as Sam jostled her down the pipeline path toward the dam. It wasn't the same voice, she was almost sure. And even—feeling a little giddy, she reached out to steady herself on the side rail—even if it were, her father couldn't have done that to Ellie. He couldn't. No one could. Yet, more and more, she felt that someone had. Someone had put on her father's red plush Santa suit with the brass buttons and slipped into Ellie's room at night and promised her the silver locket with the pearl and killed her. And now he was doing it all over again with Margie and—Tilly came to a sudden halt halfway across the dam—and he said he was coming to see her for the last time this Friday.

No, no, no. Tilly picked up a crisp yellow leaf from the middle of the road and walked over to the rail on the upstream side of the dam. These things didn't happen. She was just making them up to frighten herself. Because if something did happen to Margie, then it would certainly be her turn next. Except it wouldn't. Because her father wouldn't hurt her. He had just said so. Even though of course it wasn't him. She had to keep telling herself that. It couldn't be him. But if it was, what would happen to him if she told? And who could she tell? And if she didn't tell, what would happen to Margie? And to her? Almost on the brink of tears, she dropped the yellow leaf into the slick, dark water and watched through swimming eyes as it picked up speed and vanished beneath her under the bridge. At this point, Sam returned from an expedition under the bridge and signaled his desire to be off by making impatient huffing noises. Tilly pushed herself away from the rail and began walking again.

To tell or keep silent. Either way, there would be danger. She bit her lip. She had to make up her mind, but how could she be expected to do that when something terrible could happen even if she took the coward's way out and did nothing? It was like being caught in a game of snakes and ladders where every possible move led to a snake. Speak or hold her tongue. Left or right. Up or down. This door or that. Only one thing was certain. The choice had to be made, and she had to make it. And she had until Friday night.

Harriet Reese followed her husband into the kitchen and watched him lift his parka off the hook near the door.

"It's a good movie," she said, "And it wouldn't hurt you to be seen in public with me, just once in a while. It really wouldn't.

Edward Reese dropped his pipe into one of the parka pockets and extracted a pair of gloves. "That's not fair, dear one. I took you to the dance last Saturday."

"And hardly danced with me at all."

He grinned. "Not my fault, cupcake. We agreed to spread our favors around the floor. Noblesse oblige."

Harriet sniffed. "I noticed you managed to oblige Pamela Barlow often enough."

"Pure politics, pumpkin. If I'd let her spend any more time dancing with our bright young timekeeper, we'd have had the whole town abuzz the next day."

"You dodo. Everyone's been talking about it for weeks. Even *I* know that. I don't know how poor Dr. Barlow puts up with it."

"She's an extremely attractive woman."

"She's a common British tart, and he was a fool to have married her in the first place. Now are you going to take me to the movies or do I have to find myself a young man too?"

"Tell you what. Get your coat on and I'll drive you there. Then I'll pick you up afterward and buy you a hot chocolate downstairs."

"It's far too early. I'd have to sit around there for an hour." Harriet flounced over to the kitchen table and plumped herself down on a protesting chair. "Never mind about me. I won't go at all." She drummed her blunt, strong fingers on the table. "And I thought you liked thrillers."

Edward shook his head. "They give me bad dreams and I wake up tired. Why don't you call up Kate Taggert and go with her?"

"It's all right. I'll just stay home and practice. Give my love to the office. It sees more of you than I do."

"Cabbage Blossom . . ."

"And don't be late coming home. My nerves won't stand it. I'm making the cocoa at ten."

For a minute after the door clicked shut, Harriet felt positive that at any moment she would hear it click open again to admit a contrite Edward, an apologetic Edward, an Edward ready to humble himself and beg for her company at the movies. But all she heard was the ignition of his car and the roar of its engine as it headed off into the night. So she stamped back to the piano and played "Joy to the World" several times over, fortissimo, to relieve her feelings.

"Good night, my dear. I expect you'll be in bed by the time I get back."

The Rev. Augustus Meade addressed his daughter from halfway up the stairs leading to her room, so that only his head showed above the floor. Like John the Baptist on the platter, thought Mona when she looked up from the sewing machine. She considered making a little joke to that effect, but since her father had no humor to speak of, she merely mentioned that she would probably be taking one or two costumes over to Mrs. Holtzer's and dropping off the dish from Mrs. Jarrow's chicken casserole on the way.

"Together with my heartfelt thanks," intoned Mr. Meade, still peering owlishly over the edge of the stairwell. "Although it did contain perhaps just a hint too much onion for my taste, if truth be told." He craned his neck a little to get a better view of the room and the stack of completed costumes folded neatly in a cardboard box on the floor. "I hope, with all this work, that you are not falling behind in your studies."

"Oh, no, Daddy."

"Or imposing too much on Mrs. Holtzer's good nature."

"Oh, no, Daddy. Or at least I—I don't *think* so." Mindful that replacement bulbs cost money, Mona switched off the sewing machine light. "She's been so good to me and taught me so much. And she lets me help her. Last Thursday I gave the baby her bath and then Freddy and I pulled a big batch of taffy for Halloween."

Mr. Meade frowned. "I thought you went to sew with Mrs. Holtzer. Not to associate with that roughneck."

"I don't!" Each of Mona's pale cheeks took on a bright spot of red. "And he's not a roughneck. He's very nice and polite when he's at home. He just isn't home very much," she ended rather sadly.

"He should spend more time doing his homework and less starting fires and pushing over people's outhouses," said Mr. Meade. "I saw what happened on Halloween and I know who the ringleader was." He checked his watch. "I'm late for the beer parlor. They'll all be inebriated if I don't hurry. Take my advice and stay away from Freddy Holtzer. Good night."

Well, it was only advice, thought Mona as her father tramped regally down the stairs. At least he hadn't made her promise. Although it hardly mattered. Someone like Freddy, with his breezy manner and beautiful smile, would never look twice at a plain stick like her. Still, he hadn't exactly said no when she had offered to come and watch him bowl. That was something. Mona smiled a secret smile and switched the sewing machine light back on. And before her father had even reached the door of his car she was back at work, lulled into a harmless little daydream by the hum of the flashing silver needle.

"Dammit," said Diana Walter who, for reasons both personal and professional, hardly ever swore. She had been marking arithmetic papers at the living room table for more than an hour and had just broken her red pencil for the third time. Tight-lipped, she inserted the tip of the pencil into a little pocket sharpener and turned it savagely. The pencil lead obliged by breaking again, thereby giving her the satisfaction of repeating the process.

Having honed the lead to exactly the right shape—sharp, but not fragile—she put down the pencil and stared out the window at the empty street. It was not as if she had been unreasonable. She generally took things as they came and made few demands. But let her ask for one thing, just one—Diana folded her arms tightly against her chest and tossed her head—well, that was it. It wasn't worth thinking about. Let him go jump in the lake. She returned to her marking.

The lead snapped again. After all, was it so much to ask? They almost never went to the movies, but it just so happened that she liked Agatha Christie and she had been wanting to see *And Then There Were None* ever since she had read the reviews a couple of years ago. Now it would disappear forever and she would never see it and all because that selfish, self-centered, self-righteous *man* picked tonight to do his inventory. As if he couldn't count his bottles and cans and oranges just as well tomorrow or the next day or whenever!

If he really was counting them. She couldn't actually be positive, but that had certainly looked like Alec's car whisking past her window half an hour ago, and she wouldn't put it past him to be off at the beer parlor right now, knocking back a few with the boys from the mine. For that's what they all were—just boys. One couldn't expect them to read, or listen to decent music or even go to a good movie— "Oh, *damn*," said Diana.

She resharpened the pencil and went back to work. But it was no good. Her mind refused to focus even on the basics of grade-three arithmetic, particularly when Tilly Taggert, normally so bright, seemed intent on making so many silly, careless mistakes. Probably did it on purpose, to make my evening even worse, thought Diana, looking up just in time to see Mary and Tom Allen pass by on their way to this week's floating bridge game, which happened to be taking place next door. One could tell time by the punctual Allens and, indeed, the chiming clock on the mantle confirmed this with a short carillon display and eight melodious bongs.

Diana twisted restlessly in her chair. She knew about the Allens and their no-nonsense child-rearing policy. Which meant that poor little Margie Allen would probably be alone in the house right now, crying herself to sleep. Why not pretend that she hadn't seen Mary and Tom and drop over to their house on some pretext? Then she could comfort Margie, read her a story and stay until she fell asleep.

On the other hand, the Allens might not take kindly to the schoolteacher meddling in their affairs. Diana looked again at the clock. The newsreel would be starting right now, to be followed by a cartoon and a trailer for next week's film and probably some kind of short subject—plenty of time to make the feature if she left immediately. And why shouldn't she do just that? After all, she was a free woman, perfectly capable of putting down her own fifty cents and buying a ticket if she felt like it. And, dammit, she *did* feel like it! How stupid to sulk at home and miss something she wanted to see just because a nonentity like Alec Barrie—what had she ever seen in him in the first place?—refused to take her. And if, by chance, he happened to have been telling the truth about his wretched inventory and happened to call in later and happened to find her out—why, so much the better!

Much cheered by this last thought, Diana ran into the bedroom, collected her hat, coat and purse, and hurried off for an emancipated night at the movies.

"Not ready yet?"

Pamela Barlow chose to ignore this question. Wetting her mascara brush again, she leaned closer to her dressing table mirror and began applying color to her lower left eyelashes. In the process of doing so, however, she found herself sharing the mirror with her husband, who stood propped up in the doorway just visible over her left shoulder. Adopting a flat, offhand drawl, she spoke.

"Dougie, dear, you mustn't stand there staring. You're putting me off."

She flicked on a final touch of mascara and started to apply lipstick from one of a dozen tubes scattered about the glass-covered table-top. When her husband's reflection failed to vanish, she allowed the faintest suggestion of a frown to furrow the smooth, unmarked area between her perfectly arched eyebrows, but made no further comment. Instead, she concentrated her full attention on the task at hand until, satisfied at last that no further improvement could be made, she slipped the lipstick into its top, tossed it back on the table, and turned away from the mirror to strike an exaggerated model's pose.

Left arm down, right arm raised, feet locked together at an angle, she stood with an inquiring smile on her face, moving only the tips of her fingers, which had not yet dried after a coat of nail polish.

"Well? Was it worth the effort? How do I look?"

"Ready for dinner at the Savoy."

She raised an eyebrow. "No, thank you very much. They're probably still serving those horrid sawdust sausages in tomato sauce."

"I seem to remember you ate a great many of them."

"It's amazing what you'll eat when you're hungry." She turned back to the mirror and regarded her reflection without enthusiasm. "This neckline needs something, don't you think?"

Sliding open a drawer on the right-hand side of the dressing table, she poked cautiously among the contents of an open blue velvet box until a satisfactory object presented itself.

"Now," she said, holding out her right hand, "since I'm still wet and you haven't anything better to do, you can be a good boy and put this"—a rhinestone-studded chevron clip appeared between two bright red manicured nails—"right here." The clip hovered over a point between her breasts where two soft folds of gold lamé crossed in a plunging V. She smiled at him again. "Unless, of course, you *have* got something better to do."

Doug Barlow pushed away from the door frame and positioned himself to perform the required function.

"You smell nice. What is it?"

" 'Tabu.' It's supposed to bring out the beast in you."

"Me?" He mimicked her raised eyebrow.

"Well, somebody." She checked the mirror once more. "Yes, that's perfect. Now be a gentleman and hold my wrap."

"All this just to go to the movies?"

"The cinema."

"The movies."

"The flicks, darling." She laughed and snuggled into the thick beaver coat. "This is the closest you'll get to turning me into a Canadian."

"I just wish you didn't hate it here so much."

"Hate it?" She gave him her wide-eyed stare. "Well, I hate the climate and the bush and the town and most of the people in it. And I hate being trapped anywhere that's two days away from the nearest excuse for a city, but on the whole I thought I was adapting pretty well. Any complaints?"

"People are talking."

"Let them. They certainly haven't anything else to talk about, poor lambs."

He looked away. "Who is it tonight?"

"Vic Hughes."

"Again?"

"He's amusing. And he has a car." She picked up her gloves and began pulling them on. "We may drive over to Springford after the film for a wee drinkie in the hotel, so don't worry if I'm a bit late. Or you could meet us there, if you like."

He shook his head.

"Suit yourself. Where's my bag? Oh, there it is. Well, have a lovely evening. Maybe there'll be a nice accident to keep you busy."

He really looked awfully sweet, with that funny shock of hair falling almost over one eye. And handsome as ever. But why in heaven must he keep staring at her with that silly, hangdog look that made her want to hit him?

He said, "With so many girls wanting to get out of England and so many servicemen willing to marry them, how did we ever end up with each other?"

"God knows, love." She paused for a second at the door to pat his cheek. "It's amazing what you'll eat when you're hungry. Ta ta."

Of course there wasn't a sign of a car in front of the hospital. Pamela smiled. So like Vic to be late. But then, he was so worth waiting for. She lit a cigarette and began walking slowly down the road to meet him.

Under the merry eyes of the two soup-eating cherubs, who beamed down at him from their advertisement on the wall, Glassy Jack paced feverishly back and forth from the table at one end of the room to the door at the other. He kept his arms folded tightly across his chest, and from time to time spoke aloud, particularly when approaching the table, upon which stood a lit kerosene lamp, an unopened bottle of rye whisky and a clean uneaten glass.

"No, no, no," he muttered. "Lead us not into temptation, Lord. Don't. Don't do it."

Executing a sharp U-turn, he headed back toward the door.

"Because I'm weak, Lord, I admit it. I'm a poor weak man and I warn you, I can't hold out much longer."

Several circuits later, he stopped short in front of the table.

"Don't do it to me, Lord," he begged, his face working. "Help a poor sinner say no. Don't make me be bad."

He turned to address the two chubby children on the wall.

"I don't want to be bad," he said. "Honest to God I don't. But sometimes it gets too big for me and it's all there and waiting and I can't help it and I get so lonely and all I want is—"

He wiped his eyes and took another step closer to the picture. "Well, *you* know, don't you? And after, I always mean to be good again, but it's hard, eh?—when you got the devil in you and that wicked old son of a bitch starts whisperin' in your ear just like he's whisperin' now. And I *try* not to listen," he whimpered. "You know I do. But he keeps on and on, naggin' at me with never a minute's peace until I give in and do it. Because he knows I'm ready to be bad. I'm ready as all get-out all the time. I'm ready to say, 'Sorry, Lord, I tried. I put up a fight, but old Satan, he beat me down again and he's got me just where he wants me—ready to go out and be bad again.' And you know what?"

A broad smile spread over his face and his voice dropped to a conspiratorial whisper.

"That's just what I'm gonna do."

A bad day. Doing her best to keep the corners of her mouth from turning down into a scowl, Kate strode rapidly on toward the lights of the distant recreation hall. The worst thing about bad days was they always happened just when you could least deal with them. She should have known this morning, when she woke up feeling distinctly on the queasy side, that more would follow in the same vein. First, the vanishing kittens. It had taken a full hour of stooping down to peer underneath things, trying to imagine where Veronica might have hidden them, trying to keep last night's dinner down (breakfast had been out of the question) before she finally came across the small brood fast asleep inside an old rucksack at the back of Tilly's cupboard. Then off to a school rehearsal where she had to deal with a fretful Harriet Reese ("The 'Away in a Manger' descant still sounds awful. They just aren't trying, I know it"), a twittery Diana Walter ("There's still so much to do and we haven't even started on *Santa's Magic Toy Shop*. What if we just dropped it and concentrated on the pageant?"), and then an exasperating session with the three shepherds who giggled, forgot their lines and ended up losing their voices.

And it hadn't ended there. Plunging her hands deeper into her coat pockets, Kate walked on even faster. After another of his bad nights, Jerry had been uncharacteristically moody all day, and she had let the pudding burn and, to top it all, Tilly—looking so pale and drawn these days, poor darling, yet adamant in her assertions that she felt perfectly well and nothing was wrong—Tilly had made that ridiculous scene about not wanting to go to the movie and not wanting to stay home alone until Kate, at the end of her tether, had lost her temper and said that she could stay or come as she liked but to stop whining, for God's sake. After which, she had flung on her coat and marched out of the house with a grizzling Tilly at her heels, hating herself for being a cruel and unnatural mother while, at the same time, deriving a thoroughly unpleasant satisfaction from the unaccustomed luxury of losing her temper.

Now, just to make everything perfect, they were going to miss the start of the show. Kate considered lengthening her stride even more, but thought better of it in view of the short gasps she could hear from Tilly, still trailing a pace or two behind. Smitten by guilt, Kate slowed down and put an arm around the fur-trimmed parka hood that enveloped her daughter's head. The gasps increased in volume and became sobs.

"Tilly." Kate bent down and peered into the furred recesses of the hood. "Darling. What's the matter?"

Tilly met her gaze with shining hollow eyes, but continued to weep loudly without answering.

"Oh, sweetheart." Kate pulled her daughter off the road as Jack McCallister's ancient sedan rattled past at speed. "Tell me what's wrong."

"I c-can't," wailed Tilly.

"Of course you can. Tell me."

Tilly moved her head in little spasmodic jerks, as if seeking help from somewhere behind her mother. "I don't know what to do," she quavered. "I've been trying and I can't . . . I can't . . ."

"Why? Why can't you?"

"He'll hurt me."

A thin shaft of ice pierced Kate's heart.

"Who's going to hurt you?"

"Oh . . ." Tilly's answer lost itself amidst increased sobs. Kate crouched down to get a better view of the wet, contorted face inside the hood and tried again.

"Who's going to hurt you?"

"I d-don't know."

"Then how do you know someone's going to hurt you?"

"I can't tell. If I—if I tell . . ."

"Tilly, you must. You must tell. Please, dear." She pulled Tilly close against her. "We won't let anything happen to you. Now be a good girl and tell me everything and you'll feel better, I promise."

She felt the small tense body relax in her arms.

"Tell me," she whispered. "It's all right. Tell Mother."

With a gasp of relief, Tilly told.

21

Looking back on it, he could hardly believe how well he had managed to get through the day. He had arisen at his usual time, followed his usual routine, eaten his usual meals. He had walked and talked and appeared calm. In short, he had presented to the world the very picture of a placid, commonplace nonentity, despite a hard knot of excitement that never for a moment relaxed its grip on the center of his chest, aching and throbbing for all the world like a physical presence that anyone looking at him might see welling up under his clothing.

And now the waiting was almost over. He closed his eyes and took several deep breaths of sharp, cold air. In fact, the time had come. He could go in whenever he liked. The Allens had set out a good ten minutes ago and, even as he lingered here at the edge of the woods, staring through clumps of snow-dusted bushes at the small, vulnerable house, he could imagine Margie alone inside it, wide awake in bed, her nerves on edge, her thoughts fixed on him just as his were on her. Really, with that delicious image to draw him forth, how could he linger? But he had waited so long, it would do no harm to wait a little longer. Much as the tortured learns to love his torturer, so he had grown accustomed to the constant craving, the self-denial, the endless visions of fulfillment, all of which, when finally appeased, would leave behind only a flat, fearful inner void where once a rich nourishing sense of purpose had held sway.

He knew it would be so and he dreaded the sensation. On each previous occasion, he had suffered a death too, plunged from almost unbearable ecstasy into the most hideous depression. Because everything had a price and the question now was, could he afford to pay? Would it not be simpler, easier, better all round if he turned away while he could and went back to the dreamy half life in which he had learned to pass all but those few precious hours when his mind came alive, his senses sang, and he could be said truly to live? Could he survive another crash and the long, bleak spell of abstinence until he could permit his fancy to light on a replacement? For, in the end, there would always be a replacement, newer, fresher, more innocent—oh yes, far more innocent—than the one before. The prospect set his heart pumping like a schoolboy's. And surely the same sense of anticipation would see him through the forthcoming dark time until at last—

But there he went, running ahead of himself. First things first. And top of the list, he thought happily, was to follow the advice of the wise poet who counseled that, before taking on a new love, one had best be off with the old.

Breathless with excitement, he moved cautiously out of the woods toward the house.

Kate stood outside the recreation hall, her thoughts in chaos. Up to now she had been very good. She had listened calmly to Tilly's story, asked a few pertinent questions and spoken reassuring words. She had seen that she must do something immediately and, to that end, had asked Diana Walter, arriving providentially late, to take Tilly into the movie and stay with her afterward if necessary. She had even managed to fabricate a hitherto forgotten appointment with Augustus Meade to discuss the probable nationalities of the three kings. She had waved and smiled as Tilly followed Miss Walter up the steps. Only then had she allowed herself to panic.

Because what did it all mean? And if it meant what she thought—but it couldn't mean what she thought. Things like that didn't really happen. She had barely heard the subject mentioned, let alone discussed. It was like some terrible notion that had come unbidden in a nightmare, dredged up from her worst imaginings. And yet there had been a movie, with Peter Lorre as a pathetic little—

She tried again to sort through the fragments that whirled about in her mind: Margie, the face at her window, the Santa suit, the familiar voice, the locket, Ellie—she stopped. Had Tilly said anything about poor Ellie? Perhaps not tonight but . . . yes, last summer. Something about a locket. And Santa. Kate turned on her heel and headed quickly for the path leading to the downstairs snack bar.

Thanks to Agatha Christie and the drawing power of her stories, the room sat deserted, the jukebox silent. The pool room, too, lacked even a single customer, as did the darkened bowling alley beyond. Kate had steeled herself to make a measured, unobtrusive progress through these areas. Instead, she ran, weaving past chairs, tables and doorways until the central corridor offered her a clear final dash to Bert Nichols's office where she seized the telephone and dialed.

"Please, Jerry," she breathed, still panting a little from her run. "Please be there."

But the telephone continued to ring unanswered.

She pressed the cut-off bar impatiently and tried first the local hotel, then its rival establishment in Springford.

No Jerry.

She hung up. He could be anywhere. She needed another plan. While thinking, she hunted frantically through the papers pinned to the wall and littered about the desktop, hoping to find the mimeographed sheet that served as the town telephone directory. But Bert either did without or kept his copy in one of the locked desk drawers.

And, now that she thought of it, whom could she call, what would she say? Even if she knew where to find Margie's parents, even if she had a number to call, even if she dared pull some startled man away from the movie upstairs and drag him over to the Allen house, she had only Tilly's semihysterical account to go by. Could she bring herself to voice her suspicions and create a town scandal over something that might—probably would—turn out to have an entirely innocent explanation?

On the other hand, could she turn her back and let Margie fall prey to the monster in Jerry's Santa suit?

She retraced her steps out of the building. After following the path up to the road, she turned right and began walking toward town, all the while making a brave attempt to subdue her worst thoughts and ignore an inner voice that begged her to walk faster. From time to time, when overcome by a particularly strong surge of anxiety, she put on speed without thinking, only to be reined in by crippling waves of pain that burned down the front of each leg from knee to ankle as if she had barked both shins against a hot iron. She had experienced the same sensation many time before, when attempting to rush against time, and knew that the only cure lay in slowing down. So she bit her lip and attempted to stroll.

At the store, she made another right-hand turn and continued past three handsome old log houses, beyond which lay the hospital and the doctor's residence, both showing darkened windows. Just before the hospital, however, the road split away to the left, leading her up a hill, then straight on past a row of six identical white houses until it ended in a sandy turnaround lit by a weak yellow streetlamp.

Kate moved away from the light and came to a halt at the entrance to a narrow graveled path. Off to her left, beyond a barren uprooted vegetable plot, she could just make out the dark wall of bushes behind which, if only she had time to look, she might find a broken Celluloid doll hidden beneath a shallow layer of rotting compost. But she had no time. Directly ahead, at the end of the path, the Allen house presented its usual bland evening face. A hundred-watt light bulb burned over the porch door and, barely visible in the side wall to the right, a faint light glimmered through the thin cotton curtains on Margie's bedroom window.

Beset by feelings closer to those of a burglar than a potential rescuer, Kate stepped off the crunching gravel and, keeping to the side of the path, made her way slowly toward the window.

The best, the best. Oh, it had never been like this. Never as good. Never as richly, wonderfully, magnificently good. Never as cleverly planned and perfectly orchestrated. Never the satisfaction, the drive, the power that tapped his breath and pumped his heart and spun his head until he could barely see his creation, with its contorted features and streaming eyes, or hear the wild words hoarsely wrenched from the very depths of its being and spewed out of its twisted mouth.

During it all he said nothing. Long experience had taught him that this generally produced the best result. He merely smiled and held the locket just out of reach, alowing her to weep and scream and revile him with the pathetically inadequate vocabulary that he had taken such care not to expand.

And as she became more hysterical, he let the precious kernel of hate take root and grow within him. He watered it, nurtured it, felt it rise and swell, plucked it, savored it until his head threatened to whirl off his shoulders and his legs to buckle under him.

"I hate you, I hate you!" she screamed, her face almost purple with rage. "You hurt me and you said it would be all right and you lied. You promised! It's mine and I want it. Give it to me, or I'll tell. I don't care what happens now. I don't want to see you ever again. I wish you were dead! I wish I could kill you, you—

Oh, yes. The best. Almost subhuman now, with rivulets of moisture running out of her eyes and nose and mouth. He had frequently noticed that at this point they all began to look alike, as if all those ugly little blotchy red faces from the past rose up and converged on each other until they became no one at all, an abstraction, a convenience ready and waiting for the moment, the perfect moment when everything came together and clicked into place. The moment he had been building to so skillfully. The moment he had to have or die. Right now.

He took a step forward, causing her to retreat and trip back over the bed. She gasped and began to cry again in low, shuddering sobs. He knelt down and bent over her.

"It's all right," he said softly. "Don't cry. Look. It's yours."

He trailed the locket up her chest and let it drop in the hollow of her throat.

"Don't cry," he said. "Everything's going to be all right. Shh."

Her sobs began to slacken.

"Shh, now," he whispered.

He reached behind her for the pillow.

"Shh."

22

Really, thought Kate, what am I doing skulking about like this in someone else's yard in the middle of the night? She stopped and glanced nervously back at the road. What if someone should see her? What if the Allens arrived home this very moment and found the policeman's wife half up to her knees in the withered remains of the floral border beside their path? Worse, what if, in two minutes' time, they caught her standing among the peony bushes next to the house, peering into their daughter's window? What would they say? What would she reply?

What on earth did it matter? Kate's mouth twisted in exasperation. She would cross that bridge when and if she came to it. The most important thing, now that she had reached the corner of the house, was to move noiselessly up to the window and see if she could make out anything within the room. Choosing a spot where the path narrowed a little, she took a giant step across it, then insinuated herself slowly between crackling peony stalks until she could lean against the wall and cautiously raise her eyes and nose above the window ledge.

She could see nothing. Condensation frosted the inner window, and the curtains beyond overlapped far too generously to offer the slightest hole or chink. They did not, however, provide such an effective barrier against sound. When she placed her ear against the storm window, Kate could hear, quite plainly, the high-pitched wails of a frightened child.

Rage and shock set her head spinning. Resting her forehead against the cold windowpane, she forced herself to recover and think. The nightmare had come true, but at least Margie was still alive. She could still do something if she acted quickly and used her brain, which immediately warned her that it would not be wise to rush indoors and burst into Margie's bedroom. This would bring her face to face with a much stronger adversary. And, as a veteran of many berry-picking expeditions to sites also favored by the local black bear population, Kate knew very well that one must never get between a dangerous wild animal and its only path of escape. She also knew that most wild animals preferred to run away if given a chance. The trick lay in giving them a chance.

Accordingly, she stepped gingerly back among the dead plants and retraced her steps. She then reversed direction, this time marching loudly up the porch steps where, despite an attack of nerves that threatened to paralyze every muscle, she set the screen door rattling with a series of heavy knocks.

What if he comes to the door? The sudden thought set off a new wave of panic, forcing her to reach out and steady herself against the side wall while a chorus of inner voices begged to be carried away to some safe hiding place as quickly as possible. But the time for running had passed. Her legs refused to move. Perfect, she told herself grimly, the rescue party charges across town, then collapses on the doorstep. At which, much to her surprise, she managed to summon up a faint smile and, in doing so, sufficient courage to knock again.

Panic returned the moment her knuckle hit the door. However, she stood her ground and held her breath, hoping to hear some sound from within. But she heard nothing.

"All right," she said. "In we go."

And in she went, allowing the screen door to slam loudly behind her as she entered the porch and knocked on the inside door.

It came to her as something more felt than heard: a rapid thump of footsteps carried through the floorboards, strongly at first, then becoming lighter as they moved farther off. She began to breathe again. At least he had quit the bedroom. But where was he now? He could be waiting for her in the kitchen or hiding just around the corner in the living room. Or, if he had any sense at all, he could be letting himself out the front door this very second. Surely that was what any reasonable person would do. Unless, of course, he happened to have lost his reason. Unless he intended to kill her too. Fearing that if she waited even a second longer she might disgrace herself by fainting, Kate grasped the cold metal doorknob and turned it.

She stared into total darkness.

He's turned out Margie's light, she thought.

"Hello," she called brightly. "Anybody home?"

Silence. Then, from the far end of the house, came the faint metallic click of a latch.

Kate stepped across the threshold and closed the door behind her.

"Hello," she called again.

With the promptness of an echo, a slight noise came back to her from somewhere outside the house. She froze, straining to hear more, but heard only the beating of her own heart. In the meantime, however, her eyes had adjusted to the dark interior and she could now make out, two steps to her right, the open doorway of Margie's room where, in the far wall beyond, light from the distant streetlamp imparted a dim glow to the curtained window.

"It's Mrs. Taggert, Margie," said Kate gently. "Are you awake?"

A bulky shadow passed across the window.

In that instant, all her fear vanished, wiped out by an overwhelming torrent of rage. Did he show himself on purpose? Was he boasting? Was it a challenge? Or was he merely stupid and incompetent when faced with an adult who could see him for what he was and, if necessary, fight back? Either way, she despised and hated him with a passion that would have sent her flying out the door to do battle had she been faster and stronger and not pregnant and not so sick at the thought of what might be waiting for her in the bedroom.

"I'm coming in, Margie," she said. "Don't be afraid, dear. I'm going to turn on the light."

For the next hour Kate functioned as an automaton, running on raw nerve and instinct, unable to think of anything beyond what had to be done and how to do it. Only when it was all over, when she left the Allens at the hospital, collected Tilly and put her to bed, did the full reality of what she had been through strike home. So it happened that Jerry Taggert, on arriving home from his rounds at half past twelve in the morning, discovered his wife propped up in bed drinking neat rye from a large glass tumbler.

"It's snowing out," he said. "Hard."

He received a blank stare.

"Movie that bad?" he asked.

Kate responded to his pleasantry by bursting into tears.

"Hey, wait a minute." Jerry moved over to the bed and sat down. "What's the matter?"

"My God," he whispered from time to time as she told him. Eventually he interrupted.

"Why didn't you call me?"

"I tried." Kate helped herself to a handful of Kleenex. "But I didn't know where you were and there weren't any numbers in Herb's office."

"I meant from the Allens."

Kate took a deep breath and blew her nose. "He pulled the telephone wire out of the wall. So I ran outside, but there wasn't a house with a light anywhere. Everyone was at the show. And I was sure she must be dead by this time, but when I went back she was breathing better and she opened her eyes when I spoke to her. Don't," she said as Jerry showed signs of interrupting again. "Let me finish while I can. She didn't say anything, but I managed to put a coat on her and get her out of the house and there was Timmy Wisnicki's wagon next door, so I put her in that and hauled her to the hosh . . ." She hiccuped. "Hospital—"

"Kate! You might have—"

"Well, I couldn't leave her there by herself." Kate sank wearily back on the pillows. "Anyway, it was all downhill. Then that new nurse, I forget her name, called Doug and they went off like angels to look after Margie, which meant that I had to . . . I had to . . ." She frowned. "I had to do something. Oh, yes, I had to telephone all over town to find the Allens and then wait around to tell them what happened." She leaned forward to take another sip of rye. "That was the worsh . . . the worsh . . . it was awful. Then—oh!" A surprised look came over her face as her head fell back. "The whole room just went round!" She gave an apologetic laugh. "And I really didn't drink that much."

"You've had a lousy day." Jerry leaned over and planted a kiss on her forehead. "Try to get some sleep and we'll talk in the morning." Slipping the glass from her hand, he switched off the bedside lamp and began moving quietly toward the door.

"Ellie Hayes didn't fall down the mine shaft, Jerry." The blurred voice followed him out of the darkened room. "She was thrown. And he almost got Margie." The voice rose in pitch. "We can't watch them all the time, Jerry. Who's going to be next?"

He returned to the bed and, finding her hand clenched against the counterpane, cradled it in his. "Nobody," he said. "Nobody's going to be next. We'll tell every parent in town. We'll tell the children. We'll watch and we'll lock our doors. He won't try again. He wouldn't dare."

He squeezed her hand reassuringly and, as it relaxed open, received into his own hand a smooth, round metal object.

"Margie dropped that when I got her off the bed," whispered Kate. "Oh, Jerry, he must be mad. He'll—no." She cut herself short. "No, he won't. You're right. We won't let him. I'm sorry. I just can't think properly anymore. Good night." She tilted her face up from the pillow.

Jerry kissed her again and left the room, pulling the door shut behind him. As he did so, the metal in his hand hit the doorknob with a sharp click. He stopped and looked down. On his open palm, gleaming with a rich, mellow luster, lay a brass button from his Santa Claus costume.

"But not Tilly." Although spoken quietly, the words made their way clearly through the thin door. "Please don't let it be Tilly."

An inch of whisky remained in Kate's glass. Jerry downed it at a gulp.

Reaction struck as the first gray light of dawn stole in through the window. Having nodded off for the briefest moment, he woke up panic-striken, shaking and bathed in sweat. It had been so close, so close. A sob caught in his throat, forcing him to bite the side of his knuckle in an effort to keep from moaning. He tried to calm himself, but the cold, cruel voice of his nightmare continued to speak on in his waking thoughts. If she hadn't been alone, it whispered, if the parents had come home early, if he hadn't made it away in time, then—he bit down harder on his knuckle—then capture, exposure, disgrace. Newspaper headlines (the voice barely troubled to conceal its relish), photographs, a trial. And, depending on the verdict, either a filthy death or a worse life locked up in some jail where the twisted reports of his history would bring him nothing but the most brutal treatment from guards and fellow prisoners alike. It could have been an end to everything, said the gloating voice. And all because of her.

Her. He seized the thought greedily. Yes, it was all her fault. Because now they would take the child away from him and it was so unfair. He had been so good, so clever. He had planned and timed it perfectly. It would have been his most magnificent achievement. All he had needed was another minute, two at the most, when she, *she* had to barge in, ruining everything, destroying the slow work of months, clawing down the beautiful, fragile structure that he had built up so carefully, cheating him of his hard-earned reward at almost the very last second, leaving him with nothing, while she—

Conscious of a bitter taste in his mouth, he relaxed his jaws and sucked the blood from his bleeding finger. While she got off scot-free. Except she wouldn't. No. As the idea grew, a delicious glow of happiness wrapped itself around him, caressing his body like the smooth, liquid folds of a satin sheet. He felt very calm, very alert, in full command of himself. It would be such a satisfactory revenge, and so easy. Sooner or later an opportunity would present itself because, when one came to think of it, all he really needed were those last two minutes. Two minutes was all it would take. And he couldn't imagine anyone he would rather spend them with. He pictured her again, giggling in bed with Margie, waving in front of the recreation hall, with her round face, turned-up nose and ratty pigtails.

The little bitch who couldn't keep a secret.

Outside, the temperature dropped. Ice already formed among the bulrushes and iris stalks at the edge of the river began to spread and thicken. Small animals retreated deeper into their burrows.

And the snow continued to fall, piling up on trees and rooftops, obliterating roads and paths, smoothing out every detail of the landscape from the latest set of tire marks in a hidden clearing off the river road to the clear imprint of a stranger's foot under Margie Allen's window. Winter had arrived.

23

From THE CROW RIVER GAZETTE

Vol. XI, No. 39

NOVEMBER 19, 1947

HAIL . . .

Welcome to Mrs. Eleanor Kingly, who will be visiting her daughter Ethel Holtzer and family until after the holidays. This should give her son-in-law plenty of time to demonstrate his prowess on the curling rink while giving us that much-needed victory over Springford. Go get 'em, Frank.

. . . AND FAREWELL

We regret to announce that our popular machine shop superintendent Tom Allen will be leaving the mine. His wife Mary and their daughter Margie have already departed for Kirkland Lake. Tom will follow when a new superintendent can be found.

Pamela Barlow has returned to Winnipeg for a dose of city life and Dr. Doug would have it known that he cannot cook. Come on, ladies--we need to see that our medic eats right.

Where's everybody going? Town dances won't be the same without our most eligible bachelor, Vic Hughes. Vic will now be timekeeping and breaking hearts in Timmons.

FREEZE-UP

All of the above made it in and out on the last seaplane we'll see on Skunk Lake before breakup next spring. We're now on our own for the next two or three weeks until the ice gets thick enough to permit a landing on skis. Bert Nichols says not to worry: he's got enough movies in stock to see us through. And don't forget the library. Make Rita Griswald happy and borrow a book!

LOCK UP!

By this time, Constable Taggert should have spoken to all parents on an important matter regarding home security. If he has accidentally missed you--get in touch with him immediately. In the meantime, get into the habit of locking your doors when you go out, and under no circumstances leave your children alone in the house for any length of time.

CONTEST!

Following the success of our children's essay contest last summer, we have decided to start the snowy season off on a high intellectual tone by offering their elders the same opportunity to express themselves. The rules are simple: a composition of 400 words or less on any subject of local interest having to do with Winter. All entries to be turned in to the Office by December 12 at the latest. The winning essay will be published in our issue of December 17, and a cash prize of $5 will be presented to the author, courtesy of Bob's Barber Shop. So get moving, all you budding writers. Sharpen up those pencils and show the kids what you can do.

From THE CROW RIVER GAZETTE

Vol. XI, No. 40

NOVEMBER 26, 1947

KITTY KARAWAY'S KULINARY KORNER

Since we printed the corrected recipe for Daisy Daniel's scrumptious Marguerite cake in September, many of you who forgot to cut it out have asked us to print it one more time. We do so with pleasure, apologizing again for all the flat failures that resulted from the typing error when the recipe first appeared in our August holiday issue.

DAISY DANIEL'S MARGUERITE CAKE

1 cup white sugar
3/4 cup butter
1 cup sour milk
1 3/4 cup flour
3 eggs
2 tbs. molasses
1 tsp. soda
1 tsp. cinnamon
pinch salt
1 tsp. vanilla

Cream butter, then add sugar and beaten eggs, except for one yolk reserved for filling. Add sour milk and molasses, then flour sifted with dry ingredients. Bake in two layers in moderate oven for 25 minutes.

FILLING:
1 egg yolk
1 scant cup brown sugar
1 scant cup raisins
1 tbs. butter
1 tsp. vanilla
1 tsp. cornstarch
1 scant cup sweet milk

Cook and spread between layers. Frost with favorite icing. A spicy melt-in-the-mouth delight!

KITCHEN NOTE

Alec Barrie reminds all you bakers that Christmas cakes and puddings should be made before the end of the month so they can age properly before the Big Day. If you haven't got yours in the oven yet, the store still has a good supply of raisins, currants, citrus peel, almonds, walnuts, candied fruit and suet, all ready to be stirred up.

CHRISTMAS CONCERT

Plan now to attend on Wednesday, December 17, when the students of Crow River Secondary School will present a gala entertainment in two parts at the Community Club auditorium. Part One, a CHRISTMAS PAGEANT, will depict the story of the first Christmas in a series of dramatic tableaux incorporating your favorite carols, arranged and played by Harriet Reese. The second part of the evening, a musical extravaganza entitled SANTA'S MAGIC TOY SHOP, will conclude with an appearance by jolly old St. Nick himself. Presents for all. Time 7:30 P.M. Tickets 25 cents, with all proceeds to go toward the Crow River Community Club Entertainment Fund. Don't miss it!

From THE CROW RIVER GAZETTE

Vol. XI, No. 41

DECEMBER 3, 1947

CURLING NEWS

Well, folks, the curling is underway with 18 rinks entered in the Novelty Bonspiel. We know there were a lot of disappointed curlers last Sunday, when Old Man Weather pulled a rainstorm out of the hat to delay three of the draws. However, with the help of a little cold weather we hope to see the finish underway next Thursday and Saturday.

SKIPS--Keep in touch with the Drawmaster, because due to the many Christmas activities planned for next month some of the games may have to be changed.

PETS

The perfect Christmas present! Kate Taggert notifies us that they will have five beautiful kittens ready for adoption by the middle of December. A sixth has already been spoken for by our manager's wife, Harriet Reese, who can hardly wait to bring it home. The kittens are strong and healthy and come of good mousing stock. Kate says that although the family will hate to see them go, go they must. They're driving Sam crazy.

CHRISTMAS TREES

Throw away your saws and axes! On the 12th and 13th of the month, Buck and Snowball will be calling at each house in town with a sleigh full of beautiful Christmas trees. Choose your favorite, compliments of the mine management. Only one per family, please.

THE LOAFER'S LAMENT

August comes: a time to loot
The berry bushes of their fruit;
Time to quit our cozy dwelling,
Smeared with lotions fly-repelling,

And sally forth with happy cries
To battle snakes and bears and flies.

Many do it. Voices trill
From dawn to dusk on ridge and hill.
Yet we come limping home, alack,
With half-filled can and aching back.

Comes winter: pickers point with pride
To all those bottles side by side,
And row by row their quarts compare.
The brave, we know, deserve the fare.
But as we smile and give them credit
Do we kick us? Chum, you said it!

From THE CROW RIVER GAZETTE

Vol. XI, No. 42

DECEMBER 10, 1947

HOCKEY

The Crow River Aces are still two players short of a full team. Anyone interested in joining, please see Frank Holtzer at the mill or at practice Tuesday and Thursday nights at 8:00. Come on, guys. Grab your skates and try out. The Springford Devils are waiting to take us on. Let's get that trophy back this year!

CURLING NEWS

Well, Jack Frost came through with subzero temperatures and last Thursday and Saturday saw a two-day knockout Bonspiel run with Mike Wisnicki taking first prize and Father Boucher second. This was more of an endurance test for the winners, as they curled three games each on Saturday with the last two games one right after the other. Father Boucher's rink won the prize for the highest game score.

The banquet, hosted by the unfortunate losers, was held in the Lunch Room of the Community Club, and largely due to the wonderful supper prepared by the ladies, was a huge success. Tables for 90 guests were tastefully set out and when all was laid out in readiness, presented a very appetizing picture. After the supper, dancing, billiards, pool and bowling occupied the guests' time until the wee hours of the morning.

SKIPS--line up your rinks for next season's draws, which should start with the first shift in January. Remember, one green player to each team, and no two skips on the same team.

What's a skip? Why, any player who is too poor to play lead!

QUIET, PLEASE

Mr. Jack McCallister respectfully requests all parents to inform their children that they are welcome to stand on his dock and watch him fish through the ice as long as they refrain from asking him questions and stamping their feet. This interferes with his concentration and frightens away the fish.

From THE CROW RIVER GAZETTE

Vol. XI, No. 43

DECEMBER 17, 1947

COMPETITION RESULTS

We are pleased to print the winning entry in our essay competition. The fact that it was also the only entry in no way detracts from its literary merits. A prize of $5, donated by Bob's Barber Shop, is even now in the mail.

WINTER: A Meditation
by
Gloria Lewis

Let others sing the praises of dusty summer, soggy spring and melancholy autumn. I lift my voice to Winter. From the arrival of the first brave snowflake to the departure of the last stubborn patch of white from its shady hiding place, Winter provides our senses with a never-ending feast.

Who, on rising on a cold November morning, has not felt his heart leap at the sight of a mundane world transformed into a winter wonderland? Who has not passed hours of enchantment tracing the fantastic patterns drawn by that master artist Jack Frost on the inside of a humble storm window? And who has not trembled with delight at the beauty of a pink-and-rose-colored afternoon or a silent night sky radiant with majestic northern lights?

But Winter does not cater only to the higher senses. Heartier pleasures abound. Across the river, children careen down the toboggan slide or watch our quaint local trapper patiently seek his supper through a hole in the ice. Youthful engineers dig caverns in the towering snowbanks beside our ploughed roads. Outlines of small angels appear as if by magic in any fresh expanse of snow. And, over at the skating rink changing room, cheeks glow and merry voices ring out in a rich atmosphere of fragrant leather, damp wool, and scorched metal as childish fingers fumble with double knots while steaming socks and mittens hang out to dry on the blazing oil-drum furnace.

For Winter, like its glorious festival Christmas, is primarily a time for the young. And where better for the young to celebrate it than here in Crow River, our own dear "true North strong and free"? Not for us the City, where joy and beauty come only at a price. No. Let us take pride in our town and strive to keep it a plain, honest, upstanding community where innocence will never be sacrificed on the altar of commercialism and where trusting parents will never see their children exploited and exhibited for entertainment and profit by vain, self-promoting adults who should know better.

Truth, beauty, joy, innocence: these are what Winter means to me. If we are to stand on guard, O Canada, let us stand on guard for them!

REMINDER

For the benefit of anyone in town who has been asleep, underground or otherwise out of reach of our Entertainment Pages for the last four weeks, we would like to point out that at 7:30 tonight the curtain goes up on a gala Christmas entertainment, presented by the students of Crow River Secondary School. Sets! Costumes! Music! Tickets 25 cents at the door. See you there!

HAPPY HOLIDAYS!

In view of the coming festive season, the next issue of The Crow River Gazette will not appear until January 7, 1948. To all our readers, best wishes for a Merry Christmas and a Happy New Year!

24

Having transformed the meat on her plate into a scattered mosaic of small pieces and made several half-hearted attempts at an overly ambitious helping of mashed potatoes, Mona Meade gave up all pretense of trying to eat and set down her knife and fork.

"I'm sorry, Daddy. I just can't."

Mr. Meade methodically mashed a wandering pea onto the back of his fork, then looked up at his daughter.

"I hope it isn't my cooking," he said.

"Oh, no. It's just . . . I can't."

Mr. Meade frowned slightly. "Sad to see good food go to waste."

"Oh, it won't." With escape in sight, Mona managed a hesitant smile. "I'll cover everything with waxed paper and heat it up tomorrow. I know I'll be hungry then."

"You look pale. You aren't coming down with anything?"

"No. Nothing like that."

"A lot of flu about . . ."

"I guess I'm nervous."

The frown on Mr. Meade's face transformed itself into a look of blank surprise.

"Nervous?"

Mona fidgeted with her napkin. "Well, the pageant and everything. You haven't forgotten it's tonight?"

"Certainly not." Mr. Meade adjusted his abandoned knife and fork so that they rested precisely in the center of his empty plate. "I look forward to seeing what effect my advice has had with regard to the sets and costumes. Why should you be nervous?"

"I don't know. Getting up in front of all those people . . ."

"Pish, tush. Just keep your head up, say your lines, and don't mumble. Nothing to worry about at all. I do it every Sunday."

"It's just that"—Mona's complexion turned suddenly from white to red—"I'm not very good."

"My dear." Mr. Meade gave his daughter a reassuring smile. "No one expects you to be. You aren't a professional actress."

"And I hate the way I look," said Mona miserably.

Mr. Meade's frown returned. "Now, that is sheer vanity," he said. "You look the way God made you, and you have no right to quarrel with His handiwork. In any case, physical beauty is a totally superficial attribute and of no importance whatever. You have many other splendid qualities, so let's have no more of this nonsense, shall we?"

"No, Daddy."

"Very good. Now" Quite restored to humor, Mr. Meade flapped his napkin and resettled it on his knee with a flourish. "Mrs. Lewis dropped over a most delicious-looking pie this afternoon. I know you're anxious to set off for the world of sock and buskin, ha, ha, but before you go you might just bring me in a slice."

"Yes, Daddy."

"And don't worry about the dinner dishes," added Mr. Meade as his daughter disappeared into the kitchen. "You can do them when you get home. I might even be persuaded to wield a tea towel myself."

"Thank you, Daddy."

"Think nothing of it," said Mr. Meade, whose mind had moved on to other matters. "It occurs to me that apple pie tastes vastly better when warm. Would it be too much trouble to heat it up?"

If Mona's reply seemed to make its way back from the kitchen bearing the hint of a sigh, Mr. Meade charitably ascribed this to the effect of distance.

Harriet Reese stood in front of the kitchen counter and stared fixedly at a small juice glass placed just to the right of the sink. Decorated with an attractive stenciled design of violet plants in full flower, the innocent-looking glass had originally made its way into the Reese household filled with pimento-flavored cheese spread. It now contained about half an inch of rich amber-colored liquid, which inspired in Harriet much the same mixture of fascination and dread she might have felt had she distilled the liquor herself from hemlock of her own picking.

As a teetotaler of life-long standing, Harriet knew full well the probable path of those who indulged in the demon rum or, in this case, sherry. She knew, too, the rapid downward slide waiting for those who drank alone. Just one sip from the violet-bedecked glass might be enough to set her skidding down the road to ruin where, bottle in hand, she would soon take to smoking cigarettes and loitering outside the hotel beer parlor in a tight dress and too much lipstick.

On the other hand, she could not, no, absolutely not get through this evening without something to calm her nerves. They had tried to fool her by praising her playing at the dress rehearsal yesterday, but she knew better and she did not intend to disgrace the Reese name and the dear children by repeating that pathetic performance tonight. She should never have put herself in this hideous position again, just as she should never have promised to take one of those wretched Taggert kittens. But her arm had been twisted and it was too late to back out now. In less than an hour she would have to sit down at the piano and strike up the overture in front of a crowd of paying strangers. The very thought twisted her stomach into a knot and made her feel faint. She could only hope that Kate had kept her promise to bring over a screen from the hospital to hide her and the piano from all those eyes.

Not that a flimsy white screen would be of much help. She could imagine them there, the whole town, listening for every slip of the finger, cringing at every mistake. She could hear them gasp when she dropped her sheet music, feel them squirm and grip the edges of their seats in embarrassment when she forgot her place, imagine the nervous titters when she fumbled horribly to a halt in the middle of a song and ran out of the room to be sick. Oh, no. Nothing in the world could make her face all that with a clear head. Let the future take care of itself, she had to get through tonight. And Edward need never know. Grasping the edge of the counter tightly with her left hand, she picked up the glass and drained its contents in one swallow.

After retiring to the porch to cough and wipe her eyes, Harriet returned to the kitchen, washed out the glass and replaced it on its allotted shelf. She then switched off the ceiling light and walked carefully into the living room, where she settled down on her brocade-covered chair to wait for Edward to finish dressing and drive her to the recreation hall. While she waited, she smiled. She smiled at the mellow, polished curve of the piano. She smiled at the Dresden shepherd and shepherdess on top of the fireplace. She smiled at the silver glinting through the glass doors of her mother's corner cabinet. She smiled at dear Edward, coming through the door in his hat and coat, carrying something in his hand.

"Pumpkin," he began, looking somewhat uneasy.

Harriet continued to smile.

Edward cleared his throat.

"I was talking to Dr. Barlow today," he said. "About, hum, your problem."

Harriet nodded encouragingly.

"Nerves, you know."

"Oh, yes," said Harriet blithely.

"Now, Dr. Barlow thinks, and I agree, that a little mild stimulant might do them a world of good and help you get through tonight without making yourself absolutely miserable. So I want to you drink this." Edward held forth one of the cut-crystal glasses generally reserved for use by the mine owner and his wife on their annual visit to town.

Harriet leaned forward to inspect the glass and its meager contents.

"What is it?" she asked.

"Well." Edward became even more uncomfortable. "It's cognac. Just a little."

Harriet shook her head. "Oh, no. No, I don't think so."

"For medicinal purposes only. Ha, ha."

"Honestly, it wouldn't be wise."

"Just a sip."

"I mustn't."

"Well, if you really don't—"

"Oh, all right," said Harriet. "Bottoms up!"

* * *

"I don't know what I'm going to do," Tilly announced, huddled up between her parents in the front seat of the car. "I can't remember how the descant begins and I can't remember my part in the cooks' dance."

"Don't worry about it," said Kate, patting her on the knee. You'll remember everything as soon as you get on stage."

"You were fine yesterday." Jerry slowed down to a crawl as they passed over an icy patch in front of the refinery. "Absolutely the best angel in the line. And the best cook. I was bowled over."

"But there'll be people watching tonight." Tilly shivered and hunched deeper down into her parka. "My stomach feels funny. What'll I do if I have to be sick?"

"Join Mrs. Reese in the bathroom," said Kate grimly. "Oh, I shouldn't have said that. Please, God, don't let her go to pieces before the show is over. I thought she sounded fine last night. Jerry, didn't she sound fine to you?"

"Like Rubinstein and Horowitz combined. Your only problem is Mona Meade. Someone should give her a couple of eyebrows and a mouth and tell her that she's bringing tidings of great joy to the shepherds, not announcing a funeral."

Kate sighed. "Margaret's going to help with makeup, but it's too late to do anything more about her acting. She just won't deliver. What's so funny?" she asked as Tilly let out a giggle.

Her troubles forgotten, Tilly beamed up at her mother. "When she says that about tidings of great joy and looks down at Joey, Harvey and Walter, they're all going to cross their eyes and make her laugh."

"Oh, Lord." Kate experienced a few butterflies of her own as they approached the brightly lit hall. "Jerry, are you sure you don't want to come in and give us moral support?"

Jerry stopped exactly in line with the shoveled path leading up to the main entrance stairs. "If I don't get Gilbert into the oven tonight, we're not going to have a cassoulet on Saturday. But I'll try to catch the end of the show and drive you home. Good luck, sweetie." Pushing back Tilly's parka hood, he planted a kiss on her forehead while Kate climbed out of the car. "Be a good angel and make sure your mother doesn't tire herself out." Bending lower down, he called through the open door. "Take it easy, Kate. I hope everything goes okay."

Kate held up a gloved hand with two fingers crossed.

"Oh, look," said Tilly, pointing across the road. "Mrs. Reese has fallen into a snowbank."

The upstairs lobby presented a scene guaranteed to gratify even the most apprehensive author/producer/director. With the exception of those working the late shift at the mine, the whole town seemed to be waiting, yellow pasteboard tickets in hand, eager for the doors to open. Proud parents chattered nervously, couples without children listened indulgently, and unmarried miners from the bunkhouses across the road stood propped up against any available vertical surface, looking at once nonchalant and slightly uncomfortable in jackets and ties, with their hair slicked down for the occasion. A thick blue cloud of cigarette smoke, filling the upper half of the room, indicated that most had taken the trouble to arrive early.

Anxious to put off for as long as possible the inevitable encounter with Harriet's nerves, Kate led Tilly briskly through the crowd, heading for a door at the end of the lobby where the stairs led down to the lunchroom.

"Yoo-hoo, Kate!"

Up the stairs tripped a small, delicate woman of about Kate's age, wide brown eyes sparkling eagerly in a delicate oval face, glossy brown hair set in a careful arrangement of alternating waves and curls. She wore a deep-wine-colored wool coat, a lush stole made up of two fox pelts biting each other's tails, and neat black fur-trimmed overshoes, and in one black-gloved hand she carried several sheets of mimeographed legal-size paper stapled together at the top left-hand corner. These she waved at Kate while negotiating the last few steps.

"Kate, dear, just the person I *had* to see." Having reached lobby level, the small bright-eyed woman rushed forward with the mimeographed publication. "I hope, oh, I *do* hope, you haven't read *this*."

Closer inspection revealed *this* to be the latest issue of *The Crow River Gazette*, delivered throughout the town that morning.

"Actually, I haven't," said Kate, who actually had. "What a hectic day."

Gloria Lewis's expression, designed to simulate deep regret, rearranged itself into the genuine article. "Oh, the *relief*," she breathed. "Because you mustn't. I absolutely forbid it. You see—oh, dear, I don't know how to say this . . ."

She hesitated long enough for Kate to open the door and send Tilly backstage to get ready.

"I, well . . ." Concerned that Kate, too, might vanish through the doorway, Gloria managed to grasp her prey by the wrist. "You know the essay contest they announced last month. Well, it seems that my *silly* little composition won and there's a bit at the end about, well, never mind, but everyone seems to think I meant you when, really, *no one* could have been further from my thoughts, which were naturally on a *much* higher plane. And almost prophetic, when you think of the *awful* things that have been going on right under our very noses. So, please don't listen to any foolish gossip and promise me, *promise* me"—she pressed the offending publication into Kate's hands—"*swear* that you'll just tear this up and cast it away."

"Definitely." Wishing that she had chosen to appear in something a little more fashionable than Jerry's old parka over her sweater and skirt, Kate took a quick backward look over her shoulder. "I suppose I'd better go and see what's happening in the dressing room."

"Oh, dear, yes." Gloria put on her warmest smile. "You must make the most of tonight. Once the Little Stranger arrives, you'll be *far* too busy to do any more directing for *ever* such a long time. Heaven knows what we'll do without one of your *marvelous* productions to look forward to. I mean, I might manage to whip up something myself, but it won't be the same. I feel absolutely *bereft* already."

"Don't." Kate smiled back with equal warmth. "I've got a really terrific idea all lined up for next summer."

Gloria's face fell. "But the baby . . ."

"Oh, what's a baby? I'll just plunk it in a corner or strap it to my back."

"Kate, *dear!*"

"Why not? And wait till you hear"—Kate checked her watch—"oh, gosh, it's almost quarter past seven. I've got to go. Anyway, you'll love the idea and you have to promise to be in it."

Gloria looked bored and gave a little shrug. "I doubt if I'll have time."

"Don't say that. Such a good part."

A speck of light flashed on in each of Gloria's eyes.

"How good?"

"You could steal the show."

"Well, I *might* just glance—what show is it?"

"I'll call you."

"But—"

"Tomorrow!"

With a conspiratorial smile, Kate ducked backstage, shutting the door firmly behind her.

"Mrs. Wilson, Joey bent my halo!"

"I didn't!"

"I can't find the Baby Jesus."

"My robe's too long."

"Do I *have* to wear that gucky stuff on my face?"

The sound of general high-volume pandemonium floated out from the dressing area, leading Kate to fear the worst. Inside, however, everything seemed reasonably under control. All the children had their costumes on, filling the room with a colorful throng of overexcited angels, shepherds, townspeople and visiting royalty. A few clustered around Diana Walter requesting last-minute adjustments, but most seemed happy to strut about, enjoying the novelty of their exotic finery. Tilly, pale and nervous in her white robe and tinsel halo, stood off in a corner watching Margaret Wilson apply brown makeup to the winter pallor of the last remaining Wise Man.

"There she is! The Great Exploiter herself!" Spotting Kate from across the room, Margaret waved a stick of greasepaint in greeting. "Now don't you dare do anything. Go outside and sit down."

"Mrs. Taggert, I can't find the Baby Jesus."

Turning around, Kate found her retreat blocked by a pretty little girl in a blue robe and white mantle.

"Did you look in the cradle?"

"I looked everywhere." The dimpled chin began to tremble. "What am I going to do at the end without a baby to hold?"

"Don't worry. It was just a little bundle. We'll find some cloth and make up another. Here." Kate appropriated a reasonably clean white towel lying on a nearby chair and a safety pin from a bowl on the makeup counter. "This will do just fine. Let's go and put it where you can find it."

"You're not sitting down," sang Margaret as they walked by on their way to the wings.

"I don't want to sit down," said Kate, twirling her towel. "And if I don't make up another baby bundle, we're going to have an awful anticlimax in the last scene. Tilly, dear, you look lovely." She set off into the wings. "Come on, Josie. Where's the cradle?"

"Oh, Mrs. Taggert. There you are. Wait a minute, please."

Through the curtain at the far side of the proscenium came Nellie Holtzer, a stout gray-haired lady who, in addition to supervising the costume sewing, had also agreed to help during the performance. Although flustered and short of breath, she presented a majestic appearance in black laced pumps and a flowered crepe de chine dress of her own manufacture, pulled back at the neckline with twin diamanté clips.

"It's Mrs. Reese," she announced, fanning herself with a program sheet in an effort to recover from the exertion of crossing the stage at a jog trot. "She's sitting down in the lobby and she says she won't play a note until we take the screen away from the piano."

"Harriet said that?"

"She was very positive about it. Not like herself at all. She says she can't perform without seeing her audience. What shall I do? Everyone is waiting for us to begin and I'm not a furniture mover."

Kate put a sympathetic hand on Mrs. Holtzer's plump shoulder. "Please, Nellie. Anything to make her happy. Just ask one of the men to fold up the screen and push it over to the wall. We'll be much better off without it."

"Well, of course. Whatever you say." Nellie grasped the lower edge of an undergarment only faintly visible through the crepe de chine and gave it a firm downward tug in preparation for the walk back. "But I wish people would make up their minds. I really do." She vanished back through the curtain.

"Oh, dear. What now?"

Kate had just finished tucking the new bundle back into its cradle when a loud tremulous rumble from the piano beyond the curtain brought her head up with a jerk. The first majestic chords of "Joy to the World" brought her rapidly to her feet and propelled her back in the direction of the dressing area. She met Margaret and Diana in the doorway.

"My God," hissed Margaret. "What's she doing?"

"It's the overture," Kate hissed back. "She's started the overture."

"But we're not ready." Diana began wringing her hands. "Nobody's in place and I haven't checked all the costumes."

"It's too late to worry about the costumes." Kate put her brain into high gear and began to enjoy herself. "Frank just went upstairs to the lights, so that's all right. Margaret, you get Mary, Joseph and the Annunciation Angel into position so we can start. Diana, you sneak the stage-left angels around behind the scrim to their side so we don't have a lot of tramping about later. That's all we need to do before the curtain—oh, Lord, who's supposed to be pulling the curtain?"

"Me," said Diana. "But I'll be—"

"Just get the angels set up," whispered Kate. "I'll stand by for the curtain, then we can organize everybody else before the second scene. Thank heaven it's a long overture. What *has* got into Harriet?"

And with that rhetorical question left hanging in the air, the three ladies scurried off in different directions, intent on their various missions. Three minutes later, the curtains parted and the lights came up to reveal Mary, sewing at her simple cloth-draped card table. An angel entered. The pageant was off and running.

25

Propped up in a corner of the wings, Mona Meade hugged herself as tightly as she could bear in an unsuccessful effort to stop shivering. To the best of her knowledge, taking her entire lifetime into consideration, she had never felt worse than she did at this moment. The hour of preparation in the dressing room, although bad, had generally been too hectic for any thought beyond the problems of the moment. But now, with the pageant under way, and nothing to do but wait while one scene followed inexorably on the heels of the next, she seriously wondered if she could survive the awful moment of her entrance, to say nothing of the ensuing twenty minutes before the curtains mercifully closed on her pitiful performance.

She knew she should never have looked in the mirror. Because for just a moment after putting on her robe and halo she had been able to imagine herself transformed into someone if not beautiful (her imagination had its limits) at least not unworthy of the part. But this pleasant fantasy had lasted only about twenty seconds, or the length of time it took her to walk across the room. There, tempted by a potent mixture of vanity and curiosity, she had yielded to temptation. And there, after gravely studying her reflection in the full-length mirror by the door, she had come to the sad conclusion that it took more than a white sheeting robe and a tinsel halo to make a radiant Head Angel out of the class beanpole. Not that her father would be expecting any better. But the thought of disappointing him yet again weighed heavily on her heart.

A scuffle in the wings on the far side of the stage caught her attention. The three shepherds had arrived, ready to make their entrance. Seeing her, they stopped jostling each other and began to smile and whisper. She knew why. They intended to make her laugh when she started to speak, and she had a terrible premonition that they might succeed. With everything else going wrong, it seemed quite natural that she should disgrace herself by bursting into helpless giggles before a packed house that comprised a large percentage of Crow River's population, from her father, wearing his polite social smile in the front row, to a surprisingly large Indian contingent at the back. She longed for the courage to run away and never return.

Onstage, the action rolled on toward the hillside scene. Caspar, Melchior and Balthazar bade farewell to Herod and set off on their journey to the strains of "We Three Kings of Orient Are." The waiting shepherds tensed themselves for their entrance while, beyond them, Mona could see Margaret readying a band of small angels to climb a narrow flight of stairs that led to the raised crosswalk beneath which, at the appropriate moment, a curtain would be drawn to reveal a tableau of the Bethlehem manger. Not far away, Miss Walter performed the same function with the remaining angels whom, all too soon, Mona would be required to lead up and forward to the center of the crosswalk. The very thought set her stomach churning. She wondered if she had time to make another visit to the ladies' room.

"You haven't got your makeup on."

Mona jumped and discovered Kate Taggert standing at her side. Kate leaned forward to look closer into her face.

"No lipstick or anything," she said. "Didn't Mrs. Wilson show you how?"

Mona shook her head. "I don't want any. It wouldn't do any good anyway."

"That's what you think." Kate grabbed Mona's hand and propelled her into the dressing area. "Sit down, there's a good girl. We haven't got much time." Moving quickly behind Mona, she threw a sheet about her shoulders, removed the tinsel halo from her head and lifted her hair with both hands. "This'll be better up. I'll have to use an elastic band and pin it as best I can, but no one's going to see the back anyway. There." She turned Mona about. "Now just hold still . . ."

For the next few minutes, Kate limited her remarks to an occasional "close your eyes . . . look up . . . look down . . . mouth open . . . closed . . . head back . . . that's good" while working as rapidly as a painter with a mysterious array of tubes, pots, pads, pencils and brushes, the effect of which Mona, in her passive role as canvas, could not begin to envision. Eventually, after flicking on a final touch of mascara and brushing away some stray powder, Kate removed the sheet, replaced the halo and retired a few paces to assess the result of her labors. Mona stared back anxiously.

"How do I look?" she asked in as bright a voice as she could muster.

Her heart sank as Kate's encouraging expression faltered and failed.

"Maybe I should take it off," she suggested.

"No." Kate blinked and shook her head. "No," she repeated. "I'm sorry. You look fine. It's just . . . you look older. It reminded me—"

"Stop!" Joey Wilson's hoarse bellow traveled from the stage to the dressing area almost undiminished in volume. "See up there —in the east!"

"A new star!" roared Harvey Lewis, who had received the same lecture in voice projection. "What can it mean?"

"Oh, my," said Kate, reaching for Mona's hand. "It means you're on. Let's go!"

"It must be a sign!"

The shepherds continued their deafening dialogue, but Mona heard none of it. Half running, half pulled, scarcely able to grasp the fact that the moment for her entrance had arrived, she flew out of the dressing area into the wings, risking as she did so another glance into the fatal mirror by the door.

"Mona—are you all right?"

Kate's worried face stared into hers as they came to a halt near the waiting line of keyed-up angels. Mona nodded, too stunned to speak. It had flashed by so quickly, the figure in the mirror. She might have made a mistake. In her overwrought mood, where misery, fear and elation took turns at coming to the fore, she mistrusted even the evidence of her own eyes. The mind played tricks and, during that split second, hers could easily have seized on a chance combination of angle, light and shade to call up an image of the face she had sought and pored over so many times among the family snapshots rescued from her mother's cedar chest and certainly never thought to see staring back at her through the cracked and clouded surface of a dressing room mirror.

And yet her memory of that brief glimpse remained so vivid. She longed to run back for another look, but there was no time. Guided only by instinct, her mind awhirl, she moved toward the bottom of the ladder leading up to the raised crosswalk.

She must have made a mistake. And yet, and yet . . . there was a look in Kate's eyes that she had never seen before, and a new expression on the faces of the small angels, who stared at her with something that almost resembled awe. She smiled at one in passing and instantly received an answering smile, accompanied by a blush. This, too, was new. Mona's heart raced faster. Perhaps the mirror had told the truth. Perhaps she had only to grow up, to wait a few more years and then receive an inheritance so wondrous, so unimagined, so inconceivable, that even now she dared not think it into words.

Harriet Reese executed a trill on the piano, followed by a loud introductory chord. Once more, weeks of rehearsal came to Mona's rescue. As the angels behind her burst into song, she automatically took a step forward and, to the strains of "While Shepherds Watched Their Flocks by Night," led her section of the heavenly host up the stairs onto the crosswalk.

Her effect on Patsy Michaels, leading on the rest of the angels from the opposite side, could hardly have been more gratifying. Abandoning all signs of angelic reserve, Patsy stopped singing and gaped. Mona glowed at her. Still glowing, she turned to confront the audience, where her father's beaming face shone back at her from the front row.

This gave her all the proof she needed. A wave of gladness engulfed her, filling her eyes with tears. The song ended. When the last note died out on the piano, she bent her head and looked down at the three shepherds. They looked up at her, no longer potential tormentors, merely three very small boys with open mouths. She had a sudden impusle to laugh but just as suddenly found herself touched. This must have been how the real shepherds looked, that star-filled night on the hill outside Bethlehem; and perhaps the real angel felt toward them the same surge of tenderness that threatened to catch in her throat the words she felt welling up within her as naturally as if she had just thought of them herself.

"Fear not," she told them.

But the words emerged in a whisper. Taking a deep breath, she looked up, pitched her inner voice to the back wall and tried again.

"Fear not," she said, much louder this time, fighting to control a smile that threatened to burst out all over her face from sheer overwhelming happiness. "For, behold"—she spread her arms to embrace the entire stage—"I bring you good tidings of *great* joy, which shall be to all people."

Calmly and with feeling she continued to project the simple words out to the audience. She finished without mishap. Her father clapped. Others joined in. Freddy Holtzer winked up at her from the stage. Her cup overflowed.

Tilly heard the applause as a far-off noise that rose and faded somewhere in the shadowy regions behind the harsh, throbbing pain in her head. Although it now seemed so much a part of her that she could scarcely remember feeling well, the sick dizziness had begun quite unobtrusively as a vague malaise, lost in the general rush and bustle prior to their departure for the theater. Over the course of the evening, however, it had slowly gathered strength and tightened its grip on her until the mere action of remaining upright on the crosswalk without toppling off required all the willpower she could muster.

She stood there, her eyes turned away from the painful bright lights, fighting to keep a grip on herself while the pageant played itself out in some strange limbo on the far fringes of her consciousness. The piano tinkled and the other angels caroled something to a tune she could not quite remember. A throng of assorted shepherds, kings and townspeople marched onto the stage. Everyone sang. The song ended and the crowd below her split into kneeling groups as the curtains under the walkway parted with a swish of metal rings on clothes-line wire. Then everyone sang again, the stage curtains opened and closed several times to admit more waves of applause, and at last she was able to follow the other angels down the ladder back to the dressing area where, half dazed by the surrounding noise and flurry, she exchanged her angel's robe for a cook's apron and hat.

But even as she tied the apron she knew that she could not possibly get through the second part of the program. Joey discovered her in the outer cloakroom, struggling into her parka.

"Whatcha doing?" he boomed.

"Shh."

"You look awful."

"Don't talk so loud."

Joey moved closer and modified his voice to a hoarse whisper. "You sick?"

"I think so." Tilly began to tuck in the ends of her knitted scarf. "My head hurts."

"Didja tell yer ma?"

"I can't find her. Anyway, she'd make me see the doctor."

Joey nodded. Doctors meant cold stethoscopes, injections and sore arms.

"What about your part in the show?" he asked.

"There's lots of cooks. They don't need me." With the scarf well tucked into place, Tilly zipped up her parka, wiped an arm across her damp forehead and began pulling on mittens. "Tell Miss Walter I've gone, okay? And Mom when you see her?"

"Yer not s'posed to be at home alone."

"It's all right. My father's there."

"Maybe I better go with you." Joey looked down with distaste at the turned-up toes on his red felt boots. "I hate being an elf."

"We can't two of us leave. It'll be easier to sneak out if it's just me."

Joey shrugged. "Okay." He slouched behind her until she reached the door leading into the lobby. "But if you really wanta sneak out . . ."

Tilly paused, ready to turn the doorknob. Joey grinned.

". . . you better take off that hat."

And, before his words could penetrate Tilly's sluggish thinking, he plucked the cook's hat from her head, tossed off a "See ya tomorrow" and raced back to the dressing area.

Past caring how she appeared to anyone, just so long as she

managed to get away unhindered, Tilly cautiously pulled the door slightly ajar. A sudden influx of noise and cigarette smoke made her blink and fall back. But by half closing her eyes and restricting her breathing, she managed to approach the narrow opening again and look out.

As bad luck would have it, almost everyone in the lobby had migrated over to the opposite wall, where cool air came filtering in through chinks in the windows. Some had their backs to her—for a moment she thought she recognized her father's neat haircut and broad shoulders behind a group of miners—but the rest seemed to have positioned themselves with no better purpose in mind than to keep an eye on the door through which she had to pass. It was like being in the play again, with herself as star.

She hesitated, hoping to choose a moment when the fewest number of people would be looking in her direction. But the moment never came. The irritating audience continued to wait patiently for her entrance. Clearly, she had no choice but to brave it out. She took another look around the door just as a slight eddy in the crowd revealed her mother about to sit down on an unoccupied sofa at the far end of the lobby. Then the crowd flowed together again, cutting off her view. It was now or never. Pulling up the hood of her parka, she slipped out the door, ran downstairs, and let herself out through the lower porch into the teeth of a hard, black frost.

He stood there rapturous, hardly able to believe his luck. It only went to show. Just when his patience had reached the limit of its endurance, just when he felt unable to stand one more second of the vacuous inanities issuing from the face opposite him, the door had opened and there she was. And all at once everything changed. The talking face continued to open and close its mouth, smiling and nodding, while he continued to smile back as if nothing had happened. But something had happened, something that pulled him back from weeks of bleak depression and catapulted him into tingling life, throwing the bland, stupid face out of focus, and blotting out the monotonously cheerful voice. Now, all he could see was a small figure in a red parka and navy blue ski pants and all he could hear was a great rushing sound, as if he had placed his head inside a giant seashell. Her image filled his mind like a pale, luminous balloon, a welcome parasite that grew and grew, forcing everything else out until only its taut, thin membrane remained, ready to explode against the inside of his skull. Dizzy with excitement, he watched her close the door and run quickly downstairs.

Oh, dear, he said aloud, forcing his attention back to the tedious pudding face, which had stopped smiling and become mournful. My, my, he said. And, out of sheer generosity, tsk, tsk. He could afford to be generous, because his time had come. She was going home. Alone. The thought rang through his head like a peal of bells. In spite of everything—the warnings, the talks in school, the gossip that filtered through every age group in town—she was going home! He felt like singing. Everything was falling into place. Everything was going to be all right. A short telephone call, a quick detour, and he could be there and back before the end of the show. He willed himself into serenity. For it was now or never. All he had to do was bring the wretched bore to a halt—even as the thought came to him it was done—and make his escape.

Holding himself tightly in check, lest he break into a run, he strode downstairs to the telephone.

26

The shock of cold air outside the recreation hall cleared Tilly's head. Feeling stronger and steadier on her legs, she hurried away from the building, slackening her pace only slightly to inspect a team of Indian dogs curled up in a jumble of multicolored fur under the streetlight near the main entrance. One animal, interrupted in the middle of a dream by a vaguely remembered scent that seemed to emanate from the small passing human, lifted its smooth black head and gazed back at her with apprehensive yellow eyes. But on discovering no sign of the spitting, howling, pin-clawed devil that attacked unwary visitors from behind, Dog lost interest and went back to sleep.

Tilly walked steadily on, head down, keeping the tip of her parka hood pointed into the teeth of a rising wind until the extreme cold forced her to stop and pull her scarf up over her mouth and nose. When she looked back down the road, she saw with satisfaction that the streetlight had faded to a mere glow over a clump of trees in a bend in the road. Above her, huge banners of white, pink and green northern lights undulated silently across the stars in a broad velvet sky. And ahead, beyond the mine buildings, a growing belt of total blackness gradually blotted out this spectacular display. Black clouds at night meant that snow would soon be falling. Tilly set off again at a faster pace.

She measured her progress by landmarks: the darkened fire hall, the last of the bunkhouses, and finally the cookery, where rotating shifts of miners ate their way through a round-the-clock timetable of overlapping meals. Here, she faced a choice. She could either go forward up a long hill toward the towering headframe, now partially obscured by a light veil of eddying snow flurries, or bear left on a narrow detour that skirted the mine complex and rejoined the main road just at the point where it crossed the river. She turned left and came around the corner just in time to see twin beams from a pair of motor headlights sway down the hill on the other side of the river, then flick upward to speed across the bridge. For a moment, it seemed as if they would veer onto the detour and pass her, but in the end they held to the main road and vanished up the snow-shrouded hill in the direction of the mine.

Having crossed the bridge herself, Tilly left the road and followed the pipeline path up the hill, stopping now and then to rest against the railings and allow soft, cooling snowflakes to fall on her upturned face. Despite this refreshment, she arrived at the top panting, drenched with sweat and hardly able to move her legs. Yet the sight of home, although visible only as a gray shadow far down the path, gave her sufficient strength to move on.

She encouraged herself by dividing the distance into three laps. At the end of the first, the Reeses' darkened front windows regarded her sleepily, as if they had despaired of anyone coming home and had retired for the night. But at the Wilsons', lights shone out from both the living room, where Davy's babysitter flirted with eyestrain over a tightly printed wartime edition of *Forever Amber*, and the back bedroom, where Davy had turned on his bedside lamp as part of a failed effort to stay awake until the other members of his family came back from wherever they had gone without him. Her own house offered a more modest greeting, in the form of a single lightbulb left burning over the door in the passageway that connected Jerry's office to the kitchen. This was enough for Tilly. Gratefully, she opened the door and went inside.

Even in the passage, the house gave off a deserted air. Turning to the right, Tilly let herself into the kitchen where a rich, heavy scent of roast meat summoned up a queasy sensation in the pit of her stomach and prevented her from giving more than a cursory response to Sam's joyful welcome. The scent came from the oven, recently switched off, where Gilbert, golden brown, aromatic and, to Tilly in her present condition, perfectly revolting, had been left to cool. Averting her eyes and breathing through her mouth, Tilly shut the oven door and continued on to the living room.

Here the darkness was such that she could see almost nothing but the receding layers of falling snow that drifted lazily down past the unfrosted upper windowpanes at the far end of the room. She walked over to her parents' bedroom door. It stood open.

"Daddy?"

No answer.

She looked into the bedroom. Empty. Trailed by Sam, she retraced her steps to her father's office.

"Daddy?"

A shaft of light from the passageway surged into the room as she opened the door. It revealed only Veronica, about to seek refuge from her boisterous brood in a flat cardboard box on top of the filing cabinet where Jerry stored papers waiting to be sorted and pigeonholed.

Seeing Tilly, Veronica gave the tip of her tail a twitch to indicate that, if approached in the right manner, she might be willing to accept a few compliments and a rub behind the ears. But when the expected attentions failed to materialize, she accepted the fact without rancor. Stepping delicately into the box, she indulged in a luxurious stretch, then curled up and fell fast asleep.

Tilly, too, took to her bed, having first placed underneath it the large enameled bowl that had proved an invaluable standby during a previous bout of flu on occasions when nausea had struck too suddenly to allow time for a dash for the bathroom. Sam watched these preparations with his head on one side, aware of something gone wrong but unable to decide quite what it might be. At last he walked over to the bed, placed his head next to Tilly's on the pillow and breathed on her. The gesture failed.

"Please, Sam," said Tilly in a weak voice, "go away."

So Sam plodded off, nails clicking on the kitchen linoleum, to settle down on one of the corner sofas in the living room. Four kittens immediately swarmed up after him and proceeded to stake out territory on his tail, on his back and under his chin. Sam sighed. Children were all very well, but he longed for the day when they would flee the nest. A stabbing sensation, as of multiple pinpricks, arose in the tip of his nail. At the same time, a small body rolled down his side, then began to haul itself up again with exquisitely sharp tiny claws. Sam closed his eyes and sighed again. It was to be games before bed after all.

Eventually the merriment subsided. Sam dozed, then woke with a start, scattering kittens in the process. He pricked up his ears. Someone was coming.

Well," said Margaret, plumping down on a lobby seat beside Kate halfway through the intermission. "We've had Mona Meade turned into a swan to end Act One. What have you got up your sleeve for Act Two?"

Kate arched a knot out of her back and smiled. "Nothing. No surprises. I just want to see it through and go to bed."

"You look beat." Shifting in her chair, Margaret produced a small silver hip flask. "I brought this in case of emergency. Care for a little pick-me-up?"

Kate shook her head. "I'd drop off right here and now. If you want to be a real friend, go pick Harriet up. We still have to get her through *Santa's Magic Toy Shop*."

"I'm way ahead of you." Margaret sloshed the contents of her flask. "I offered her a shot just a few minutes ago."

"You didn't!"

"And she took it like a lamb!"

They both laughed.

"Actually," continued Margaret, "she didn't seem all that nervous."

"She didn't *sound* all that nervous. The piano in the finale—"

"Kate! Dearest Kate!"

Harriet's ample form appeared across the lobby.

"I've been looking all over for you. Isn't it going well? Aren't you happy?" Harriet clasped her hands to her bosom. "Weren't the children splendid?"

"Yes, they were," said Kate, disregarding a pointed cough from Margaret. "And so were you. I'm sorry your lovely descant got a bit mangled in 'Away in a Manger.' "

"Oh." Harriet unclasped her hands to dismiss the thought with an airy wave. "It couldn't matter less. Now, before I go back and play another note, I want you to promise me something."

"Well . . ."

"Has anyone seen Alec?"

Diana Walter bore down on them, her eyes flashing.

"I'm furious, just furious," she announced, when no one volunteered any information. "First he said he wouldn't play Santa, then he said he would, and now just when I had him all ready to go on, he's vanished, God knows where. Oh!" She beat her fists in the air. "He's the most impossible man I've ever—he's probably wandered over to the store to count oranges or cereal boxes and if he forgets to come back, who's going to give out the presents? I wish I'd never started this. I wish I'd never got him involved. I wish . . . oh, never mind!"

She whirled away.

"Love and show business," said Margaret dryly. "What a combination!"

Harriet, who had not appreciated being pushed out of the limelight, became animated again. "That's just what I want to talk about," she said.

"Love?"

"No." Turning her attention from Margaret, Harriet perched cautiously on the arm of Kate's chair. "We must do another big musical next year," she told her.

"Oh!" Having steeled herself for an argument on the subject of nerves, Kate fell silent while her brain took time out to change gears.

Harriet bent closer to Kate and continued in a conspiratorial stage whisper. "Edward had such a good time last year in *The Mikado*. I was thinking we might follow up with *The Pirates of Penzance*." She giggled. "And not tell Mr. Gilbert and Mr. Sullivan."

"As a matter of fact," said Kate. "I thought we might do something newer, like *Oklahoma!* And not tell Mr. Rodgers and Mr. Hammerstein."

"Oh!" Harriet gave a delighted shriek. "You're terrible! I'll order the piano score tomorrow. Gloria Lewis will have a fit. Exploiting childen, indeed! Well"—she hopped lightly off the chair arm as the lobby lights began to flash on and off—"I get to tickle the ivories again. What is it they say in the theater? Oh, yes: *merde*, girls. Now, don't forget, Kate—I'm coming over in the morning to collect my dear little kitten-cat! Ta-ta." She trotted off eagerly into the auditorium, leaving behind her a bemused silence.

At last Kate spoke.

"Exactly what did you put in that flask?" she asked.

"Whisky." Margaret held up her right hand. "Plain old Hiram Walker, as God is my witness. And she only had a drop."

"Well, whatever it was, I'm laying in a case of it and we're doing *Oklahoma!* next summer."

Their eyes met. They both laughed.

"And Gloria *will* be livid," said Margaret.

"Mmm," said Kate, still grinning. "But I think I'll do it anyway. Whoops, there goes Harriet."

At the first buoyant notes from the piano, the few last-minute dawdlers remaining in the lobby stubbed out their cigarettes and hurried away. Margaret prepared to do likewise.

"I suppose I'd better see if there's anything to be done backstage. Are you going to watch?"

"Not yet." Settling deeper into the chair cushions, Kate stretched out her legs and made circles with her feet. "I can listen from here and go in when the cooks come on. Did you see Tilly anywhere after the pageant?" she asked, as Margaret stood up to leave.

"Wasn't she backstage?"

"Not while I was there."

"She probably went downstairs for a drink."

"I guess so. Maybe you could ask Joey."

"Joey." Margaret rolled her eyes. "I don't know what's got into the boy. Did I tell you? I came into the bathroom yesterday and found him drowning Davy. Head down in the bathtub, with ice cubes. Oddly enough, they both seemed annoyed when I pulled him out." She shrugged. "I'll ask about Tilly, if I see him."

And with a departing wave, she headed for the door by the stairs, leaving Kate to swing her legs up onto the sofa, close her eyes, and attempt to ignore the seductive melodies drifting up from the lunchroom jukebox in favor of the bouncy ditties being offered by a succession of elves, toys and teddy bears in the next room. Eventually she gave up the struggle and hummed along with the jukebox until the cooks' entrance music forced her to abandon Irene Dunne halfway through "Smoke Gets in Your Eyes." She reached the auditorium just as the cooks began their song, backed by an accompaniment to which Harriet, on the spur of the moment, had added the merest hint of a boogie bass.

"Six little pastry cooks are we," they sang,

"Busy as pastry cooks can be . . ."

Slipping into an empty seat beside an impassive Indian matron swathed in a colorful multiplicity of layered cardigans, stockings and skirts, Kate cast a critical director's eye over the stage picture. It seemed in order. The scenery had been set up correctly, the dolls and toys were in their assigned places, and the singing cooks looked charming as they stirred yellow mixing bowls in their gingham aprons and tall white hats.

"Baking a cake as you can see-ee.

Six little cooks are we!"

Except there were only five. Kate counted again to make sure, trying to recognize the distant faces beneath their starry painted eyelashes and bright red cheek spots. Certainly only five and, unless she was very much mistaken . . .

"Joey," she said on discovering that disconsolate elf staring mournfully at his pointed toes in the dressing room. "Where's Tilly?"

"Gone home."

"Home?"

"She felt sick."

"But she knows better than to go home alone!"

"Isn't her dad there?"

"Yes. Yes, I hope so." Feeling that she had taken out her sudden alarm on the innocent messenger, Kate made an effort to smile. "You were a very good shepherd."

Joey nodded in agreement. "Yeah. But I wish I didn't hafta be an elf."

"You'll be a good elf too. Don't worry." Kate pulled on her galoshes and scooped up her parka. "I think I'd better go home. Tell your mother and Miss Walter, will you?" And, without waiting for an answer, she hurried into the corridor and out into the lobby.

Here she hesitated for a moment, unable to decide whether to set off immediately or seek the reassurance of a quick telephone call. Logic came to her aid. There was really no question about it. If she skipped the call, she would worry. And if she worried, her legs would seize up and she would have to walk slowly. Descending the stairs, she passed into the deserted lunchroom where the glowing jukebox had been left to play on softly. A lush orchestral introduction followed her through the pool room, down the corridor and into Bert Nichols's office, where she dialed and waited. The introduction ended and the singer began. By some quirk of reverse logic, she found his calm, crooning voice vaguely irritating.

"I wonder who's kissing her now . . ."

The telephone continued to ring. Kate bit her thumbnail. Jerry must have been called out. But what about Tilly? If she had gone to bed, she might be asleep. She might also be too ill to reach the living room. Kate replaced the receiver and, pulling on her parka, walked back to the lunch room, where the record had begun to play again.

"Wonder who's showing her how . . ."

She halted abruptly and stared at the glowing jukebox.

"Wonder who's looking into her eyes
Breathing sighs, telling lies—"

Please, God, no. Seized by a panic so complete that it overpowered every other thought in her head, she rushed out of the room, through the downstairs porch and up the path. Even before she reached the main road, the familiar pain had clamped down on the front of her legs.

Deserted by Sam, Tilly rolled over in bed, closed her eyes, and drifted away to a strange land where reality became indistinguishable from dreaming and danger lurked like quicksand, waiting to entrap her wandering mind as it flitted erratically from one topic to the next. For a while she skimmed over the trouble spots, touching down lightly and springing away before they could get a grip on her. But at last she became hopelessly bogged down, lost in a vain, obsessive attempt to seek out answers to questions that continued to turn back on themselves in endless circles until, reduced to a state of helpless anguish, she found herself spinning dizzily, going past the same signposts over and over again.

To divide a fraction by a fraction, did one multiply across or diagonally? She tried both methods, but the top numbers kept slipping off onto the floor, and no sooner had she scrambled to put one back than the other fell, which meant that she had to keep running back and forth, back and forth, always arriving a little too late because the sheet under her had stopped behaving like a sheet and taken on a fluid quality, now flowing gently, now heaving up and down in a sickening, oily roll. At the same time, its surface texture altered, changing from rough to smooth to rough, except that wasn't it at all, those weren't the right words, it was something quite different—she began to gulp down deep drafts of air as she hunted for the right words. It was, it was—but she could think of nothing but rough and smooth and rough and rough and rough and—

The first instant of waking brought with it an awareness that she must either reach the bathroom in the next few seconds or take the extreme measure of using the bowl by the bed. She ran. Afterward, when she had regained sufficient strength to move, she stumbled over to the washbasin and rinsed out her mouth with tooth powder. Then, thoroughly weakened, she sank down beside the bathtub and laid her forehead on a folded towel thrown over its porcelain rim.

She began to feel better. A pleasant weakness replaced the nausea, soothing her brain, relaxing her muscles, and gently easing her into sleep. Gradually she slumped against the side of the tub, while her right arm slipped down its inside wall. In a dream she heard the creak of the porch screen door, followed by a bark from Sam. A second bark woke her in time to catch the scrabble of Sam's feet on the kitchen floor and the click of the inside door latch.

Tilly's heart leapt. Her father had finished his rounds. Her mother had missed her and come home. Now someone would take her back to bed, smooth the sheets, tuck her in, and lay a cool hand on her brow. Now she could stop taking care of herself and let others shoulder the burden. She could stop being brave. If she felt like it, she could even cry. And since she did feel like it, she allowed a few tears to well up in her eyes.

Around the corner, Sam bounced up and down making happy huffing noises. Tilly waited in an agony of impatience. Would her turn never come? Her parents always started talking the minute they came in the house. Why did no one say anything? With the questions came a grain of doubt, accompanied by a cold, clenched knot in the center of her chest. On the very point of speaking, she stifled the words and listened.

From the kitchen came a twang of springs as the oven door hinged downward, followed by a slither of metal roasting pan against metal rack, a low whistle, more eager panting, a quiet opening of doors and, almost simultaneous with the scramble of padded feet down the porch stairs, a soft double thump as the roasting pan and its succulent contents hit a nearby snowdrift. Then, in rapid order, the screen door springs creaked close and an indignant bark arose from outside. A short silence followed. Then the inner door clicked again.

Tilly pressed the folded towel hard against her mouth. There could be no doubt. The horror she had dreamt of nightly for the last five weeks had come at last, as it had to Ellie and Margie before her. Unlike them, however, she knew what lay in store for her. If she could gain some time, hold out until one of her parents came home . . .

The telephone in the living room began to ring. She longed to answer it, to hear a friendly voice, to scream for help. But no one could reach her in time, not even poor little Miss Baines, with her bad leg and cane, minding Davy next door. The ringing stopped.

Hunched over on her knees, her brain racing, Tilly strained forward to catch the next sound from the kitchen. It came as a light footstep. Then a distant tap at the half-open door of her darkened room. Then a familiar voice, deep and low, yet somehow as clear and close as if it were right beside her.

"Ho, ho, ho," it said. "Look who's come to see Tilly."

It seemed to be whispering directly into her ear. But it was in her bedroom. It had made a mistake. Tilly struggled to her feet and ran.

27

She waited in the dark, unable to stop shaking, partly from fear, partly from the icy draft rolling across the floor. Somewhere nearby, John Henry began to recover from the collapse precipitated by her sudden arrival in the middle of his evening nap. The tiny asthmatic gasps became shorter and less frequent and finally, much to her relief, stopped altogether. In the black silence that followed, she began to feel as if her senses, too, had faded away and ceased to function. Then it came to her, more as an awareness than a sound. He had left the bedroom and moved closer.

Nothing in the bathroom. To make sure, he checked behind the curtain at the end of the tub, but found only shelves and, on the floor, a cardboard box with a hole in the front for the cat. So much for the bathroom. He stroked one more possibility off his mental list, then did the same for the office and the cellar, neither of which could have been reached without his notice. Enjoying himself hugely—why had he never before thought of hide-and-seek?—he moved on to the living room.

Light from the bathroom streamed in behind him. No need to switch on a lamp. He looked about. Built-in sofas with wooden bases, freestanding chairs, nothing under the dining table, nowhere to hide. Except, perhaps . . .

He strode over to the far end of the room and threw back the lid of the cedar-chest coffee table. It contained only blankets, sheets and towels.

The room seemed very cold. A loud bark made him look up. Sam looked back at him through the front screen door and barked again. The inner door stood open. He moved around the cedar chest and squinted through the wire mesh. Has she really made a run for it? Impossible to tell—the dog had tramped down all the snow on the steps. No matter. He could soon pick up her footprints on the ground outside.

Much to Sam's joy, he reached toward the door handle. But where would she go? She couldn't outrun him. Why would she—? He paused and laughed to himself. Yes. It was a trick. Better and better. Strike off the great outdoors, on to the bedroom. He could always look outside afterward. Cutting Sam off in midbark, he closed the inner door and moved over to the bedroom.

A flick of the wall switch lit up an overhead bulb, sending a wash of flat yellow light over the cramped arrangement of furniture. He bent down and checked under the combined twin beds. Flat cardboard boxes, old paintings and dust. That left only the closet.

It had no curtain. Hanging clothes filled it from side to side: her clothes to the left, his to the right. Underneath these, a forest of shoes, galoshes, rubbers and boots followed the same arrangement. He felt his hands clenching. The game had ceased to amuse. Using his full strength, he racked the hangers viciously from side to side without meeting any resistance beyond what might be expected from the bulky coats, dresses, pants and jackets. He bent down again and pushed some shoes aside. Something stirred. His heart missed a beat as a small brown mouse shot out from behind a pair of black suede pumps and disappeared under the beds, where it proceeded to make a high-pitched warbling noise like a distant penny whistle. He swore and stood up. Clearly no one had been there before him. The little idiot must have gone outside after all. He turned on his heel and made for the door.

Hunkered down against the corner of the closet, her legs lost in her father's tall rubber boots, the rest of her enveloped by the suffocating naphthalene-scented folds of his woolen city coat, she listened to the footsteps recede and, by sheer effort of will, forced strength back into her body. It had almost collapsed from sheer terror when the hangers began scraping along the rod and the clothes piled up against her. But luck had come to her rescue in the unlikely form of John Henry. Now she must do her part and do it quickly. When her pursuer found no footprints leading away from the house, he would return for a more thorough search. Only one really safe place remained for her, and she had only seconds to get there.

In the living room, the screen door twanged open, then slammed shut. She heard the crunch of snow on the outside stairs. This was it. Stepping lightly out of the rubber boots, she disengaged herself from the coat and tiptoed past the beds to the door. The room beyond stood empty. She quailed, but there was no going back. With one swallow and one breath, she darted across the room, closed the front door, and released its spring lock. The sound of his boots thumping up the stairs followed her into the kitchen and the rattle of the knob accompanied her as she fled through the passage into her father's office.

She wasted no time switching on the light. Her father always left the lockup door open with the keys in the lock. Once inside, with the door shut and the keys in her possession, not even the longest arm could reach her. It would be terrible, but it would keep her out of his hands long enough for someone to come to the rescue. Panting, she seized the barred door and pulled. It refused to move.

She pulled again, straining back with all her might. The door stayed shut. Almost numb with shock, ready to cry out in her helpless frustration, she rattled the door as hard as she could. Her stillborn cry became an audible gasp when something stirred in the shadows under the bracket bed that hung on the rear wall of the lockup. Something in heavy boots and a red jacket. Groaning, it stood up, stumbled two paces forward and thrust a bleary, grizzled face between the bars.

"Wha'?" Jack McCallister made a mighty effort to focus his eyes. "Who'sh there?"

"It's me, Mr. McCallister." Tilly's hoarse whisper threatened to crack with every word. "It's Tilly. Please let me in. There's someone after me."

"Tilly!" Jack fell forward against the bars, expelling a potent blast of vaporized alcohol. "Wha'cha doin' here, Tilly? No place for li'l girls."

"I want in, Mr. McCallister. Please. Open the door."

"No, no, no." Jack flopped one arm through the bars and wagged a reproving finger. "Only bad people in here. Only wicked sonsabitches like me."

"The door's locked. Where's the key?"

"Wicked!" Jack's eyes caught fire as his voice rose. "Oh, yes, Lord, I've been wicked. I've sinned, and I've tasted strong waters and I've let you down again. Show no mercy, Lord," he bawled. "Lock this poor sinner up forever. Let him rot."

"The key, Mr. McCallister!"

"Lock him up," mumbled Jack. "Throw away the key," he howled, miming a loose overhand cast with his extended arm. "Never fin' it in a mill'n years."

Tilly whirled about. She had no doubt as to the location of the key. Her father had frequently complained about Jack's unfailing ability to lob it into the narrow gap between the filing cabinet and the wall. Fighting to keep her head and subdue a renewed attack of dizziness, she staggered over to the cabinet and heaved her shoulder against its outside corner. The cabinet shifted very slightly. At the same time, a heavy object behind it toppled over, slid down the wall, and landed on the floor with a thump. She looked down. A smooth, metallic cylinder about three inches long stuck out from behind the cabinet. It was the barrel end of Uncle Max's hunting rifle.

You load it, cock it, and . . .

Her father's words came clearly back to her. But she had nothing to load it with, and it was so heavy . . .

Her ears caught the soft click of a lock in the kitchen, sending her into a nosedive behind the desk, where a lithe tippet of sleek, soft fur brushed across her cheek. Startled, she pulled back, just in time to see the last few inches of Veronica's tail disappearing into the partially open lower right-hand drawer of the desk.

In a house of few rules, one alone had been drummed into her. Under no circumstances must she ever touch the lower right-hand drawer. She had tried, of course, but always found it locked. Now it stood open. Hardly daring to hope, she pulled the drawer farther out and removed Veronica who, with an indignant flick of her tail, bounded back into her box on top of the filing cabinet. Tilly held her breath. It all depended on her father. Had he removed his revolver or, by some wonderful stroke of luck, had he put it back and neglected to turn the lock? Her eyes could tell her nothing. The inside of the drawer lay in dark shadow. But when she thrust in her hand, it encountered cold, smooth metal.

She immediately snatched her hand back. Frightened as she was, she could not bring herself to pick up the gun. There must be some other way. Perhaps if she explained how ill she felt, or pretended to faint, or—

In rapid succession, the overhead light went on and Glassy Jack uttered a loud cackle of laughter.

"Hey, whaddaya know!" he yelled. "It's Sandy Claus!"

Davy woke up to discover the lamp beside his bed still lit. He found this puzzling. Under normal circumstances, it ought to have been turned off while he slept. Someone had slipped up, and badly. By way of protest, he clambered out of bed and stood defiantly in the middle of the room, waiting for the exciting moment when a parental thunderbolt would send him racing back under the covers. It failed to materialize. He then checked Joey's bed and found it empty. He listened for the sound of the radio in the living room, but heard nothing. A thrilling sense of adventure stole over him. Everyone was still out. Miss Baines would certainly be asleep. The house belonged to him.

Since no true adventurer would set forth into the unknown without the correct clothing and equipment, Davy took time to tie a warm blanket robe over his flannelette sleepers and pull his feet into fleece-lined bunny slippers. He also armed himself with a small soiled cushion, whose plump contours and comforting aroma of ketchup, cocoa and strawberry jam had supported its owner through many a dark midnight moment. Thus prepared, he opened his door and marched through the kitchen with a bold step, occasionally tripping over the toes of his slippers as the result of an unlucky guess in the matter of which bunny fitted which foot.

At the entrance to the living room, he stopped to look in on Miss Baines, who, as expected, had received a visit from the sandman. Her book and cane lay on the floor. He therefore forged ahead into the bathroom where his eye immediately came to rest on a controversial object set atop the open toilet seat. Equipped with arms, a back and a small but alarming oval opening in its flat base, the object had been painted an inviting shade of bright blue and decorated with colored decals of ducks and rabbits in an effort to win its way into his heart. Davy gazed at it with dislike. Despite frequent brightly phrased invitations to sit in it, he had thus far managed to remain firm in his refusal to do so. It occurred to him, however, that with no witness at hand to spread word of his capitulation he might risk a brief visit. Accordingly, he struggled up on the seat and, after much precarious turning and twisting, managed to occupy it in the correct fashion.

He sat there kicking his heels, noting how different the room looked from this new elevated perspective. After a while he began to sing.

"*Potty, potty, potty,*" he crooned.

"*Potty, potty, potty.*"

But with no one about to suggest how much fun it would be if he sang something else, the ditty soon palled. He therefore slid down onto his feet and set off for the living room, where Miss Baines slept peacefully on, heedless of the glare from several lamps and the sound of Sam Taggert's regular, agitated barking next door.

Davy could do nothing to quiet Sam. He could, however, extinguish two low table lamps by placing his cushion down on the floor, standing on tiptoe, and pulling at their beaded metal chain switches. A third rather taller model in the corner presented more of a problem, which he solved by climbing up on a nearby chair. Now only the standard lamp by the window stood between Miss Baines and a decently darkened room. Davy ascended an adjacent sofa and pulled the switch.

A second later, the barking outside came to a halt. Peering through the window's spreading frost patterns and the swirling snow beyond, Davy could see Sam jumping about on the front steps of the Taggert house, welcoming a visitor. The visitor ignored the greeting and, coming down the steps, began searching for something in the smooth, unbroken snowdrifts between the two houses. On finding nothing, he climbed over the pipeline and vanished into the Taggerts' back porch. Sam, locked out again, immediately resumed his barking while Davy, with nothing further to look at, climbed down from the sofa, picked up the languishing cushion, and walked thoughtfully back to his room.

On a wall, at the end of his bed, Joey had fastened a large colored picture cut out of *Life* magazine. It showed a jolly gentleman with red cheeks and a white beard seated at a wooden workbench amidst a stack of toys. The gentleman wore a red jacket, red trousers and black boots and appeared to favor a particular brand of soft drink. More to the point, according to Joey, this very same gentleman, if contacted by letter, could be relied upon to show up very soon in a sleigh drawn by animals with horns bearing wonderful presents for good little children like Joey and perhaps even Davy.

Davy studied the picture closely. It had been too dark outside to tell about the red cheeks or the soft drink, but all the other details seemed to correspond. No doubt the animals had been tethered on the other side of the house. Buy why, he wondered, were they there at all? Was this the night for presents? Or was the gentleman, unaware that Tilly would be out being an angel, merely stopping off to ask about some mistake in her letter? Davy hoped that his mother had made no such mistake in the writing of his own terse note. After taking a moment to plot out a course of action, he left the room, let himself out through the kitchen porch and, burying his face into Cushion's soft, warm center, set off through the snow to pay a call on the man in the red jacket.

28

He stood in the doorway, considering what to do next, while the imbecile waved wildly at him through the bars.

"Hey, Santa!" yelled the halfwit. "Merry Christmas! Merry fuckin' Christmas, eh? I bet I know who you wanna see." He swung his head about and spoke into an area between the desk and filing cabinet at the far end of the room. "C'mon out, Tilly."

Ah.

"C'mon meet Santa, Tilly. Don' be shy. He w'nt bitecha. Ah, she's shy, Santa. C'mon, Tilly, say hi to Santa."

With the tiresome wheedling voice came the odor of cheap whisky. The man was drunk. Worse, he was a witness and a distraction.

"Look, Tilly. Don'cha see who it is? He w'nt hurtcha. Come on, Santa. Show Tilly. Shake hands with y'r ol' pal Jack. Put it there. See, Tilly, it ain't no real Santa at all, it's only—"

He reached the lockup in an overwhelming rage. Seizing the proffered hand, he thrust its owner as far away from the bars as he could reach, then pulled back with all his strength. The grizzled head struck a metal rod with a richly satisfying crack. The bloodshot eyes rolled up and the rubber-jointed legs buckled. When he released the hand, the entire body keeled over to one side and collapsed on the floor. Dead, with any luck. One down, one to go, he thought. Totally restored to humor, he put on his best fatherly smile and turned around.

She stood facing him, her hand grasping the top of the desk for support. She had on a full-length cotton nightdress with a scalloped collar, short puffed sleeves and a sprigged pattern of faded pink rosebuds. Very good. She had undone her braids and her feet were bare. Oh, yes. And her wide, round eyes stared back at him from out of an ashen face, lightly beaded with sweat. She was terrified. Oh, God, yes. The blood sang in his temples.

"Hello, Tilly," he said kindly. "You're a hard little girl to find."

She continued to stare at him.

"Do you know who I am?" he asked

An almost imperceptible shake of the head.

"I won't hurt you," he said. "You know that, don't you?"

No reaction.

"I want to give you something."

He let the locket dangle temptingly from his hand, swinging it back and forth to display the polished metal and the tiny pearl.

"Isn't it pretty? Wouldn't you like to wear it to school?"

Her mouth began to work. She was trying to speak. He moved his foot slightly forward. She retreated.

"Won't you let me put it on for you?" he asked.

Again her mouth moved.

"You'll have to speak up, Tilly. Santa can't hear you."

"I'm sick."

The words came out a mere whisper.

"Oh, no. You poor baby." He knelt down and opened his arms. "Come to Santa, dear. He'll make it better."

It almost worked. Her eyes misted over and a look of weary longing passed over her face. She wanted to let go, to be held. But she shook her head again and backed farther away, out from behind the desk. Was she going to bolt? Moving quickly but casually, he placed himself between her and the door.

"You wouldn't run away from Santa, would you?" He allowed his voice to take on just the slightest touch of mockery. "When he's come such a long way to give you this lovely necklace." He took a short step toward her. "You've been such a good little girl, you deserve a little extra something." Another step. "I'll just . . ."

The gun appeared from nowhere. The sly little bitch had been holding it behind her back. Outside, the dog began to howl. He clenched his teeth. When he finally got his hands on her, what a pleasure to bring this little episode to a close. He pocketed the necklace and shook his head sadly.

"Oh, Tilly, Tilly. You wouldn't hurt old Santa, would you? Think about all the poor little girls and boys who'd never get their presents. Think about what your father would say when he found out you've been playing with his gun. And you don't even know if it's loaded, do you?"

The sudden alarm in her eyes told the story. He began to talk very softly.

"Because it's empty, Tilly. It has to be empty. He wouldn't leave it loaded. You know that, don't you? Now why don't we just put it back where it came from, before anyone finds out, and we'll pretend that nothing—"

"Twactor!"

He jumped and whirled around. A small boy in sleepers and a checked bathrobe stood in the doorway clutching a stained, lumpy cushion to his chest.

"Well, it if isn't my friend Davy Wilson." He knelt down and swiftly pulled the child so that he stood between himself and the gun. "Is that what you want for Christmas, a tractor?"

"Twactor. Big."

"Oh, ho, ho. A *big* tractor. I'll have to work on that. But"—he heaved a dejected sigh—"maybe we won't have any presents at all this year. Tilly there wants to be a bad girl and shoot poor old Santa dead."

"Dead?"

He nodded.

Davy glanced back over his shoulder at the gun wavering in Tilly's hand.

"Bad Tilly."

"Yes, I'm afraid she is. Now look what I have for you." Digging into the pocket of his jacket, he extracted a sleepy kitten, the little tortoiseshell, who blinked, yawned and started to squirm in his hand. Davy crowed with delight, gently stroking the tiny ruffled head.

"Do you like that? Isn't it nice?" He turned the boy around and stared over his head at the girl's startled face with its tired eyelids and pale, parted lips. "And you know what?"—he reached around the boy to give both children a clear view of the small, struggling creature—"I think if we ask Tilly very nicely"—cradling the kitten in one hand, he grasped its head in the other—"very nicely"—he tightened his hand just a little—"I think maybe we can make her change her mind."

The last drop of color drained from the girl's face as she made a small sound of protest.

"And if she doesn't want to watch something very nasty, she'll throw down the gun . . ."

He tightened his hand a little more. The kitten cried out.

"Throw . . . down . . . the . . . gun . . ."

The gun hit the floor with a sharp thud.

"And kick it over here . . ."

The gun slid several feet toward him.

"Thank you." Thrusting the boy aside with sufficient force to topple him off his feet, he dropped the kitten, picked up the gun, and checked its cylinder.

"Empty," he announced pleasantly, tossing the useless thing away.

She made no move, except to place her left hand on the side of the filing cabinet in an effort to remain standing. Davy, having recovered from the shock of his fall, began to wail. Outside the window, Sam's howls rose to a high-pitched warble.

Instead of rousing him to fury, the noise fed his mounting excitement. What a satisfying encounter, he thought. So rich in surprises. First a game, then a gun. He could hardly wait to get home and replay it in his head. But first he had to provide a satisfactory conclusion.

"Well, Tilly," he said, "I think it's time for you to thank Santa for your present."

She recoiled from the locket as if he had come to her bearing a snake.

"Now, let's not spoil everything by making a fuss," he said, gently backing her into a niche formed by the filing cabinet and the wall. "Just let me slip this over your head . . ."

Her strength came as a surprise. Kicking, struggling, screaming, she hit out blindly and, by the suddenness of her attack, actually managed to slip past him. But before she could take more than one step, he caught her arm, wrenched her back against the cabinet and, making a cool assessment as to the exact amount of force necessary, struck her sharply on the side of the face.

The blow won him a moment's silence, during which the boy attacked his back with small clenched fists while the girl stared up in shock, her left hand pressed against her cheek.

"Don't make it hard for yourself," he said. "Try to relax and it'll be all over in a minute."

Again she lashed out, uttering hoarse choking sounds that died down to grating gasps while he forced her arms behind her back and pinned them there with one hand. She screamed again as he began to move his free hand upward, heedless of the feeble blows that continued to strike his lower back. And her scream mingled with the howling of the dog and the cries of the boy and a shrill screech that pierced his ears and traveled onto his shoulder and sent him reeling backward as sharp talons raked his face, lodging some in his forehead, some in his cheek and one in the corner of his right eyelid where—oh, God—if it moved once more, just a fraction of an inch to the left . . .

He had to act quickly. Releasing the girl, he reached up to soothe the snarling, spitting animal wrapped around the back of his head. And ignoring the pain and the rage and the blood welling up in his lower lid, he stroked it and spoke to it by name in a soft, reassuring voice. All right, Veronica, he murmured, keeping everything in check with an image of the foul creature hanging helplessly by its tail. Nice Veronica, as he pictured the clawing body arching through the air. Good girl, as he watched the flat serpentine head split open against the wall. That's it, Veronica, as he slowly, carefully and with infinite skill unhooked each claw until at last he stood—weak, shaking and bloody, but free—with his fingers around the thin, sinewed neck, ready to reap his reward with a quick, deft—

"Don't."

A new note in her voice made him turn around.

"Don't hurt her."

He let the cat drop to the floor.

"Go away."

The rifle weighed too much. She leaned back against the filing cabinet to balance it better, but its barrel continued to waver in the air, pointing now at his head, now at his knees.

"That won't be loaded either," he said, as a surge of elation rendered him suddenly short of breath. "You know it won't."

"It might be." Her voice came out unnaturally high, from the back of her throat. "Go home, Davy."

"And even if it were"—he wiped his sleeve across the congealed blood on his eyelid—"you couldn't pull the trigger."

"I could."

And if she did, would he really care?

"You have to cock it. You don't know how."

"I do. I did." Her eyes never left his. "Go away."

No, he thought. Play it to the end.

"I don't believe you." He took a step toward her, stopping short when she gasped and gripped the rifle harder. "Look, you can't even hold it." Another small step. "You're sick, Tilly. You need help. Let me help you." Three more and he'd have her. "You don't want to hurt me. You don't want to hurt anybody."

The shaking rifle barrel wandered off to one side. His foot slid forward. The barrel moved back.

"Be good, now. Be a good little girl." Just two more steps. All he needed was—"Listen!" He jerked his head as if he had heard a noise. "It's your mother."

Hope leapt into her eyes. Her head moved. He had her. He lunged for the rifle.

She pulled the trigger.

Jerry leaned across the steering wheel and squinted through the small patch of cleared glass that trailed the frail rubber blade of the windshield wiper as it moved to and fro in a vain attempt to keep up with the fast-accumulating snow. Ahead, the beams of his headlights picked out an unbroken trail of white bounded on each side by snow-laden trees, all receding into a dense haze of swirling flakes. Behind lay total blackness. And inside, an overenthusiastic heater bathed him in a rush of scorched air that mingled with the drone of the engine, the rattle of tire chains, the roar of the heater fan, and the whine and slap of the wipers to produce a confused jumble of sound made even more intense by the thick, dead silence outside the car.

Blinking, Jerry wiped his forehead and flexed his shoulders. He had developed a pain in the center of his chest where it rested on the steering wheel, his back and eyes hurt, and his head ached. According to the faint white digits of the dashboard odometer, he should be within three miles of Springford; but in this strange blank landscape, free of any discernible landmark, he could not be sure. Nor had he time to consider the matter. For, totally without warning, the tone of the engine changed and the car began to revolve sideways in a slow, sickening skid. Following well-drilled instinct, Jerry steered into the skid and recovered traction. He mopped his brow again and took a deep breath. It had been a near thing. All he needed was to run off the road and freeze until the snowplow found him. Not for the first time, he began to harbor doubts about his chosen profession. Who else would be idiotic enough to drive on a night like this?

As if in response to his thought, two points of light appeared in the distance. Jerry slowed the car to a crawl. The dots grew larger until, almost at the last moment, they attached themselves to the headlights of a truck looming out of the dense whiteness directly abreast of him. Both drivers rolled down their windows.

"Hi!" yelled Jerry as he recognized the anxious faces of Dick Orton, the mill superintendent, and one of his assistants. "What's it like up ahead?"

"Pretty bad!" Dick yelled back. "Whatcha doin' all the way up here?"

"Got a call. Some drunk with a gun is shooting up the beer parlor."

The two men in the truck traded glances. Dick leaned out of the window.

"We just come from there," he said. "It's as quiet as a tomb. Someone's played a joke on you."

Jerry felt his mouth go dry. "Looks like it," he managed. "Let me turn around, and I'll follow your tracks. I've got to get back fast."

Sick with fear, fighting to keep control of himself, he followed the truck as far as the recreation hall and ran into the auditorium. Here he found Alec Barrie, his Santa beard slightly askew, just beginning to hand out presents from an enormous gift-wrapped bin. He rushed backstage to the dressing area, where a number of children still remained struggling out of their costumes.

"Where's Mrs. Taggert?" he asked. "Where's Tilly?"

Gone home, they thought.
Separately? Together?
They shook their heads.
He raced back to the car. At the cookery, he had to choose between traveling straight ahead up the main road or turning left at the cutoff. He turned left. Kate, Kate, he thought. Oh, Kate, where are you?
His headlights picked her up, hunched over on her knees, sobbing by the side of the road.
"My God, what happened?" He pulled her up and staggered as she collapsed into his arms. "What's wrong?"
"My legs," she gasped. "They gave out. Oh, Jerry get me home. He's got Tilly."

They found her lying by the filing cabinet next to some splashes of blood, Uncle Max's hunting rifle and a heart-shaped silver locket with a pearl on its cover. Near her head lay a small soiled cushion, and Davy Wilson in bathrobe and bunny slippers knelt by her side patting her cheek and saying, "Tilly, Tilly, Tilly," over and over. On hearing them come in, he turned around and frowned into their shocked faces.
"All right," he said.
They stared at him in astonishment.
"Tilly all right."
His face broke into a broad beam.
"Tilly dead Santa."

29

Cold. He had never felt so cold. Crouched in the deep shadow beside the path, he listened and waited as the rowdy adolescent voices grew louder and nearer. And, waiting, he began to feel afraid. Not of the boisterous teenagers, who had evidently passed up the dramatic offerings of their juniors in favor of an evening on the toboggan slope. The night was too dark and they sounded too involved in their own concerns to notice the trail of unsteady footprints that stumbled toward them, then veered suddenly off the path into the bushes. It was the pain, the appalling pain in his left shoulder. It seemed to be spreading.

Slipping his right hand out of its leather mitten, he unfastened the top button of his coat and reached carefully under the overlap, where he encountered a thick, warm, saturated wetness, as if he had plunged the hand into a living wound. Shocked, he rebuttoned his coat and pushed his hand back into the mitten, already half frozen stiff. It was worse than he had thought. He must hurry.

But not yet. They came tramping around a corner, picking their way along the path with a flashlight. He ducked lower behind the bushes, suppressing an involuntary moan as his knee struck the wounded area.

"Hey, Chris! Bet you're sorry you aren't singing at the concert.

Hey, guys, remember Chris when his voice broke and he started bawling?" The voice slipped into a piping falsetto. "*While shepherds watched their flocks by night*—"

"Shut up, Barry!"

"*All sleeping on the ground . . .*"

"You're gonna get it!"

"Oh, help. I'm so scared. *An angel*—auk!"

The song broke off in a screeched note, general laughter and a scuffle that brought the two wranglers crashing into the bushes a bare two feet from his hiding place. Clumps of falling snow thumped down on the back of his head and a stray beam from the flashlight revealed a deep red stain on the pure white drift directly beneath his bent shoulder.

"Quit it, you guys!"

"Let's go look in at the rec hall. Maybe we'll get a present from Santa."

"Oh! Golly-gee! Gary wants a tangerine!"

"Or maybe a yo-yo!"

"What are we waiting for?"

"Let's run!"

"I like tangerines . . ."

"You're such a jerk, Gary!"

Their voices faded as they turned another corner and disappeared from sight.

He straightened up slowly and looked back down the path. Far off, a diminishing spot of light flickered among snow-laden branches and a final burst of laughter diminished into inaudibility. For a moment his heart sank as he thought of the carefree, happy party and its enviably easy route home. But no, he told himself sternly as he set off again. He could never have risked returning to the car and meeting anyone in his present condition. He had done the right thing. The only thing possible. And now, luck had come his way and gained him an advantage. With fresh footprints on the path and snow coming down hard, even if her parents came home early and started looking right away, they would never pick up his trail. And once across the river, he would be home free.

If he didn't bleed to death first. Pulling off the false white beard that still clung to his face, he stuffed it into the sodden area under his jacket, where a sudden agonizing spasm set his head spinning. Idiot, he told himself. Leave it alone. Pass out and you're done for. Hurry.

He stumbled on, forcing his legs to move and his eyes to focus on the trail of footprints, toboggan tracks and sled runners. Soon he must get down to the river. But he must choose the right spot. An image of stars and water and a distant light in the window sprang into his head. That was it: the end of the swimming dock pointed directly across the water to that drunk McCallister's shack. If he set out in the opposite direction, he could finish the last third of his walk across the river on good firm boards rather than deep snow. And not only that—

He studied an oddly shaped object looming out of the swirling snow on the river side of the path. It resembled a giant candy cane but it was, in fact—yes, another stroke of luck—a toboggan jammed end-down into a snowbank. Things couldn't be working out better if he had laid out the plan ahead of time. Now all he had to do was coast down the recent toboggan tracks, work his way along the sheltered riverbank to McCallister's dock and follow its line across the river. Then they could search this side of the river all night long and never find a trace of him. Grinning savagely in an attempt to ignore the surging waves of pain in his shoulder, he pulled at the toboggan with his good arm until it slid free of its mooring and toppled into position at the top of the run.

With the moment of departure upon him, he fell prey to second thoughts. He would be launching himself into utter blackness, quite out of control. If the toboggan veered off course, he could end up shattered against a tree. Then there was a matter of technique to consider: did one go down headfirst or on one's back? And, even if all else went well, there was the ride itself. Could his shoulder stand it? Could he? Coward, he thought grimly. You haven't got a choice. And, tucking his feet under the front curve of the toboggan, he lay back, grasped one of the side ropes, and tipped forward.

He should never have done it. He had forgotten how fast a toboggan could travel. Clinging desperately to the side rope, he fought to keep his feet in place and his weight evenly balanced. But every jerk, twist and undulation threatened to topple him off. How much longer could he hold on? The thought rattled wildly about in his brain as freezing wind whistled past his ears and a spray of fine snowflakes rained down on his face. How far had he traveled? Where was he?

At this point the toboggan shot over the edge of a rocky outcrop, took to the air, and landed on the ground with a slap. He followed suit a split second later, striking his left shoulder against a metal eyelet on the side of the toboggan. The searing pain struck with the force of a high-voltage shock. He shrieked, fainted, and lost his grip on the rope. The toboggan continued to hurtle forward. And as it took to the air once more, this time over the edge of the riverbank, he flew off on a trajectory of his own, regaining consciousness just in time to experience a soft landing on his back in the deep snow covering the frozen river.

How comfortable it felt. If it weren't for the tiresome voice in his head urging him to move, he might be tempted to lie there and catch his breath and enjoy its embrace just a little longer. For it was warmer than he might have supposed. Get up, said the voice. And quite seductive in the way it molded itself to his body. It reminded him of those winters on the farm, before it all went bad, when he would make angels in the snow, one after the other, until he had populated the front yard with an entire squadron. Flock. Host. Get up. And as pleasant memories of the distant past drained away the pain in his arm, he began to feel as light as a drifting snowflake and deliciously drowsy. Because what he really needed was sleep. Just a short nap. Five minutes would do. Get up! Even one.

Get up!

Catching his breath in short, high sobs, he struggled to his feet, staggered over to the toboggan and pulled it out of sight under the projecting ledge of matted vegetation at the edge of the river. The snow seemed shallower here and walking easier. Weary and half asleep, he set forth again, left foot, right foot, heading blindly into the whirling storm, guided by the line of the river that would lead him to—where? He racked his brain. So ridiculous. He had known once. He knew still. It was right there, hanging just out of reach, ready to pop into his mind when he least expected it. But perhaps it didn't matter. Perhaps this was how it ended, left foot, right foot, left arm hanging useless, right eye swollen shut, on and on, until he dropped or gave up or came to—yes, how could he have forgotten?—the ramshackle dock straight ahead, rising like a ghost out of the night, black on black, until at last it took on solid form and became a friendly sheltering guide that took him in hand and said stop here, turn left, follow me.

Which he did, making his way along its length slowly and with difficulty (for the snow grew deeper with each step) until at last its comforting presence came to an end and he stood alone, exposed to the full force of the downriver wind, squinting into the wall of shifting snow through which he had to pass before he reached home and rest and safety. It all seemed very far away. He longed for a beacon, something that would give him heart and draw him forward, but he could see no farther than the snowflakes that whirled about his head and whipped against the surface of his eye. He longed to sit down and rest, but dared not. He had only one choice, to gather his strength and begin again, left foot, right foot. It would be easier once he got started. The first step was always the hardest. He took it and plunged feet first through the paper-thin layer of ice covering Jack McCallister's fishing hole.

Inky darkness engulfed his head before he could gasp for air. Frigid water streamed into his mouth and nostrils. Agonizing cold forced him to close his eye as his soaked clothes dragged him down. Blind, weak, lost in the grip of panic, he could do no more than kick off his boots and flail with his uninjured arm until his brain recovered from its initial shock and began to grasp the facts of his present situation. How far had he sunk? How much longer could his aching lungs hold out? Which way was up? Panic returned with the realization that he had lost all sense of up or down. He could be propelling himself away from the surface. He could be wasting his last minute of air.

Just at that moment, his heel struck a solid object. Failing hope flickered back into life. He had landed on a submerged log or rock. Instantly regaining his bearings, he brought both feet together, sank into a crouch, then pushed himself off the firm base with as much force as he could muster. Up, up, he could feel his face cutting through the water. Or could he? The water was so cold, his face almost frozen. Perhaps he only imagined it. Perhaps he had come to a halt and begun to sink again. He kicked and raised his arm. His hand, still encased in its leather glove, encountered a firm, unyielding surface. He had come up under the ice. The thick midwinter ice. Forcing himself to open an eye, he twisted about in a circle and despaired. He had lost the way out. He was going to die. With his lungs threatening to burst, he began to paw feverishly along the rough underside of the ice.

"Are you sure?"

"Pretty sure." Jerry sank wearily down on the sofa beside his wife. "We found his car behind the old Springer house. No sign of him. God, I hate my job." Throwing his legs up on the cedar chest, he slumped back into the cushions and closed his eyes. "How's Tilly?"

"Better." Kate's heart expanded in a burst of warmth as Jerry, still with his eyes shut, managed to slide his hand gently over hers. "She drank some cocoa and I put her to bed in our room. Do you want anything?"

Jerry considered. "I wouldn't mind a stiff drink, if you happen to have one in your pocket." His hand tightened. "No, don't go away. Come back."

"Sorry, this is all we have," said Kate as she returned bearing an inch of whisky in a tumbler. "I drank the rest on Halloween." She resumed her place on the sofa and gave back her hand. "What will happen when you catch him?"

"If I catch him, I'll make an arrest. Cheers." Jerry downed half the whisky in a single gulp. "But we couldn't find a trace of him anywhere. He may have wandered off into the bush."

"He won't last long out there," said Kate, surprised to find herself shivering at the thought. "Not with a bullet wound and bleeding. He may be dead."

"I hope so." Jerry succumbed to a huge yawn. "Oh, hum. Excuse me. Did you say something?"

"I said Amen," said Kate.

30

Here, boy. Here, boy. Whee-oo.

The voice, although soft, floated clearly out of the storm, followed by the familiar low whistle.

He smiled. No, no, no. Not this time. He was a grown man now. Besides, he needed to rest. Just a little longer, supported by his good arm thrown over the edge of the ice, and he would try again to pull himself out. It would be hard, with the opening so small and no strength in his other arm, but he would do it. He remembered swimming classes in the city school, where one learned to propel oneself up out of the water, twist about and sit down on the edge of the pool. That was what he would do in a moment.

Here, boy.

But not yet. He felt so comfortable and warm, with the underwater nightmare behind him and his breath back and the ice-fish no longer nibbling at his feet and legs. He could hold out for hours now. All he had to do was keep his eyes open.

Whee-oo.

The whistle. How he hated the whistle. It made everything worse. Right from the first time, that first Christmas in his grandmother's house, when he passed the door and heard it.

Whee-oo.

And he had looked in and seen him, only half dressed in the red suit, his crisp yellow hair shining like a halo above the white beard.

Here, boy. Whee-oo. Come and get it.

And there it was, the almost-silver pocket watch from the pawnbroker's window that he had yearned for every day since September. There it was, shining, twinkling, swaying, gently twisting to and fro at the end of its almost-silver chain. And it could be his. He knew what he had to do. It had been suggested on several occasions, very casually, in the easiest, most natural manner. He had shaken his head and run away. But now, with the watch . . .

How lovely it looked, with its cover design picked out in time-blackened etching, its warm, friendly tick, its tinkling chime when one pressed the hidden button. And to get it—would what he had to do be so terrible? Just once, to gain such a prize? He stared entranced as the silver circle continued to sway back and forth.

Hey, get a move on up there! Where's Santa?

The raucous voice from downstairs made him start and look away. When he looked back, a golden eyebrow arched in a question mark above the white beard. The blue eye beneath the eyebrow twinkled. The almost-silver chain began to shorten. He understood. It was to be now or never. Never to see the watch again. Never to hear its magical chime. Never to own anything as desirable, as rare—

Come on, boy. Whee-oo.

The whistle became almost a whisper. And he had gone in, smiling a little, his eyes fixed on the watch, like an obedient dog to a bone. It sickened him, even now, to think how he had gone in. Oh, how he had loathed himself that first time! And the next, after it had been explained what would happen to him if anyone found out and what would be said if he dared to tell. And every time thereafter, no matter how hard he tried to escape. For what could he do? They were all against him.

Guess what, darling? Uncle Max is going to take you on a fishing trip! You'll get to sleep in a tent . . . Sorry, dear. Mother and Granny have to go out to dinner, but don't worry. Uncle Max will stay home and look after you . . . Sweetheart, what's keeping Uncle Max? Just run upstairs and see.

Again and again, in love and trust, they handed him over to the enemy. Poor foolish innocents. Even after it had ended, they never let him forget.

Dearest, I wish you'd do better at sports. Look at all those trophies in Uncle Max's room . . . Precious, can't you study just a bit harder? Look at Uncle Max—when he gets back from overseas, he's going to be a doctor.

Until at last—

Darling, Granny and I have something very sad to tell you. It's about Uncle Max . . .

He had looked down at the floor as they told him, his heart welling with joy at the thought of those frank blue eyes and perfect features and shining curls dropping out of the sky in a ball of fire to be consumed and reduced to ashes and wiped off the face of the earth forever. And then he had begun to cry, not for Uncle Max but for himself, left behind with their secret, the secret he could never lay down, never forget, never share because of what would happen if any one found out, if anyone told. And he had resolved . . . he had resolved . . .

What had he resolved? It didn't matter. He was too tired to think anymore. And the voices made it harder, crowding in on him, whispering out of the wind . . .

Here, boy . . . Hello, Joe, you got gum? . . . Sorry, darling, I'm getting out . . . No, I don't want to . . . Guess what, dear? We're going to live in the city with Granny . . . You got cigarettes? . . . Oh, that hurt! . . . With purity and holiness I will pass my life and practice my art . . . I'll have a little fling with Vic, then get a job . . . And you can get to know your Uncle Max. Won't that be nice? . . . Stop, stop, please stop . . . Whee-oo . . . I'll let you know where to send the money . . . Come on, kid, just once . . . and will abstain from every voluntary act of mischief and corruption . . . Why don't you want to go fishing with Uncle Max? . . . and about the divorce . . . Pane, signor. Pane, per piacere . . . *It's the least you can do, considering what I think I know . . . and from the seduction of females or males . . . Whee-oo . . . Oh, that's so pretty! Can I have it? . . . Here, boy . . . You lied . . . I hate you . . .*

But at last they died away, setting him free to drift up through the falling snow like a balloon reeled slowly out at the end of an invisible string. And when he came to rest high above the sleeping town, he looked down on the winding river where, at a point near its northern shore, a dark speck of life still clung to the edge of a small black circle hacked into its smooth white surface. The sight troubled him, as did the constraint of the invisible string. But the speck soon vanished, slipping gently down into the water, and the string snapped and he soared away, higher and higher, leaving the town and the river and the snow to coalesce into a vast, white globe hurtling from him at tremendous speed, shrinking, contracting until, at the very last, it dwindled down to a single point of light that flared up for a moment, burned bright, then went out.

Long after the Taggert family had settled down for the night, with Kate, Tilly and Veronica on one side of the bed, Jerry and Sam on the other, and John Henry underneath, Jack McCallister regained consciousness on the lockup bunk where he had been hurriedly deposited several hours earlier. Disregarding the ill effects of a throbbing head and aching shoulder, he pulled himself to his feet, wove across the floor to the barred door and gave voice.

"Hey, out there!" he yelled. "Why'd nobody tell me what day it was? Merry Christmas, folks. Happy New Year."

Staggering back to the cot, he arranged himself under its blanket, then sat up again.

"Oh, yeah!" he roared. "God bless us every one, eh?"

And with that, he fell into a deep and dreamless sleep and peace descended on the house once more.

31

On a fine mid-April afternoon, at that time in spring when poplar trees sported a light green haze on their branches, mud-soaked roads showed signs of drying out, and snow had vanished from all but the darkest woodland hollows, Tilly and Joey pushed a large blue baby carriage out of the Wilson yard and proceeded to trundle it down the narrow pipeline path in the wake of Sam's jaunty plumed tail. Handsomely outfitted with heavy springs, oversized wheels and a quilted satin lining, the carriage had recently been brought up from the cellar in anticipation of that happy day in May when it would receive into its lush interior a pink and smiling infant Taggert, Isabel or Anthony as the case might be. At the moment, however, it contained Davy Wilson and an assortment of recently gathered twigs and branches, all bound for a game of Pooh-sticks at the bridge.

"All right, Davy," said Joey, when they had achieved their destination and unloaded their human cargo, "this is how we play. We each take a stick and drop it over this side of the bridge at the same time. Then we run to the other side and see whose stick comes through first. Okay?"

"Okay," replied Davy, who had recently turned three and made several welcome additions to his vocabulary. He marched over to the carriage and hauled out a long forked branch. "My stick," he announced. "Ow! Sam. Leggo."

"Hold on." After rescuing Davy's branch and placating Sam with an acceptable substitute, Joey helped himself to a short, thick stick, then regarded Tilly with a look of concern. Leaning against the railing of the bridge, she seemed half asleep, with her eyes closed and her drawn face turned up toward the sun. "Come on, Til. Take a stick."

Tilly started up and, in smiling, erased something of her gaunt expression, although not the dark shadows that seemed to have taken up permanent residence under her eyes. She picked a thin twig with brown bark and a patch of pale green lichen still clinging to one side.

"Who's going to say 'On your mark'?" she asked.

"Me." Joey moved to the side of the bridge where glistening river ice, piled up behind the upstream log boom, gave way to a glassy-smooth expanse of black water. Holding his stick out past the top rail of the wooden parapet, he waited while Tilly took up a similar stance and Davy, straining on tiptoe, thrust his arm over the middle rail. "Okay," he announced when they had all achieved the proper form. "On your mark. Ready. Set. Go!"

Without waiting to see their sticks hit the water, they dashed across the road, closely followed by Sam, who joined them in peering eagerly over the railings.

"Mine! Mine!" yelled Davy as his forked branch sailed triumphantly out from under the bridge and vanished over the edge of the dam just slightly ahead of its competitors. "I win!"

"Davy wins," echoed Tilly.

"He cheated," Joey protested. "He dropped his stick before I said 'Go'!"

"Didn't," said Davy.

"Did too."

"Didn't."

Wrapped in a serene innocence that never failed to infuriate his older brother, Davy collected another stick and returned to the starting line.

"Okay for you." Joey marched back to his original position, stick in hand. "Come on, Tilly. And this time watch him! If he lets go early, we'll do the same. Okay. On your mark . . ."

They continued to play, adjusting the release of their sticks to Davy's unpredictable timing, and in this manner managed to achieve an acceptable number of wins each. Eventually, however, the unaccustomed warmth of the sun and the heady scent of sap and warm earth on the breeze took their toll. While Davy continued to drop the last few sticks by himself, the two older children crouched down on a dry patch of ground by the side of the bridge and leaned dreamily back against a heavy wooden cross beam.

In the silence that followed, far-off sounds, previously unnoticed, advanced and became louder. Davy continued to patter to and fro from one side of the bridge to the other, while Sam, having tired of the game, amused himself by flushing newly arrived birds out of the willow bushes under the bridge. A rousing piano rendition of "People Will Say We're in Love" floated down the hill from Harriet Reese's open window, to be joined every few seconds by the high, wailing song of a ripsaw slicing planks in the nearby sawmill. Across from the mill, on the opposite bank of the river, hammers banged out a rhythmic counterpoint as repair work continued on the old Springer house where Diana Walter and Alec Barrie would be taking up residence after their wedding at the end of June. Over at the mine, a sudden "gonk, gonk" from the hoist signal elicited a number of enthusiastic echoes from a band of ravens on the lookout for lunchbox scraps near the entrance to the cage.

As usual on these occasions, Tilly appeared to fall asleep instantly. Joey shut his eyes too, but soon wearied of silence and inactivity. Letting his head fall sideways, he inspected Tilly for signs of consciousness. She remained quite motionless. He wished that Sam would come and disturb her, but the sound of distant snuffles, followed by a wild flutter of wings, informed him that this was not likely to happen for some time. At last, pressed beyond endurance, he spoke.

"You see him again last night?"

Tilly appeared not to have heard him. Then, without opening her eyes, she nodded.

"Same place?"

Another nod.

"Didja run into bed with yer ma?"

"No." The word came out in a whisper.

Joey nodded sympathetically while racking his brain for some words of comfort.

"He's gotta be dead by now," he observed.

"I know."

"Even if they never find him. He couldn't last the whole winter."

"I know."

"And at least you got to keep the locket."

Tilly lifted her hand to touch the heart-shaped pendant, running her finger over the hummingbird and pearl on its cover.

"It should have been Ellie Hayes's," she said quietly. "She was going to let me wear it sometimes."

"Now you got it for always."

"Yes." Rising briskly, Tilly brushed the back of her skirt and kicked the toes of her rubber boots to resettle her feet. "Let's walk on and see if they're pouring gold today."

"Yeah!"

Everyone in Crow River had heard how the mine's first casting team had overshot the mold and spread a layer of molten gold over the refinery floor. A few, like Joey and Tilly, never ceased to hope that history would repeat itself.

Calling Sam, Tilly walked over to the empty carriage, leaving Joey to collect his brother, who had just dropped the last stick into the river.

"Come on, Davy. We're going."

"Bye-bye."

"Don't you wanna come?"

"Bye-bye."

"Tilly!"

Tilly turned and looked back. Joey stood staring out past the top rail of the parapet. Davy waved. From behind the chunks of ice piled up at the log boom, an arm waved back. Encased in a pink sleeve that had once been red, and terminating in a brown leather mitten, it moved stiffly from side to side in a gentle arc, then sank slowly out of sight behind the ice.

Everyone ran across the road to the other side of the bridge and peered down into the water. Nothing stirred in its inky shadows.

"Look!" yelled Joey.

A shapeless form, pink and livid white, hovered on the edge of the dam, then toppled over and vanished.

"Bye-bye."

They continued to study the rapids at the base of the dam, but nothing broke through the surface of the white foam. At last Joey turned away from the railing.

"Wow," he breathed.

Tilly attempted to speak, but found that she could not. Relief surged through her, bringing with it a blissful mingling of hope and comfort, as if she had just emerged from a feverish illness. She looked about, dazed, at a shining world that seemed to have emerged newly minted from behind a dull storm window, left on too long after the winter. Overwhelmed with joy, she burst into tears.

The two boys stared at her in astonishment.

"Tilly, Tilly." Davy seized her hand and began pulling at it.

Joey shuffled his feet. "You okay, Tilly?"

Tilly brushed the back of her hand across her eyes, smiled down at Davy and nodded. Joey smiled too, then looked down again at the churning rapids.

"I guess we better tell somebody."

"No." Tilly's voice returned with surprising force.

"But shouldn't we . . . ?"

"No. Let's—" Tilly stopped and searched for the right words. "It's gone now. It won't come back. If we don't tell anybody, we'll be the only ones to know."

"A secret?"

"Yes. A secret."

Joey, long rankled by his lack of participation in the dramatic events of last Christmas, broke into a delighted smile. "Swear?"

"Swear."

They raised their right hands and spat.

"Okay, then. Let's go." Taking a firm grip on his brother's hand, Joey set off to collect the carriage. "Come on, Davy. Maybe we'll see them splash that gold all over. Come on, Tilly."

Tilly stood for a moment, watching the river as it sped away to lose itself in the vast network of lakes and waterways that she seemed to have seen once, spread like a silver web across the great northern woods.

"Come on, Tilly."
"Coming."
The sun struck her eyes as she turned to follow. Dazzled, she headed blindly across the bridge into an explosion of dappled light, bird song and green buds bursting into leaf.